International Praise for Shakedown *(Las Chicas de Palacio)*

"…brings the reader into the inner-circle of power."

—*Maxim*

"…the author is very familiar with her subject (politics from the inside) with an amazing skill to write between the lines…"

—*Eve Gil, Siempre*

"…accurate portrait of Mexico's political life"

—*El Informador*

"…blurs the border between the political world and its actors, defining these in a multihued plot…"

—*Fabiola Palapa Quijas, La Jornada*

"Intrigue, conspiracy, corruption, danger, secrets and the hidden face of power..."

—*El Porvenir*

"It is an interesting novel, a must read…"

—*Eduardo Ruiz Healy*

"…weaves an interesting yarn that keeps you reading."

—*Elisa Robledo, El Financiero*

Also by Erica Fuentes

Island Dreams

A Window to Paradise

Miguel's Cantina (First Love)

Hearts Ahoy!

Loving Deceit

Salve Regina
(with Annemarie Stonewater)

SHAKEDOWN

(Las Chicas de Palacio)

a novel by

Erica Fuentes

Casablanca 2010

Barcelona • Los Angeles • Mexico • New York
www.editorialcasablanca.com *www.casablancapublishing.com*

Cover design: Erica Fuentes
Adapted to English by Erica Fuentes.

First English Edition: December of 2010

Second Spanish Edition: December of 2010

First Spanish Edition: © 20007 Santillana Ediciones Generales SA de CV

ISBN: 978-607-8125-00-5

Spanish version released simultaneously. Also available in ebook.

2 4 6 8 10 9 7 5 3 1

Publisher's Note:

Casablanca Publishing is proud to present

Erica Fuentes'

SHAKEDOWN

which original Spanish First Edition
Las Chicas de Palacio
was misteriously and abruptly discontinued
despite ranking among the top 10
best-selling books in Mexico.

Prologue

1982

Tanya

Tanya lifted a tray from the arm of the elegant leather recliner seat and placed it on her lap, to make room for the chest that contained all of the essential bases and cosmetics to turn a face showing the hackneyed results of too many late nights, into a veritable brilliance of freshness and beauty. The mission she'd been given just a few hours earlier that day would not only require her greatest efforts and talents, but also her internationally recognized and radiant beauty.

Opening the case, she fanned out all the little compartments full of eyeliners, eye shadows, blushes and lipsticks to uncover the bottom compartment containing her bases, liquid make-ups and powders. She took a small wet pad, and resting her head on the back of the recliner, she washed her face with the soft cold cream impregnated in the pad. From the other side of the case, she took a cotton ball, and after soaking it with astringent, she rubbed it over her face. Without opening her eyes, she tossed the pad and the cotton ball on the still half-full plate of cheeses and fruits that the military flight attendant had served her after take-off from the Presidential Hangar in the Benito Juarez International Airport in Mexico City, en route to Cozumel.

After resting a few minutes, she opened her eyes, and studied herself carefully in the built-in mirror under the cover of the chest. She grimaced, annoyed with the dark circles that revealed her fatigue, and she sighed. In her youth, she had never noticed any dark circles, nor had her eyes been puffy, in spite of the crazy life she'd led from party to party, and from bed to bed.

Now, nearing forty, any late night seemed to stamp its mark on her face.

She frowned again with disgust, and sat up in her seat.

"Better get to work, Tanya," she said aloud.

The military flight attendant shot out from behind the curtains that separated the passenger cabin from the small galley in the Sabre Liner assigned to the Chief of Staff's Office of the Presidency.

"May I bring you something, Miss? he asked politely.

Tanya flashed him one of her smiles that the media always described as "the sexiest smile in Mexico."

"No Lieutenant, thank you," she said as she lifted her gaze toward him, "I was only thinking out loud."

The young lieutenant could feel the heat rising to his cheeks and knew he was blushing. Murmuring his apologies, he withdrew to his post.

Tanya returned her gaze to the mirror, and after taking a small jar from her case, she began the long process of making-up by applying a thick base to cover any imperfection in her skin.

From his vantage point on a little bench behind the curtain, the young lieutenant watched her with the singular fascination only comparable to that of a wild feline enjoying every moment while stalking its prey. Tanya reeked of power.

Lorena

"Jesús, we need to go by the construction site before heading for the Hangar," Lorena told her chauffeur after throwing her suitcase on the backseat of the car that had been assigned to her by her lover, the chief of police in Mexico City. "They're having problems with the garage door because of the weight of the bulletproof panels.

"But Madame," her chauffeur responded with a worried tone in his voice for fear of displeasing the most tyrannical major in the Mexican Army, now the police chief of the biggest city in the world, "what if you miss the plane?"

Lorena threw her head back, letting her long auburn hair fall over the back of the leather seat of the luxurious Mercedes Benz, and she laughed.

"So what?" she said with a mischievous tone. "So we'll commandeer the Grumman and we'll go anyway, right?"

Jesús Galindo was trembling, but he dared not change the expression on his face. He had been working as the chauffeur and bodyguard for his commanding officer's lover for more than three months; long enough to figure out that any capricious whim that His Lady wanted, His Lady got, was the order from the top of the organization.

Carolina

The bar in the Ritz Carlton Hotel in Washington D.C. was dark, and so filled with smoke that Carolina had to cover her nose with her hand as she entered. She squinted her eyes to try to accustom them to the dark, and took a few steps into the cocktail lounge. She stopped at the bar, near the cash register, and leaned against a bar stool. She searched the room with her gaze, desperately trying to find her colleague, a major in the Mexican army who had accompanied her on her long journey from Mexico City the night before. Their mission had been to attend a meeting at the White House in which they were to discuss a number of aspects surrounding the summit meeting which was to take place in Cozumel three days later. The President of the United States would confirm his attendance depending on the outcome of the discussion, and on the documents that she carried as the officer in charge of protocol for the Presidential Chief of Staff's Office.

Determined to get to the meeting on time, and after having discovered that their shuttle flight to Washington D.C. had been canceled, the young military officers had rented a car at Kennedy International and had driven all night.

They had walked into the meeting with seven minutes to spare, despite a long series of mishaps which had culminated in front of Gate Four of the White House when the engine on the rental car threw a rod and died.

But despite everything that could possibly go wrong, they had accomplished their mission, and had called the General to give him the good news after the meeting at The White House as soon as they'd arrived at the hotel where the rest of the advance team had been registered for the past few days.

Jet-lagged and tired, Carolina had gone to her room after talking with the General. After soaking in a hot bubble bath, she had drifted off to dreamland the entire afternoon until the dinner hour, when much to her displeasure, she'd had to get up. She had accepted an invitation from one of the military attaches to the Mexican Embassy to dine with the entire advance group from Mexico, as there had been little choice.

However, upon their return to the hotel after a nice dinner in a downtown Chinese restaurant, she had run into a potentially scandalous situation which could seriously damage the public image of the presidential staff.

She needed Alejandro's help. Through the conversations they'd enjoyed during the long ride to Washington the night before, the young Major had inspired Carolina's confidence, and now she would have to count on his discretion and ingenuity to solve the problem that had come up.

She finally found him at a corner table with a very attractive woman, but Carolina didn't think twice about interrupting him. She approached the table, and the Major looked very surprised to see her there.

"You were so tired that I thought you would sleep until tomorrow," Alejandro said to her as he rose to his feet, and then he turned to his table companion. "Carolina, I'd like you to meet my friend, Candy."

Carolina held her arm out to shake the hand offered by the woman.

"I'm Carolina Suarez and it's a pleasure to meet you, Candy," she said, "and I'm sorry to interrupt you, but a little problem has come up that I need to discuss with Alejandro. Could I steal him away from you for just a couple of minutes?"

"Of course," the voluptuous woman said, "as a matter of fact," she said as she rose from her chair after releasing Carolina's hand, "you can have my place for a few minutes, because I was about to go to the powder room, anyway."

Carolina thanked her and took the young woman's chair. Alejandro sat across from her, his brow creased with sincere concern.

"What's wrong?" he asked. "Is there a problem in Mexico?"

"No," the lieutenant said, "we have a problem here, and I don't want to cause a scene. I need your help."

"Count on it."

Carolina smiled at him appreciatively.

"Thank you, Alex," she said smiling. "What is happening is that I went out to dinner with the group, and we just returned."

"Yes, I knew about the dinner," Alejandro said, "and I'm really sorry for cutting out on the group, but it's just that..."

Carolina laughed when she realized that Alejandro thought that his absence at dinner could be the problem.

"That has nothing to do with it. Don't worry."

Now she felt ridiculous. A thirty five year old woman who traveled the world over like a gypsy in the service of her country should certainly have been quite capable of taking care of herself without any help from anybody. But this problem involved a general. Her superior. In her ten years at the presidency, she had never gone through anything like this. She took a deep breath and continued:

"It's about General Santiago. When we got back to the hotel, I went to pick up my room key and started off toward the elevator when the disgusting old goat came up to me." She noticed that Alejandro arched his eyebrows in a silent question as his body tensed. "He told me not to worry because he already had the key to my room, and he would be up to visit me in a while with a good bottle of champagne!"

Alejandro sat up straight and his expression showed his anger.

"That son of a bitch!" he spewed.

Then he sat back in his chair, pensively. Carolina remained silent, watching her colleague's face and hoping for a word of advice that might resolve her dilemma.

All of a sudden, Alejandro stood up. Carolina followed his lead. Alejandro put a hand on her shoulder and smiled.

"Do you trust me?" he asked with a serious expression on his face.

"Yes, of course I do. That's why I came to you," Carolina responded, intrigued.

Alejandro took the key to his own room from his pocket and pressed it into Carolina's hand, and then he smiled at her.

"What are you going to do, Alex?"

"Don't ask. Just go to my room and go to sleep. I'm leaving at five in the morning for the airport, so I'll be there after I teach Santiago some manners," he said, and putting his hands on Carolina's shoulders, he spun her around facing the door to the lobby bar. "So go on, woman, off to bed!"

Carolina went upstairs to Alejandro's room, and she only removed her shoes before falling exhausted into bed. She was sound asleep until there was a knock at the door.

She got up and crossed the room, but stopped before opening the door.

"Who's there?" she asked before unlatching the door.

"Alejandro. Let me in," the Major answered.

She opened the door to find Alejandro doubled over in laughter. He held a bottle of champagne in his hand.

"What's that?"

"Just a little present from the General."

"You're kidding... Alex, what did you do to him?"

"Just wait until I tell you!" he said, unable to contain his laughter as he crossed the room to the table to sit down. "When the son of a bitch came into your room, he sat on the edge of the bed calling me *blondie*, trying to wake me up. You should have seen his face when I sat up and said, *What's going on, Sir?* He ran out of that room so fast that he forgot his little bottle of champagne!" He held the bottle up and began to loosen the cork. "Would you like some?"

Hours later, aboard the commercial flight on their way back to Mexico to transfer over to a presidential flight to Cozumel, Carolina had to dig for a bottle of aspirin in her briefcase. She took the third tablet of the day. She had a headache to end all headaches, paying dearly for the triumphal drinks she had enjoyed with her new and apparently loyal friend.

General Santiago was seated in the back row of the first class section, pretending to read one magazine after another. He had been too embarrassed to look Carolina in the eye, which couldn't have pleased Carolina more.

The General knew perfectly well that if he were to be reported for his indiscretion, it would mean a court martial.

What the General didn't know at that moment was that Carolina had absolutely no intention of reporting him; not because she forgave him, but rather because in not reporting him, the old goat would owe her a huge favor.

And who knew? Someday, the jerk might just be in the right place at the right time to collect on that favor.

Chapter 1

"Please don't pet the dog, Miss!" Carolina heard the stern words of the Secret Service agent from the United States Treasury Department in the precise moment that she was reaching in the direction of the German Shepherd dog that just moments earlier had been rubbing against her left leg.

"Sorry, Sir," she responded apologetically as she took a sideways step to distance herself from the dog.

Upon entering the lobby of the hotel which would be housing the global summit meeting, she had stopped momentarily to get her bearings and to study the layout of the place before reporting with the Fourth Division of the Presidential Staff's Office that was in charge of the room assignments for the working staff of the presidency. She was tired and a little annoyed because no one had bothered to send a car for her at the airport, and against her strongest protests, the customs inspectors had pawed through her luggage. Fortunately, they hadn't recognized nor confiscated the documents she carried in her briefcase, but Carolina felt that her colleagues had exposed her to an unnecessary security risk.

As she visually scoped out the lobby, her gaze finally rested on the registration desk of the Presidential Staff's Office. Without diverting her gaze, she walked firmly toward her colleagues, her face scowling with contempt. As she approached them, she forced a sardonic smile.

"Thanks for dispatching a car to the airport," she addressed a uniformed lieutenant who had greeted her in a friendly way.

The lieutenant blushed, and rose to his feet.

"A thousand apologies, Lieutenant, but..." the young lieutenant stammered, immediately remembering that Major Mendoza had ordered him to dispatch a car to the airport a few hours earlier.

"It doesn't matter," Carolina said, interrupting him, "but if you would be so kind as to give me the key to my room, I would be extremely appreciative."

The lieutenant quickly checked his room list, and then found the key to the room which was assigned to Carolina.

"Both Lorena Araujo and Susana Aragon have already registered, and they said that they will see you later for lunch. The three of you are sharing room 403."

The lieutenant noticed that Carolina seemed confused, and hurriedly explained.

"Don't worry. It is a junior suite with a bedroom, and the living room converts to another bedroom at night."

"It's all the same to me," Carolina said, forcing herself to smile.

The lieutenant gave her the key to her room, and then he pointed to a door on the other side of the lobby.

"Before going up to your room, you'll have to register with the Fifth Division, in the Command Center on the other side of the lobby. They will give you your security badge for access to the summit."

"I'd prefer registering later," she told the lieutenant, "because I have a headache that is killing me and I'd like to go up and rest a while before unpacking."

The lieutenant smiled kindly, but his words were firm.

"They won't let you out of the lobby, Lieutenant... so you will have to register."

She glanced out of the corner of her eye toward the elevators, and indeed, noticed that there were two security guards checking the security badges of every person before allowing them access to the stairs or elevators.

She shrugged her shoulders, and turned on her heels to cross the lobby toward the door indicated to her. When she opened the door, she immediately felt at home.

The room thundered with the raised voices of her work companions, yelling orders and whispering blasphemies as they worked on connecting the computer banks they were installing behind the partitions of sheet rock and glass that would separate the Security Command Center from the rest of the working sections of the Presidential Staff's Office.

"*Hola, hola,*" she greeted the group in general. Some of her colleagues lifted their eyes toward her and smiled, and others ignored her sovereignly, focused only on the task at hand. They were all dressed in civilian clothes, and she wondered if they hadn't had time to go up to their rooms, either.

Expecting to help with the work, she piled her luggage in the closest corner, and went behind the counter to offer any help she could give them.

The Chief of the Fifth Division approached her, and shook her hand.

"You are a welcome sight," he said as he let go of her hand. "You are just the person that we needed," he said, and noticed that Carolina raised her eyebrows in a silent question. "We need the interpreters' assignments and the booth hours for each of them."

Carolina smiled, amused by the Colonel's ignorance.

"Well," she mused, "I don't know if what I have will do you any good, because I can't really assign anyone until the summit begins, and the length of time that anyone interprets in the booths depends on his or her mental endurance and on the topics discussed in the summit," she explained to the Colonel, but she detected something akin to panic in her superior's eyes. "But I can give you a list of sorts anyway; so that you can you can do whatever you have to do with it."

Colonel Treviño's face revealed his displeasure.

"All right. I guess that will have to do," he said with exaggerated cordiality.

Carolina went back to the reception area and took out a list of the names of the simultaneous translators who would be working the summit. She circled around the counter again, and gave the list to the Colonel.

"Here you are," she said as she held out the list. "As you can see, next to each name is the security clearance at which the interpreter can work."

She noted that the Colonel was wearing a more curious expression, and she explained.

"This is why I can't assign schedules, neither can I designate for whom they'll be translating nor in which languages. The topics of conversation dictate which translator will interpret, all according to the security clearance of each translator. I often have to substitute one translator for another with a higher security clearance... you understand what I mean, right?"

The Colonel took the list from Carolinas hand, and he studied it carefully. Finally, he sighed.

"That's enough. I understand what you're saying, but I don't have to like it."

"Of course not, but there is no other way. If it helps, I can try to get you a list with the approximate schedules every morning when I receive the list of topics to be covered, but only in the understanding that it can change at any time."

"Do you mean to say that you can switch an interpreter at any given time? How do you do that without interrupting the summit meeting?"

Carolina laughed.

"It is completely transparent. That's why I wear the multi-frequency headphones constantly... to listen to everything going on in the summit enclosure, and to see how the translations are going. If I notice that one of the interpreters is so tired that he or she is making mistakes, I call for an appropriate substitute, and I go in to take his or her place until the replacement arrives. By the same token, if I notice that the conversations are beginning to focus on subjects requiring higher security clearance, I personally replace the disqualified interpreter until a translator with a higher security clearance can arrive."

"And what happens if you have one fatigued interpreter, and another with too low a security clearance, at the same time? What do you do then?"

"I commit suicide," Carolina responded, laughing. "But changing the subject, what do I have to do to get a security badge? I am told that I can't even go up to my room and unpack if I don't have one."

"That's right," colonel Treviño answered, signaling in the direction of one of his aides. The aide approached them. "Captain, the lieutenant needs her security badge so she can go up to her room and freshen up."

He turned toward Carolina, who only then realized that she probably looked as tired as she felt.

"Carolina, why don't you go upstairs and rest a while? We'll all get together in the main dining room about three thirty to eat, and then we can schedule everything." He studied Carolina's face, which showed deep, dark circles under her eyes. She looked emaciated. "As a matter of fact, why don't you take a nap? You look tired, and remember that we are doing the security sweep at five. You need to be there to translate between all the foreign security teams."

Carolina gave him a weak smile, nodding her head in agreement.

"Thanks," she said. "That is precisely what I plan to do. Furthermore, I have already met one of the security agents from *Gringoland*; a rather unpleasant guy, but he has a simply divine dog."

Just minutes after snapping a photograph of her, the captain handed her a badge which identified her as an officer at the highest security level on the president's staff.

With the badge hanging from her neck on a chain that looked like the one she'd used as a child to avoid losing the key to her house when she went out to play with her friends, Carolina headed for the elevators. The security guards, zealous in their duty, checked her badge before allowing her to enter the upper floors of the hotel, even though they had known her for years.

"*Hola, hola*," she greeted the empty space upon entering the suite that she would be sharing for the next week.

There was no response, which was nice. At least she wouldn't have to make conversation with her roommates. The living room was nicely furnished with rattan furniture upholstered in bright colors, and it had a small dining room in a little niche that led out to a terrace with a beautiful view of the sea. She peeked through the open door into the bedroom, but her colleagues had arrived earlier and were already installed in the room.

So I guess I'll be sleeping in the living room, she thought to herself.

She placed her luggage on the floor next to the couch, and immediately picked up the phone. She heard the three clicks that meant that the telephone system was controlled by the Presidential Staff's Office, and pushed the three, which would give her a direct line to Mexico City without having to dial the area code. She dialed the number for her home in Mexico City, and the governess answered.

"Hi Lupita," she greeted her. "How is everything going there?"

"Carolina, it's so good to hear from you!" exclaimed her housekeeper.

Lupita had worked for the family since the birth of Mauricio, Carolina's youngest. Her son was about to turn ten. Lupita was part of the family, and Carolina acknowledged the fact that she depended far too much on her, but she had no other choice. She had been widowed at the age of thirty with two small children, and her work required a great deal of travel.

"I'm already in Cozumel, girlfriend."

"You're kidding... I thought you'd be in Mexico City for at least a day between trips. What happened?" Lupita couldn't mask the disappointment in her voice.

"Just part of the job, Lupita. I had no choice, believe me. Are the kids home? I am really short on time, but I wanted to talk to them..."

"No, they're not home. Mauricio had a Boy Scout meeting, and Margarita had her ballet class. Thomas came for them just after lunch, and he's bringing them home about seven this evening. But Miss Robin is here. Do you want to talk to her?"

"Yes, Lupita, if you'd put her on... we'll see you soon, *amiga*."

In a couple of minutes Robin answered, a dear friend of Carolina's who had lived with her since the death of her husband three years earlier. She was an American, but had lived in Mexico since her days as a student at the University of Guanajuato, where the two women had met.

"Hi there, lady, where are you?"

"Already in Cozumel. I only had about three seconds to change planes in Mexico City and they didn't give me a chance to even run by the house. How are the children?"

"A pain in the butt, but they're fine. Don't worry about them.

Between Lupe and me, we've got them toeing the line. When are you coming home?"

"With a little luck, either Monday night or early Tuesday."

"How did it go in Washington?"

"I'll tell you all about it when I get back. You have no idea, friend of mine... no idea."

"Sounds interesting. A guy?"

Carolina nearly doubled over laughing, despite her exhaustion.

"Not exactly. An old, decrepit and disgusting wolf, that's all."

"Yuck... you'll have to tell me all about it. You sound tired." Robin's voice showed concern for her friend.

"A little bit. You know how flying affects me. But I better go, because I haven't even unpacked and I need to be in uniform and ready to go to work after lunch."

"Well, you take care of yourself, and we'll see you the beginning of next week."

"Okay, but Robin, thanks for being there."

"Gee, yeah... it's so difficult! You leave me with a house, food, servants, chauffeurs and two children that adore me. You have no idea what a sacrifice it is to be here!"

Carolina laughed.

"I really appreciate it anyway, girlfriend. Ciao..."

Before allowing herself the luxury of getting homesick, she decided to unpack her clothes, worried that everything would be too wrinkled to use it, and she didn't have time to iron anything.

She hurriedly unpacked her things, but there was no closet in the living room that would have to be her bedroom for the next few days. She hung her uniforms on a hook on the back of the bathroom door and put her underwear and nightgowns in one of the drawers under the television stand. She was relieved to find that her things weren't too wrinkled. She put her purse on the same television stand, but first removed her gun, which she placed under a cushion on the sofa bed where she planned to rest her tired head a few minutes later.

At least I have the television, she thought out loud, and without bothering to open the sofa bed, she lay down on the couch, using the cushions to elevate her feet because they were swollen from the flights. She picked up the remote control and turned on the television, and immediately lowered the volume. She found a news channel, and the sound of the mellifluous voice of the reporter talking about the latest terrorism attack in Israel lulled her to sleep.

Her dreams took her to a place she avoided remembering when awake.

The lights of the ancient city sparkled in the night fog which lay like a blanket over picturesque plaza during the cold months of autumn and winter, but the city's symphonic orchestra played a beautiful waltz despite the snowflakes that still fell lightly. The ground was lightly dusted with a powdery snow that had fallen earlier, and as they crossed the plaza, they stopped to watch a puppeteer with some intricately carved wooden puppets dressed in the typical outfits of Old Brussels. The dances that the woman made them do made Carolina laugh, but suddenly one of the puppets turned toward her, with a grotesque face.

Carolina tried to get away, but the puppet's face became more and more sinister; it was baring its teeth and jumping against Carolina's leg, trying to bite her.

Carolina screamed, but both Mauricio and the puppeteer had turned toward her with the same grotesque faces as the puppet...

Carolina awoke to the sound of the key in the lock of the door to her suite. Through pure instinct, she grabbed the gun from its hiding place, and with a snap, she loaded the chamber before greeting the intruder:

"Who's there?" she asked with a hoarse voice, pointing the gun toward the front door.

"Calm down, woman! It's just us!"

"Good God! I am so sorry!" she said feeling mortified, as she lowered her gun, put the safety on and hid it discreetly. "I'm turning into a trained seal."

She rose from the couch to greet her two colleagues. Lorena was elegantly attired in a white pant suit and a sky-blue blouse with a low neckline. She was the first to approach Carolina, and gave her a hug.

"We were beginning to give you up for dead, woman," she said as she kissed the air next to both Carolina's cheeks. "How did it go in Washington?"

"It went well, thanks," she responded, wondering how she knew about her trip to Washington, and then she turned to Susana.

Susana was a majestic woman. She was nearly six feet tall, but with a nice body and not awkward at all, despite her height. She always dressed demurely, but regardless of her modest wardrobe, she gave off an intangible sensuality that seemed to be a magnet for the opposite sex. She was wearing a simple outfit that was the same color as Lorena's blouse.

"Did you two get together on what to wear today, or do you both play in the same orchestra?" Carolina asked after hugging her other friend. "I'm sorry I don't have anything in that color, so I guess I'll just have to go buy something to fit into the trio.

Her two roommates looked at each other from head to toe, and they laughed.

"I swear I hadn't even noticed," Susana said. "How charming we must have looked at lunch!"

Lorena stood on her tippy-toes to kiss Susana's cheek.

"They'll just think we're Lesbies, darling..." she said in an exaggeratedly sexy voice.

"You're both crazy!" Carolina said laughing, and then she stopped suddenly as if someone had dumped a bucket of ice water over her head. "Did you say lunch?"

Susana and Lorena nodded their heads.

"Oh my God!" Carolina exclaimed. "I was supposed to meet Treviño for lunch to accompany him on the security sweep at five o'clock. What time do you have?"

"It's five before five," Lorena said, looking at the gold Rolex that her paramour had given her the night before as a remembrance of a lovely evening.

"Nice little watch you have there, *amiga*," Carolina said over her shoulder as she ran to the bathroom to put her uniform on and get to the security meeting on time, since she hadn't shown up for the lunch. "Dare I ask what bank you robbed to buy it?" she asked with a diabolic laugh.

"It's just a knock-off," Lorena lied. "They sell them for a hundred dollars all over the duty free zone."

Three minutes later, Carolina came out of the bathroom freshened up and uniformed, still tying her hair into a regulation bun.

"I won't even say goodbye," she called out to her two companions who were then seated at the dining room table drinking some beer they'd found in the minibar. "but be nice, *Chicas*. Save me one, okay?"

As she walked out to the hallway, she stretched the neckline of her uniform blouse to pull out the chain with the coveted security badge, and she placed it over her chest where anyone could see it. She glanced at herself in the mirror that lined the entire wall between the elevators while she was waiting, and she realized that too many skipped meals had made her lose a few pounds that she had needed to lose anyway. She was only five foot two, so every pound showed far too much. Satisfied with her appearance, she turned to wait for the elevator.

When the doors opened, she took a step inside and found Colonel Treviño, also in uniform. She saluted him, and waited for the Colonel to return her military salute before lowering her arm.

"Good afternoon, Colonel," she said formally. Even though she spoke informally with most of her military superiors when alone with them or when they were dressed as civilians, she always addressed them formally if they were uniformed or in public.

"Good afternoon, Lieutenant," the Colonel responded with an apologetic tone. "I hope you will forgive me for not coming down to lunch as we had planned, but the truth of the matter is that when I went upstairs to my room to change, I fell asleep."

Carolina couldn't help but laugh.

"I did the same thing, so we're even."

The Colonel smiled at her, and they rode the elevator to the lobby in silence.

When the elevator doors opened, the Colonel waited for Carolina to exit first, and then he followed her. As he followed her across the lobby toward the Security Command Center, he couldn't help but admire his subordinate. He calculated her to be, at the most, thirty five, but she had the figure of a teenager. Her step was light, but firm and her posture erect. By the way she wore her hair, the Colonel imagined it must have been long, but he couldn't remember ever having seen her with her hair down in the four years that he had known her. Inexplicably, at that moment, he would have given anything to see Carolina with her hair down.

When Carolina opened the door to the Command center where all of the others were waiting, the Colonel was jolted from his fantasy back into the real world. There were officers there from The United States, France, Spain and Mexico. They were all carrying their own electronic explosive detection equipment. The officials from Spain and the United States had their dogs with them, as did the Mexicans who had their star sniffer, Venus, leashed and ready, but the the French officials had the most sensitive of all the detectors on earth: an authentic terrorist.

Carolina had met him a few months before in a summit meeting in Nice, but she realized that the Colonel hadn't been on that trip, so she hurriedly and discreetly explained what was going on before the Colonel recognized the man's face from the political jackets that all presidential security personnel had memorized.

"Colonel," she whispered to him, "I am certain you have recognized the man who is with the French, but I assure you he is here to help." The Colonel looked in that direction and Carolina sensed his body becoming tense. "He often finds things that neither the electronic equipment nor the dogs find, and he has been brought here and has been paid by the French. They firmly believe that a sane mind cannot possibly predict what an insane mind will do."

"And what if someone else pays him more than the French have?" the Colonel mused.

"To tell you the truth, that had never occurred to me," Caroline said, "but I know that he is accepted all over the world when there are summit meetings where France is involved. But if you're uncomfortable with his presence or his particular expertise, we can organize one last sweep with Venus after he has left. I understand that he never sticks around for the summits. He always leaves a couple of days before they begin, after declaring the place clean."

"Normally, I wouldn't care at all," the Colonel whispered, "but normally we aren't hosting the summit. Twenty two heads of state under the same roof is an unusual situation, and I think we will be doing another sweep after he has gone.

"Unusual? It might be more accurate to say it's a nightmare, but okay. We'll have to tell the Americans, the Spanish and the French before doing it," Carolina reminded him, "because they have the same right as we do and they may want to participate."

"And they are more than welcome to do so," the Colonel said, and then he addressed the group on the other side of the Command Center. "Gentlemen, welcome to Mexico!"

After the necessary introductions for which Carolina interpreted, the group divided the hotel in four parts. Each team would sweep all four parts, but not at the same time.

If any one of the explosive teams were to detect a hot zone, they would notify the rest of the teams to locate and disarm any explosive artifact that might be there.

During the entire week before the arrival of the foreign security teams, the officers of the Fifth Division of the Presidential Staff's Office had interviewed every one of the hotel employees. They had disqualified more than fifty; some of them because they were Central or South Americans illegally in the country; others because they had no documents to prove their citizenship even though they were obviously Mexican; others because they had criminal records... and some others just because the officer in charge deemed it necessary. None of them had been fired, but they had been given a week of vacation time, fully paid by the Presidential Staff's Office.

Soldiers from the closest military base to Cozumel had taken over for the workers that had to be replaced, and the change had been done in a completely transparent manner. The soldiers were all using the hotel uniforms; from the bellboys to the waiters, maids and kitchen helpers. Fortunately, the hotel chefs were Mexican citizens and had no criminal records, and were recognized internationally only for their culinary abilities and talents.

The sweep went on for more than three hours, and none of the teams had found anything. After each team had swept their particular fourth section, they all gathered in the hotel lobby, and were lounging around on the rattan couches with their tropical flower print covers.

The French chief of security rose to his feet.

"Gentlemen," he said with a strong British accent, "if only the security chief from each country would car to accompany us, I would like our terrorism expert to conduct a walk-through inspection of the building before we consider it secured."

Carolina leaned toward the Colonel and explained that the French security chief had invited him to do the last sweep through the hotel with his terrorism expert.

As soon as the four security chiefs had gone off with the terrorist expert, Carolina got comfortable in her seat and rested her head against the back pillow. She looked around, and realized that over half of the teams present had done the same, and two of them were asleep.

She was thankful for the moment of peace brought to them by one considered to be one of the more blood-thirsty terrorists in the world.

Suddenly the lobby became a beehive of activity. Carolina didn't have her radio with her. She stood up and searched until she found a captain from the Fifth Division.

"Has something happened, Captain?" Carolina asked.

The captain held his hand up with his palm outward to quiet Carolina as he listened to the transmission through a small earphone. Then he lowered his hand and spoke to her:

"They've found an explosive on the fifth floor of the hotel, two stories below Potus' suite. They are about to disarm the bomb," he said in a low voice.

"Who are?"

"The French that found it, us and the Gringos, I believe..."

But Carolina was already walking toward the elevator bank, aware of the tragedy that could ensue if the different groups disarming the bomb couldn't understand one another.

The security agents were waiting for her with the elevator doors open.

"They are waiting for you on the fifth floor, Ma'am," one of them said as he took her arm to help her board the elevator.

Carolina hesitated in the doorway. Another security team member was inside, holding something that looked like the astronaut gear that he seemed to be wearing just like the other young explosives expert. It was only at that moment that Carolina realized that she could be running a risk by going up to the floor where the bomb had been discovered.

She gulped, and mustered up some courage. *It is just an astronaut suit; it is only a costume, and nothing will happen!* she repeated to herself over and again, in silence.

"Good afternoon," she said to the astronaut who was holding out the suit to her." The suit is really very pretty, but don't you have it in a more feminine color?" Her joke fell on deaf ears, and the young officer didn't respond. She was very nervous, but kept it up. "Could you help me put it on? I'm not used to these weird things. It's my first trip to outer space."

At least she got smile out of him this time.

Before reaching the fifth floor, she had the suit on. She felt like the suit weighed as much or more than she did, but she didn't complain.

When the elevator doors opened, two men were waiting for them, and Carolina followed them to the suite. At the suite door three men were awaiting her: one was French, one American and a Mexican that she recognized as an officer from the Fifth Division that she only knew by sight.

"Captain," she said to the Mexican, "how may I help you?"

"Please, explain to them that I fully acknowledge the fact that they are familiar with C5 plastic explosive, and if the bomb were only made of *plastique,* I would be happy to let them disarm it," he explained. "However, the detonator is digital, and it is connected with a catalyst that they are not familiar with because it is something that was invented in Mexico: it's called Mexamon. It is odorless, which is why none of the dogs detected it, and electronic detectors only detect nitrates, so they didn't work, either.

Carolina translated the Captain's words, first to French, and then to English. The two foreigners admitted that they had no experience with the explosive the Captain had mentioned, although they were aware of its existence.

The Captain continued the explanation:

"The problem with disarming this is in the instability of the Mexamon. In its inert stage, it looks like somewhat like coarsely ground rose quartz. When mixed with water, it becomes very unstable. Whoever made this bomb knew exactly what he was doing. He placed the *plastique,* then the detonator, and then mixed the Mexamon. He only had a few seconds to cover the bomb, because just ten seconds after it is mixed, it explodes if it's moved. By the same token, to move it in order to get to the detonator, we run the risk of detonating the bomb. The terrorist left it as an insurance policy of sorts.

Carolina translated his explanation to the Captain, and the two other foreigners nodded in agreement. The higher ranking officer of the two took a deep breath, and addressed the Captain through Carolina's translation:

"We are familiar with Mexamon, but we have no experience dealing with the substance. What is the disarming process?"

The Captain shook his head, and his face took on an expression that bordered on irony.

"To tell the truth, this is the first time we have dealt with the explosive armed this way," he said, but upon noting the alarmed expressions on all faces present, he hurriedly continued: "Of course we have disarmed simulations, but the truth of the matter is that this is the first time that we'll be doing it for real, so I suggest that we evacuate this entire part of the hotel, except for absolutely essential personnel. Among those is the French expert, who has offered to help. Although he won't admit it openly, he seems to have some experience with this particular explosive."

No one moved. The French chief of security seemed slightly amused by the paid terrorist's accomplishment is discovering the artifact, and the other foreign officers exchanged looks. Carolina felt paralyzed by this unexpected and unusual evacuation of a hotel. Finally, with a trembling voice, she addressed the foreign officers.

"I believe the best way to proceed would be for us all to return to the Command Center in the lobby to coordinate an orderly evacuation, without causing panic," she said and then she turned toward the Captain. "Captain, are you staying?"

The Captain only stared at Carolina, appreciating her intervention. *The fewer people on this floor, the better,"* he thought.

"Yes," he answered. "I will give the evacuation order, but I don't want anyone in the Command Center, either. No one. I mean it," he said with a nod in the direction of his subordinate who was standing near the elevator doors.

Carolina was relieved to realize that she wouldn't have to stay in the hotel while they disarmed the bomb, but she made a special effort not to show the urgency that she felt to get on the elevator that would take her to a much safer place.

She quickly gave the necessary explanations to the foreign officials, and then she accompanied them to the elevator. They rode down in silence, and all of them had removed their protective suits before they reached the ground floor.

When the doors opened, the lobby was empty with the exception of two officers from the Presidential Staff's Office waiting for them next to the elevators.

Carolina stooped down to pick up the suits while her companions rushed out, but one of the officers hurried her.

"Don't stop to pick up the suits, Carolina. We're the last to exit the hotel and they can't give the *all clear* until we're out of here."

Carolina didn't understand what the problem was since they were seven floors from the bomb, but she dropped the suits. The officer smiled at her.

"Come on, woman!" he said as he took her by the arm. "As far as we know, whoever planted the bomb will detonate it as soon as he's figured out that we found it."

Carolina hastened her step and followed the officer as fast as she could.

Chapter 2

The group gathered next to Cozumel Bay less than one hundred yards from the Hotel Melia looked like the cast of extras in a bad international intrigue movie. Each and every race and ethnicity in the world seemed to be portrayed by its own traditional garb, and there was a humming whisper of different languages clashing together in an off-key chant.

The entrance to the facility which was to house the summit meeting was cordoned off to block its access to both vehicles and pedestrians, and a platoon of uniformed military men had mounted a security blockade around the evacuees that were gathered in small groups, talking.

A few waiters from the hotel wandered through the group with trays of refreshments, serving beers with slices of lime, Rum and Cokes, High Balls, Margaritas, and Mojitos to the hot, thirsty guests sitting out under the Autumn Caribbean sun.

When she reached the security zone where the rest of the evacuees were, Carolina had found her roommates quickly, and was now seated with them. Susana gave her a cold beer, and Carolina accepted it gratefully. She took a long sip of the icy liquid, and sighed.

"You have no idea!" she exclaimed. "Few things have tasted quite as good to me in my entire life! Thanks, *amigas*."

Lorena was lying on the grass, using her purse as a cushion. Her white pant suit was already stained, but she didn't seem to care.

She was drinking her third beer as she enjoyed the afternoon sun. She stared at Carolina intensely.

"We figured you'd be with the guys from security," she said to Carolina, "but sooner or later they were bound to get you out safe and sound," she said as she held her beer high without sitting up. "So here's to your health, dear friend!"

Susana also raised the High Ball she was drinking in Carolina's direction to toast to her safety.

"Cheers!" said Susana, clinking her glass against the Carolina's beer bottle. "And now, would you like to tell us what in damnation is going on? Was there a bomb, or what?"

Carolina hesitated. She hadn't even thought about asking anybody about what cover they would be using to explain the sudden evacuation of the hotel. But as she looked around her, she realized that it would be ridiculous to invent an excuse with a group of people as accustomed to summit meetings all over the world as this one was. Furthermore, they all seemed so perfectly at ease that it seemed to Carolina that they were obviously either informed about what was going on, or they simply had figured it all out for themselves.

She smiled at her colleagues.

"Yes, apparently there is a bomb on the fifth floor."

"Who is programmed for that room?" Lorena asked lackadaisically.

"I have no idea," Carolina answered, "but it's *plastique* with some other strange thing, and the impression I got was that it would have blown a number of floors up and down if it had detonated."

Susana laughed.

"What I do know is that Potus is being housed on the seventh floor, so among others, he was probably the target," she said as she stretched her legs out in front of her. "Have you noticed how white I am? I really need a tan."

Lorena lifted her head slightly.

"Yeah, so I see. You look like a *gringa*." She laid her head back against her purse again, and yawned. "Who is Potus?"

"President of The United States," Carolina and Susana sang out together.

A number of heads turned in their direction, but soon returned to their own conversations.

At that point, a limousine was approaching the entrance of the hotel. It parked in front of the hotel entrance that was cordoned off, and the shrill voice of a woman arguing with the military guards got the three women's attention.

"Who's that?" Susana asked.

Carolina shrugged her shoulders and focused her attention on the voice of the mysterious woman whose tone of voice was rising by the minute.

Lorena sat up and took off her dark glasses to better observe the cause of the noise. She gazed at the woman a moment, and then lay down again.

"It's Tanya Monteblanco," she said dryly. "You can bet she is on one of her missions."

"What missions? Is she going to sing here?" Carolina asked.

The two other women laughed with marked sarcasm. Lorena faked a very innocent tone and said:

"I don't think so. As a matter of fact, I think she's going to dance!" She laughed again, with Susana.

"Yeah, she's going to dance, all right," Susana said between giggles, "the horizontal tango, that is!"

"Meeeoooowwww!" Lorena added, "Careful... here she comes."

Tanya was headed directly for them, swaying her hips as she walked as only she knew how to do. She was wearing while silk flare-legged slacks, with a shawl in the same material that barely covered her voluptuous torso. Carolina rose to her feet, and walked out to meet the diva, not without realizing that everyone there, both men and women alike, had turned their heads to admire her. The actress looked beautiful, and her mere presence commanded attention. Her long raven-black hair floated in the air as she walked, and her posture was regal.

Tanya held her arms out to Carolina as the woman neared her. Carolina hugged her and kissed the air next to the actress' cheek.

"How nice to see you, Tanya!" she said sincerely. "What a surprise to see you here!"

The actress returned Carolina's kiss. She felt infinitely more comfortable in this place having found someone she knew.

"You have no idea how happy I am to find a friend!" she answered. "With all this nonsense about not letting us into the hotel, it is kind of hard for me to discreetly hide out without anyone knowing I'm here!" Noting the confused expression on Carolina's face, she continued: "Porfirio had told me that you'd be here and he said he was going to call you later, but you know how I hate crowds of people."

Carolina smiled at her. The bit about their being friends was just a bit exaggerated since they had only seen each other three or four times in the past ten years, but she had always liked the actress, and she liked the fact that she would refer to her as a friend. On the other hand, her referring to the Presidential Chief of Staff as "Porfirio" had seemed strange to Carolinas, as had her friends' remarks about Tanya Monteblanco's horizontal tangos.

But Carolina had always considered good manners to be of the highest importance, and she put her curiosity far from her mind.

"I'm sure they'll let us back in soon," she assured the actress, "but in the meanwhile, why don't you join us for something nice and cold to drink?"

Without waiting for an affirmative or a negative answer, Carolina took the actress by the arm and guided her toward her roommates.

"Girls, look who I found!" she announced as she approached them. The two women stood and cordially greeted Tanya.

After greeting them, she turned to Carolina again.

"I would give my first born for a beer," she said.

Carolina laughed, and took a Tres Equis beer from the tray that a waiter was carrying near them at that moment, and a slice of lime.

"Here's a beer for you," she said cheerfully as she handed the beer to Tanya, "but you can keep your first born. I have more than enough children, but thanks for the offer."

Tanya accepted the beer, and took a long drink of it, and then sucked on the lime.

"Aaaah!" she exclaimed. "There is nothing as wonderful as an icy cold beer."

She sat on the grass without giving a second thought to perhaps staining her exquisite white silk suit. The three other women followed her lead, sitting on the grass as she had.

After another long sip of her beer, Tanya leaned forward, making a movement with her hands to tell the other women to gather close. They did.

"And now, who is going to tell me the gossip? Why are we being corralled outside the hotel?"

Carolina hesitated a moment, but then she shrugged her shoulders. The rumor had probably been spread everywhere among the different groups, so it didn't seem necessary to hide that which was no longer a secret, anyway.

"They detected some rather dangerous explosives on the fifth floor, and they won't let us back in until they have disarmed the bomb." She noted the alarmed expression on Tanya's face, and she hurriedly assured her. "But don't worry about it, *amiga*. This is normal around here. Believe me when I say that nothing out of the ordinary will happen."

Tanya's face relaxed. Lorena and Susana laughed and Lorena held out her hand to then take Tanya's forearm.

"Don't be alarmed, sweetie... this is something like our daily bread. Believe me; nothing even remotely strange is happening."

Tanya's face relaxed. Lorena and Susana laughed and Lorena held out her hand to touch Tanya's forearm.

"Don't worry, *amiga*," she assured her, "Porfirio's three *chicas* will take good care of you!" She laughed again good-heartedly, and then became more serious. "Don't tell me this is your first summit meeting?"

Tanya nodded her head. "Yes, I'm afraid it is. So you'll have to forgive me if I'm a little nervous." She turned to stare at the strange crowd of people who were forming different small groups that you could only tell apart by the regional dress of their countries. Her gaze rested on one of the members of the Saudi Arabian entourage who was staring at her intensely. The guy was attractive, but he had a somewhat mysterious and frightening air about him. Tanya felt as if his stare was burning a hole through her, and she had to avert her eyes.

Susana had noticed the exchange of gazes, and she laughed.

"Careful with that one, sweetie," she said in a low voice, "that is Abdul-Al-Horny."

"Who?" Tanya let out an involuntary chuckle.

Lorena drew closer with a Machiavellian grin.

"We call him that because the first time that we met him at a summit in Switzerland, the guy made indecent propositions to every one of us, one by one."

"And which of you accepted?" she asked, giggling, but she noticed that the question had not amused the three women, so she corrected herself promptly. "It's just a joke, girls, just a joke!" she added.

"Well, if you had seen how Carolina had breakfast with him alone in his suite one day, you could probably guess," Susana answered with a teasing sing-song in her tone of voice.

Carolina slapped her arm.

"Only because he is my counterpart in protocol, you naughty bitch," she said to Susana, who was now rubbing her arm and laughing uncontrollably, "and for your further information, he was a complete gentleman."

"Of that, I have no doubts," said Susana, "because I'm quite sure not a hair on his head is gay."

Carolina continued, paying no attention whatsoever to Susana's teasing.

"Actually," she continued, "I find him quite efficient, and of all the royal protocol directors, he is the most accessible and reasonable when we have to accommodate the rules of royalty with international governmental protocol when dealing with a mixture of heads of state and royalty," she turned in the direction of Susana to throw her an snooty look for all her roommates teasing, "and furthermore, he is a very nice guy who has never even tried to get fresh with me."

"Well, you'd be the only one in the Presidential Staff's Office that he hasn't tried to seduce, my dear," said Lorena.

Carolina ignored her colleague's remark, and she addressed Tanya again.

"If I'm not being too indiscreet, what is it that brings you to the summit meeting?" By the expression on Tanya's face, she realized that her rather direct question had bothered the chorus girl, and she tried to back out of it. "What I mean is..." but she didn't know what to say, and knew she was blushing right up to the tip of her ears.

Tanya laughed.

"Don't try to fix it," she said between peals of laughter. "The truth of the matter is that I have absolutely no idea why I'm here. I only know that the General sent an officer to invite me to the summit, and he said that perhaps I could help him with the Prime Minister of Canada, because he wanted to have some private conversations with him, and of course, I speak Canadian French."

"You do?" Lorena interrupted.

"Well, being that I'm Canadian by birth and only naturalized as a Mexican, yes. Didn't you know that?"

"No," Lorena said, surprised, and she sat up straight on the jacket that she had been using as a blanket on the grass. "But you look Mexican."

"My father was Argentine, and my mother is French-Canadian, so I grew up speaking as much French as Spanish, and the Mexican accent was something I just picked up as a young girl when we came to live in Mexico."

"So I see," Lorena said, and lay down on the grass again.

Susana and Carolina exchanged looks, as if they had both been thinking exactly the same thing. The General wouldn't call an actress of questionable repute to be an interpreter. It just wasn't his style.

What neither of the women knew was if Tanya suspected what her real mission was at the summit meeting.

Carolina became pensive for a few moments, pondering whether or not to prepare the woman for what might be going on. All her friends and colleagues always told her that she suffered from a mother hen syndrome, because of her constant warnings and sermons regarding the licentious behavior they could and should expect from all the powerful people that surrounded them. But she decided not to say anything to Tanya. Tanya was quite a bit older than Carolina, and should certainly know how to take care of herself. Furthermore, Carolina wasn't altogether convinced that the woman didn't know exactly where she was headed. She was no innocent child, unlike so many of the military and civilian women in the teams of interpreters, pages and flight attendants from the Presidential Staff's Office.

They realized, suddenly, that the forced evacuation was over. People were beginning to leave the gardens, so the four women got up to follow the crowds back to the hotel.

Standing at the door of the lobby waiting for the people in front of them to file into the hotel, Lorena turned to the other three women.

"Listen! Just in case we are all so busy the next couple of days that we don't even have time to make plans, why don't we plan to get together in the *Up Wheels* to have a drink together?"

Tanya laughed. "The *Up Wheels*? What's that?"

"The *Up Wheels* is a party we have when the planes carrying the heads of state have taken off and their landing gear is raised, because there's no longer any danger of a magnicide. All the staffs get together in the different presidential suites to have a few drinks out of the bottles left in the suites. It's sort of a tradition. Furthermore, if we don't drink it, what are they going to do with it? Throw it out? There are even wonderful, gourmet goodies to eat, too."

"Well, you can count on me," Tanya said. "Do you know which suite you're having it in?"

"There are always a few to choose from," Lorena said. "But just so we don't break the tradition, how about it if we meet in President Santos del Alba's suite? And then from there we can run around and say our farewells to everyone in the other parties. Sound good?"

The four women agreed on the time and place to get together to toast the accomplishments of the summit meeting, and then went off to their rooms to get ready for the official events that ensued.

Chapter 3

"Does anyone need the bathroom in the next half hour?" Carolina asked when she and Lorena and Susana were back in their room. She was taking off her shoes and felt like her clothes were glued to her body because of all the humidity out in the hotel gardens. "I urgently need a bath, and a bubble bath would be heaven about now."

"I couldn't agree more," Lorena said, "and I know a place where all three of us fit! Put your bathing suits on, and let's go, ok?"

"Where?" Susana asked. She was much too tired to take part in one of her friend's antics.

"Well, let me tell you, girlfriend," Lorena said in a sing-song. "There is a suite being used as a lounge for the interpreters and pages that aren't staying here in the hotel, and it turns out that it has a hot tub big enough for about ten people. We're interpreters, aren't we? And since there aren't any official activities today, who is going to tell us we can't use it? And let me tell you that I went by to see it this afternoon, and it is fully stocked with hors d'oeuvres, drinks and anything else a self-respecting interpreter could possibly want. Let's go!"

Susana and Carolina exchanged looks, and they smiled. Finally, a truly pleasant idea had occurred to Lorena, who normally came up with things that were so crazy, that sooner or later they would get them all in trouble with the high command.

They quickly put on their bathing suits, and went out into the hotel hallway after donning long caftans to hide their bathing suits. Susana and Carolina had started out for the elevators when Lorena stopped them.

"No! It's better if no one sees us, because if they do, we'll have half the Presidential Staff's Office in that suite with us, and that will defeat the entire purpose of being able to relax a while. We'd better take the service stairs, because the suite is right next to the concierge's office, so we can get in through the service entrance."

Carolina laughed. "Boy, Lorena! One can hardly tell you're going with a cop. You are getting more mysterious every day."

Lorena spun around on her heels, and bowed before Carolina. "Please, my dear girl. Not with a cop, but with the Father of all cops."

"Yes," Susana added, "with Poppa Smurf."

"What do you mean, Poppa Smurf?" Lorena hissed, feeling very offended.

"Haven't you noticed that ridiculous uniform that the cops in Mexico City are using? With that sky blue suit and the little white boots, I swear they look like smurfs. So the supreme boss has to be Poppa Smurf, doesn't he?"

Lorena threw her head back and howled despite herself.

"You're absolutely right!" she said between howls of laughter. "I have to tell Arnulfo about that one. He'll love it!" She turned and opened a door at the end of the hallway. "Here we are."

Lorena held the door open for her friends to enter the service stairs, and soon they had climbed down the four floors to the Concierge's office, where they discreetly found the lounging suite.

It was even better than how Lorena had described it. The hot tub was out on the terrace with a beautiful view of the ocean, and the afternoon breeze had cooled things down to the point where the hot tub was very inviting.

The suite was nicely furnished with a number of groupings of couches, desks and computers, and Carolina walked around the whole room, checking the sound system to the interpreting booths and the main summit enclosure. She couldn't test the system until the following day when she could turn the equipment on in the booths and in the meeting room, but she had checked enough equipment in the past to be able to immediately recognize if the technical team had done a good job or if it had been done sloppily.

This time it had been done well, and she smiled, satisfied with their work. She went to the refrigerator and took out three mineral waters, and she opened them to take them out to her friends.

When she came out onto the terrace, she breathed deeply to enjoy the fragrance of the tropical night air.

"Mmmm... it smells like Hawaii!" she said nostalgically as she handed a drink to each girl.

"That's because of the Night-blooming Jasmine, which smells a lot like Pikaki from Hawaii," Susana said, and then she laughed. "And that is something I know thanks to Alejandro."

"Alejandro who?" Lorena asked, visibly bothered by the fact that her friend hadn't taken her into her confidence regarding any new love affairs with anyone by the name of Alejandro. "What secrets have you been hiding from me, *amiga*?"

"Yeah," Carolina said as she removed her caftan and got into the hot tub. "Tell us all about it, and don't leave out any details," she added, sighing deeply as she enjoyed the bubbly water that seemed to soften her tense skin after so many days on the road. She scooted down in the seat on the opposite end of the tub from her friends, rested her head on the marble edge, and closed her eyes. "I need to hear a good romantic story to revive my spirit. You have no idea the hell I have been through the last few days."

"So tell us about it," Lorena said.

"Nope. It's Susana's turn first," Carolina responded lazily, "and then I'll tell you about it."

Susana hesitated a moment, but then decided to take them into her confidence. After all, the three women had been working together for years, and they had shared their stories about so many loves and ex-loves, breakups and make ups. What harm could it do for them to know that she was dating one of the most powerful men in the country?

"It's Alejandro Sansores," she said, and waited for her friends' reaction.

"The old goat that's Secretary of Foreign Relations?" Lorena asked with a shrill in her tone that bordered on hysteria. "Yuck!"

"And I suppose Poppa Smurf only appears old and decrepit? And at night he turns into a beautiful and sensual young man?"

Lorena shook herself without feeling really offended.

"The truth is that I had never thought about it, but you're right. Arnulfo is not exactly an Adonis, is he? Sorry, girlfriend. Go on telling us."

Susana went back to telling them what was going on in her life.

"Do you remember after the trip to Switzerland, I took some time off alone to go to Andorra?" Lorena and Carolina nodded their heads. "Well, on the commercial flight that I took to Barcelona to go on from there to Andorra, Alejandro Sansores sat next to me... and before either one of you says one word, I can assure you that it was a pure coincidence. He was going to Barcelona on a mission for Mr. President, and from there he was to return to Mexico."

"And then?" Lorena wanted every juicy detail.

"Well, we got to talking about a thousand insignificant things on the plane while we drank quite a few Mimosas, and the truth of the matter is that both of us had a little too much to drink. When we arrived in Barcelona, instead of renting a car, as I had planned to do, Alex invited me back to his hotel to get something to eat and rest for a while until the effects of what I had been drinking wore off before driving a car."

"Hah!" Carolina said with her eyes still closed. "So that's when the old man began the art of seduction?"

"As a matter of fact, no," Susana said, and then she laughed. "This is precisely what I find so attractive about him. He's not a flirt, nor is he a Casanova, and he is anything but vulgar. On the contrary, he is a total gentleman. After having lunch in the restaurant at the Hotel Princess Sophia, he took me to his suite, and I lay down on the couch with the idea of taking a little nap before leaving for Andorra, to the spa, you know."

"And you never made it to Andorra, right?" Lorena spoke in the mischievous tone that defined her personality.

"On the contrary. I didn't awake until the next morning, and I found myself alone in the suite. Alex had gone out, but not before leaving me a wonderful breakfast. On the breakfast tray, he had left a note attached to a beautiful white rose, and it said that he had sent for my luggage so that I could bathe and change comfortably. Then he said that once he had completed his mission at one o'clock that afternoon, he would feel honored to drive me personally to Andorra."

"And then the romance started. Right?" Lorena prodded for details.

"No, not really. I had my breakfast, bathed and dressed, and then he came for me at one. He had rented a car without a driver, which made me suspicious because I thought that he had done it to be discreet. You know, with all intentions of discreetly screwing me without a limousine driver as a witness."

"But it didn't turn out that way, did it?" Carolina knew Alejandro Sansores very well, and she considered him to be a true gentleman, incapable of committing any type of transgression.

"You know him well, don't you? Well, nothing improper happened. We arrived in Andorra around the dinner hour, and he had already reserved two connecting rooms in the best hotel in town. We enjoyed an exquisite evening, and then he accompanied me to my room, gave me a kiss on the cheek, and wished me a good night."

"And that was that?" Disillusion overwhelmed Lorena's tone of voice. "How boring!"

"Not by a long shot," Susana said. "On the contrary. It was something like an old fashioned date, like when we were teenagers and went out on dates with our little boyfriends who barely held our hands. He is a terribly sweet and romantic guy, but incapable of trickery with a lady."

"So then, what happened?"

"Well, that was, what? Two months ago? We spent that night in Andorra, and the next day we returned to Barcelona to catch our plane for Mexico. We sat together again, shared the deepest secrets of our lives, and arrived in Mexico. Period. Each back to our own lives, and all that, or at least that's what I thought," she said, smiling at her friends, "but it didn't turn out that way. He has invited me out at least twice a week since then, and we have had a wonderful time."

"But, no hanky-panky?" Lorena asked, stifling a yawn. "You bore me, girlfriend."

"Well, not until last week, when he invited me to Hawaii."

Carolina sat up straight and widened here eyes. "As far as I know, there was nothing official going on over there, because I'd have seen something on the President's schedule if there had been anything in Hawaii."

"No, there was nothing official. It was just super romantic, and he invited me one night while we were having dinner at the Mauna Loa Restaurant, in Mexico City. I was thoroughly enjoying the show, and he asked me if I had ever seen the show at the

Halekulani Hotel just at sunset on Waikiki Beach. I said that I hadn't, and just like that! He invited me to spend a week with him in Hawaii."

"Wow!" Lorena exclaimed. "What a place to spend a honeymoon!"

Carolina was very serious. She knew the whole story on the Secretary of Foreign Relations, and she knew he would never leave his wife. The poor woman was a paraplegic, the result of an automobile accident years before, and Alejandro Sansores was known for his absolute and sincere dedication to his wife. It was said that he had been driving the car, and because of his guilt feelings, he had never left his wife's side. Carolina feared that her friend would come out of her new romance deeply hurt.

"Ah, Susana," she said, "I can only imagine what a romantic and beautiful week you had, but do you know what you're doing? Everyone knows that Alejandro Sansores will never leave his wife, and I am so afraid you're going to get hurt, sooner or later."

Susana laughed.

"Carolina, I am perfectly aware of what I am doing. Take a good look at me, dear friend. I couldn't be less interested in marriage nor in a formal relationship with anybody. On the contrary. What I want is exactly what I have with Alejandro. He treats me like a queen, and we have a marvelous time together... and when we get home, we both go on our merry ways and live as we please."

"Yes," Carolina said with an embittered tone to her voice, "I know the syndrome very well. Each to his own home, each to his own life, each to his very own loneliness. He to his accompanied loneliness and you to your loneliness in solitude. Your children are with their father. And what about you, Susana? Don't you deserve more than this?"

"More than a man who really loves me, and treats me incredibly well? Look, Carolina. In this life, there are two types of women: Those left behind at home while their husbands run around with a lover, or the lovers who run around with another woman's husband. I have lived in both roles, and I prefer being the lover, not the one left behind."

Carolina reflected a moment before responding. She was the widow of a man who was very likely to have been unfaithful on their very honeymoon. By the same token, she had been the girlfriend of a married man; a brief affair that hadn't lasted, precisely because of the overwhelming loneliness she'd felt during their romance. Susana's words made a lot of sense, but she wasn't entirely in agreement.

"I don't know, Susana. I guess I would love nothing more than to find a man who could accept me as his wife and his lover at the same time. Don't you think that such a man exists in this world?"

"Yes, of course there are men like that," Lorena interrupted. "I have known many of them, and so have you. The only bad part is that they tend to be ugly, boring, poor and nerds."

The three women cracked up over Lorena's remark, but then turned serious.

It was absolutely true.

Carolina forced a smile.

"I truly am happy for you, Susana. If you're happy with him, that's all that counts."

"Thanks, Carolina, but now it's your turn. How did it go in Washington? What happened with the Potus problem?"

"The same as always," Carolina sighed. "If Castro came to the summit, Potus wouldn't, and at meant that the summit would be over before it began."

"And so he's coming?" Susana asked, but she knew the answer because they wouldn't be there if it were not the case.

"Yes, of course, but that means that Castro's participation has just been canceled, which did not please Mr. President in the least. Tomorrow there is a meeting between Castro and Santos del Alba in Cuba so that Santos del Alba can speak for Fidel at the summit."

"Are you going?" Lorena asked. "Can I go with you?"

"I still don't know. I imagine they'll tell me tonight when I get to our room if I have to go, but who knows? With everything that's happened this afternoon, they may just take Santos in a helicopter instead of the hydrofoil that was programmed, and if that happens, fewer people will be going. And no, Lorena, I am not in a high enough position to enjoy the privilege of inviting my friends on trips."

"What else happened in Washington? You seemed rather pissed when you got here," Susana's concerned had creased her brow in a frown.

Carolina told them all about what had happened with general Santiago, not leaving even the most minor of details, and their peals of laughter reached the ears of the hotel's concierge.

He entered the room and found the girls in the hot tub, and far from being disturbed by the encounter, he offered them a special supper of salad, fruit and cheese.

"Just what we need!" Carolina said, still stifling her laughter after remembering Alejandro's description of the General's facial expression when he found him in Carolina's bed, "but could you possibly send it to our suite? It's getting pretty late, and we have to get up at the crack of dawn with the birdies."

"Yes, Miss, I'd be happy to," the concierge responded as he discreetly exited the sweet, closing the door behind him.

In their suite a little later, the three women were in their pajamas enjoying the supper sent up by the kind concierge, when the hotel phone rang.

Carolina got up to answer it, and after a short exchange of words, returned to the table.

"Santos del Alba just arrived, and I am going to Cuba at nine in the morning. Potus will be arriving at eight tomorrow night, so we'll barely get back in time to receive him."

"Did you ask them if I can go?" Lorena never gave up.

"No, Lorena, I didn't ask them. It wasn't an option... I can assure you of that. But I have a mission for you, if you want it."

"Of course I want it."

Lorena quickly realized that it was a personal favor, because Carolina's expression changed. Her lips twisted into a half-smile, and her eyes twinkled.

Lorena laughed. "What's it about? By the look on your face, I have the feeling that it is something very personal. Am I going to follow some guy? Seduce a foreign dignitary?" She got up and lifted her right hand to her forehead as if giving a military salute, but not correctly. "Your wish is my command, Captain."

"Lieutenant," Carolina said giggling as she returned the girl's salute with an aired gesture, "but that's okay. Let me tell you that I am extremely curious about Tanya's mission, but it would be very indiscreet on my part if I were to ask her."

"And it would be even more indiscreet if she were to answer you," Susana added.

Carolina continued: "So," she said with a Machiavellian smile, "since you get along with her so well, watch her carefully, would you?"

Lorena seemed to think about it for a moment, but then she smiled at her friend.

"Okay, but why don't I just simply ask her? She is a very candid person, and I don't doubt that she would spill the beans with very little provocation from me. Remember when she was running around with Arzate Bachi, they would go out with Arnulfo and me. And even though they aren't seeing each other anymore, that doesn't mean that our friendship ended." She furrowed her brow in a worried expression. "Now that I think about it, girlfriend, why are you so interested in finding out what she's up to? Like I don't think she would ever meddle in your affairs, would she?"

Carolina hadn't really thought things through very well before asking for Lorena's help. It had completely slipped her mind that Lorena and Tanya really were friends. She apologized hurriedly.

"Gosh, Lorena, please forgive me! I would never put you into an uncomfortable position. I assure you that it was nothing more than simple curiosity on my part. It's just that for a while now, I have been forming a hypothesis on how things are manipulated, and when I discovered Tanya here in Cozumel; I could only imagine what her mission could be. If the Prime Minister of Canada actually comes, then it means my theory is one step further in being proven."

Susana and Lorena exchanged looks that bordered on laughter, but neither of the two broke up. Susana, the more contained of the two, turned in Carolina's direction.

"That sounds a little like the Chinese Secret Service, Carolina... you know, very mysterious but really dumb, because they see phantoms and assassins behind every bush and tree."

Carolina couldn't help laughing in spite of herself.

"Maybe," she said between giggles, "but what if I'm right?"

"Right about what?" Lorena asked, now intrigued by it all.

Carolina hesitated for a moment not sure if she should take her friends into her deepest confidence. They were civilians, after all, and she would never think of confiding classified information to them, but this was about something that was probably only an unfounded suspicion. Finally, she decided to confide in them.

"Right about general Porfirio manipulating the heads of state of foreign nations through everything he can possibly use in order to make them vote with Mexico against a lot of things, and in this case, the North American Free Trade Agreement that the *gringos* are going to propose at the summit meeting."

The two women studied Carolina's face intensely, and they realized that she was quite serious. Susana, the oldest, was an attorney who had served as a minor diplomat in the foreign service. She was well aware of the significance of such an accusation.

"Carolina, I think you have let your imagination get away with you," she said severely. "Our country is an unyielding enemy of intervention in the policies and sovereignty of other countries, so what you are talking about is a violation of at least six international treaties."

"I know and acknowledge that," Carolina said, "and I hope I am completely mistaken. However, if I were to tell you..." She looked at her watch. "But that is another long story, and we had better leave it for the *Up Wheels*. If I don't get to bed pretty soon, I won't wake up in time to go to Cuba."

Chapter 4

As the hydrofoil gently glided over the waves of the Caribbean, Carolina had the sensation of floating instead of sailing. She didn't feel the queasiness she'd felt on other crossings on any other ship of any size, and she was actually enjoying the trip.

Her orders had calculated a two and a half hour trip, which had seemed impossible to her even given the short distance between Cozumel and Cuba, but noting the hydrofoil's high speed, she was beginning to understand.

A Cuban navy officer approached her and introduced himself.

"Good morning!" The young officer smiled at her, showing off the whitest and most perfect teeth that Carolina had ever seen in her life. "Are you enjoying the cruise?"

The Cuban government had sent this hydrofoil, *El Kometa*, to Cozumel to transport the presidential entourage to the Isle of Youth, about a hundred kilometers from the main island of Cuba, and therefore much closer to Mexico than any of the other ports in the island nation.

Carolina returned the smile, glad to have someone to talk to for a while.

"Tremendously," she answered, and she reached out her hand to shake the officer's. "I'm Carolina Suarez, at your service."

"It's nice to meet you, too," the officer said, "and I'm Roberto Vallejo, *a los pies de usted.* I noticed you up here all alone on the observation deck, and thought that perhaps you weren't feeling well."

"On the contrary, and the pleasure is mine. I feel marvelously well, and that is a miracle, because I normally get seasick even before sailing. The dock itself moves far too much for my taste, I assure you. But this ship feels entirely different."

"May I get you something to drink? or to eat? There's a buffet in the main dining room with an exquisite selection of breakfast dishes."

Carolina hadn't eaten breakfast in preparation for what she had feared would be a long day of queasiness and dizziness.

"The truth is that I didn't have breakfast because I was afraid of getting seasick..."

"I didn't have breakfast either, Carolina." The officer paused before continuing: "May I call you Carolina. Since we're both lieutenants, I just thought..."

Carolina laughed.

"Of course you may, Roberto. So if you're inviting me to breakfast, I am happy to accept. The fact is that I am starving. But first, one question: Can you feel the ferry's movement more on the lower decks? I have no desire whatsoever of getting seasick."

"I promise you that it feels the same down there as it does here. Let's go, because I can promise you that the breakfast buffet is wonderful."

The lieutenant took her by the arm very properly, and helped her down the winding staircase to the lower deck. Before them was a huge passenger lounge, with brightly colored benches along the entire length of both sides that looked out toward the sea through glass partitions. The view was just as beautiful as on the observation deck, since the ferry had no draught at all. The enormous inflated pontoons that glided above the ocean waves made the ship look like a space ship, and certainly not a ferry.

The officer guided Carolina to the other end of the passenger lounge, where there were two closed doors. She knew Mr. President was in the cabin with a sign on the door that said "Private," because when she had boarded the ship and had excused herself from going down to the lower decks for fear of seasickness, her commanding officer, The Chief of Staff, had teased her goodheartedly, and then he'd told her where they would be during the cruise.

The officer opened the left door which led into the crew's dining room. Some of Carolina's colleagues were finishing their breakfasts with other officers from the Cuban Navy, and they turned to see her entering with the Cuban lieutenant.

Colonel Treviño was the first to applaud, and the rest followed his lead.

"So the lady has decided to grace us with her company... congratulations! You have finally overcome your phobia for ships!"

The Colonel's teasing was well intentioned, and Carolina responded laughing.

"Be careful, Colonel," she said between peals of laughter, "because it is not a phobia. It's called seasickness," she said as she twisted her face into a fake grimace. "Would you like me to sit with you? Just in case?"

The Colonel stood to his feet, still laughing.

"You may sit wherever you want," he said pleasantly, "but I must take my leave in order to coordinate our arrival with my counterparts in Cuban security. Enjoy! I'm glad you're feeling better."

The Colonel left, and Carolina asked herself again why they'd included her on this trip. Normally she only accompanied them as an interpreter with a high security clearance, so for the life of her, she couldn't figure out why they would need her presence during a meeting between President Santos del Alba and Fidel Castro.

The Cuban officer's voice startled her.

"Do you feel well?"

"Yes, perfectly. Why?"

"Because you seemed sort of "out there" for a minute and I thought..."

Carolina laughed.

"No, I'm really fine. But the weird thing is," she said as she sat at the table, "is that I have absolutely no clue as to why they brought me along on this trip."

At that moment the waiter approached with a coffee carafe in his hand, and Carolina turned the cup that was at her place on the table. Her mouth watered from the rich fragrance of her favorite drink as the waiter poured her coffee. She smiled and thanked him.

Roberto sat beside her as he turned over his cup also, and thanked the waiter for attending to them. The waiter cleared his throat, and proceeded to give them a run-down of the menu:

"Folks, today we have an exquisite selection of sweet rolls and breads, eggs and omelettes, Eggs Benedict with Hollandaise sauce and Canadian ham, cereals and oatmeal with fresh fruit and yogurt."

"Hmmm," Carolina furrowed her brow, "I would love to try the Eggs Benedict, but I'd better not," she admitted, not altogether trusting her stomach with such a food attack, "but if you'd be so kind, I think I had better stick to a bit of yogurt with some fresh mango, and toasted Cuban bread with butter."

The waiter nodded his head in acknowledgement.

Roberto ordered the Eggs Benedict, generously remarking that he would be glad to share them with Carolina if she felt like trying them after caressing her stomach with the yogurt.

Their orders arrived almost instantly, and the two of them nearly devoured their food. They barely spoke a word; their conversation was limited to commenting on the food.

After their plates were cleared from the table, the waiter offered them more coffee. The dining room was almost empty; the other guests had left one by one and were probably now in the passenger lounge or on the upper deck enjoying the view or smoking on the only deck where it was permitted.

Roberto broke the silence.

"Before breakfast, you said something about not having any idea why they had brought you along on this trip."

It wasn't a question, but Carolina decided to answer as if it had been.

"Yes, actually, that's right." She clearly noted the confused expression on Roberto's face, so she explained. "It's just that I deal with protocol and media communication. Cuba follows the same protocol as we do, as we both follow French norms, so they certainly don't need my services there, and insomuch as communications are concerned, I suppose our Presidents speak the same language, wouldn't you think?"

"I see," the Officer agreed, and then he laughed. "So it affirms that our commanders in chief are the same in both countries. They don't give explanations, just orders. Our duty is to simply obey and not question."

"Something like the old saying: *Slow thinking, quick acting.* However, given that I will probably have absolutely nothing to do here, please tell me about the island we're going to. I have heard it mentioned before, but I must admit my ignorance regarding this particular Cuban tourist attraction."

The Cuban Officer seemed pleased for the opportunity to talk about his country, and smiled widely.

"It's in the Batabanó Gulf, about a hundred kilometers from the main island, and this hydrofoil is the ferry that takes passengers between the port city of Batabanó and the Isle of Youth. It's about the size of Trinidad, but the population isn't over about 60,000 residents. It used to be one of the favorite haunts of pirates, and actually, it is thought that its legends were Robert Louis Stevenson's inspiration in writing *Treasure Island*. From the nineteenth century until the Revolution, its only official use was as a prison, and not only Juan Ignacio Marti, but Fidel Castro both served out sentences there. Castro closed the prison in 1967," he explained, his voice becoming more enthusiastic as he spoke, with a tone showing a mixture of emotion and sadness, "but my grandfather lived there until his death a few years ago."

"Oh, I'm sorry. But what brought your father to live on the island, if there was only a prison there?" she asked, fascinated over the idea of actually visiting Treasure Island.

"Precisely, the prison. He was jailed there at the same time as Commander Castro, for being a sympathizer. He was a professor when he was arrested, considered a dissident," he said, almost proudly.

"And was he?" Carolina asked, her eyes widening with curiosity.

"No. He was just a free thinking man."

"So, when he got out of prison, he loved the place so much that he couldn't bear to leave it?" Carolina asked, giggling.

"No, not quite. No, he had other interests, which take us back to the history of the island. Remember, Stevenson called it Treasure Island for a reason. My grandfather was a professor of Geology and because of the legends that some of the local guards and other prisoners had told him; he was convinced that there was gold on the island. After his release, he got a job teaching at a local school in New Gerona, and from then on, he spent all of his free time prospecting for gold."

Now Carolina was truly intrigued by the island, and she hadn't even seen it yet.

"And did he find it?"

"In abundance. The main veins of gold in Cuba have been discovered on the island, and as we speak, there is a project called "Delita," for gold and silver exploration, and they are beginning operations toward the end of the year with Canadian investment."

"And your grandfather discovered it?" she asked, with amazement and respect in her voice.

"My grandfather and many others," Roberto answered.

"How impressive!" Carolina exclaimed. "Tell me more."

Roberto continued talking about the Isle of Youth and its legends, but they were soon interrupted by colonel Treviño.

"Lieutenant, you're needed in the Command Center," he called out to her from the dining room door.

Carolina immediately rose to her feet, and held out her hand to the Cuban lieutenant.

"Duty calls," she said as she shook the young Cuban's hand when he, too, stood up, "you have no idea how nice it has been to chat with you. I hope to see you again before our return to Mexico."

"The pleasure has been mine," Roberto answered. "Don't you want me to accompany you?" he added noting that the Colonel hadn't waited for her at the door.

"No, thanks, Roberto," she replied appreciatively. "I know the way."

Upon entering the private cabin used as the Command Center, Carolina noticed another private office on the far end of the cabin, where she was certain the President and the General would be.

Colonel Treviño was waiting for her, alone in the cabin.

"Please take a seat, Carolina," he said informally, since they were alone in the room.

Carolina sat at the table feeling intrigued by all the secrecy as she waited for her orders. She could sense the Colonel's tension, and tried to lighten the atmosphere with levity.

"Don't tell me I'm finally going to find out why you brought me?"

The Colonel laughed.

"That's right, Carolina, but it is a rather delicate matter."

Carolina sat up straight in her chair, and fixed her attention on the Colonel's face as she listened to the details of her mission.

"Very discreetly, you are going to attend the private conversation between President Santos del Alba and Commander Fidel Castro."

"Yes, Colonel," Carolina answered, without knowing why, but it would have been imprudent for her to ask.

"In that meeting a number of issues will be discussed that have as much relevance for Mexico as for the United States, and you will have to pay particular attention to the issues and messages that Castro wishes to communicate to the United States. Do you understand?"

"I suppose so, Colonel, but what shall I do with the information?"

"I'm getting to that, Carolina, so please don't interrupt me until I finish." He realized that the lieutenant was literally biting her tongue, and continued: "There will be very little time between our return to Cozumel and the arrival of the North American President; most definitely not enough time to have an entire two or three hour meeting transcribed and translated through the normal channels, not to mention the fact that these are very confidential issues and there are far too many reporters around the hotel in Cozumel. So what you will have to do is to take notes on the main points, translating them into English as you go. Can you do that?"

"Of course I can," Carolina assured him. "And then what?"

"And then on the way back to Cozumel, I want you to transcribe it all, in English. There will be only one copy of the document, and you will not give it to anyone. Understood?"

"Yes, Colonel." Carolina was beginning to feel like a schoolgirl. She had carried out similar missions many times in the course of her career, and it offended her that the Colonel would question her acumen for security regarding official documents. "And of course, I must destroy the typewriter ribbon from the machine I have used, right?"

"Of course."

The Colonel was quiet for a moment, and Carolina stood, glancing at her watch. From the Cuban Officer's description, they should have been docking at the Isle of Youth any minute.

"If that is all, Sir, I would like to freshen up a bit before we dock."

"You may be dismissed," the Colonel told her, and then he stood to observe his subordinate's exit. "And Carolina..." he said, and Carolina turned in his direction, "thank you."

"No thanks needed," Carolina said. "That's why I get paid so many millions of pesos."

She could hear the Colonel chortling as she entered the rest room.

After refreshing herself, Carolina went upstairs to the main deck. A few minutes later, she saw the island for the first time. Although she could see about a third of it, she began to understand why the island was so legendary. The lower areas were blanketed in a soft haze, and the higher elevations stood majestically above with their thick green forests. It had never occurred to Carolina that the island would be mountainous, although now that she thought about it, it made perfect sense because the island had gold mines, and gold was found in mountains.

While the Kometa was docking next to the pier and its pontoons were slowly deflating, Carolina set out to find Colonel Treviño, who surely would be the one to accompany her to the meeting between the two presidents. A group of military officers was waiting for the entourage on the pier, and she was pleased to see that their uniforms were very similar to the tropical uniform that she was wearing, so much so that her presence at the meeting would be very discreet.

As she disembarked, Carolina followed the Colonel, who helped her into a military jeep. She obeyed, and joined two other officers from the Mexican delegation on the rear seat.

From there, she watched as President Santos del Alba disembarked with General Porfirio Caballero Castillo, the Presidential Chief of Staff. The General glanced directly toward the vehicle where Carolina was, and Carolina noted his almost unperceivable smile.

The General was a man of a rough and serious nature, and seldom showed any expression. In the beginning of her military career, Carolina had been scared to death of him, but over the years she had discovered him to be a wonderful commanding officer with a deeply sentimental essence. After all the years, she had come to appreciate him as the dear friend he had proved himself to be again and again.

The confident look from the General dispelled all the nervousness that had taken hold in her, and she felt far more comfortable. At that point she began listening to the military tour guide who was driving the jeep.

"We are on the side of the island known as the "*Hotel Colony,*" a popular tourist resort with spas and hotels that offer all their services at an all-inclusive rate," the young Cuban petty officer explained. "We are on the opposite side of the island from the city of New Gerona, the most populated town on the island, but this place is a much better choice for a summit meeting, because of the quality of its services and because it is so isolated from the rest of the island. As for security, all the guests from the different hotels have been moved to a hotel on the other end of the colony, which will give us freedom of movement within the summit location. If the presidents so wish, they can swim in the sea or walk through a tropical rain forest. Everything has been duly secured."

While the others laughed, Carolina thought about the two possibilities, neither of which pleased her, given the duties she had to perform. Despite herself, she laughed at the idea of taking notes underwater while the two presidents made like Flipper.

Soon they arrived at the lobby of a huge hotel, which looked like any deluxe hotel in Cozumel or Acapulco. The lobby was open-air, luxuriously decorated and attended by uniformed employees. The Jeep's driver invited the Mexican military officers to sit at a grouping of rattan couches, and immediately called a waiter over to take their orders.

Carolina leaned toward a colleague and whispered. "They are treating us like royalty."

Her colleague smiled, pleased.

A few minutes later, the car in which President Santos del Alba and General Porfirio arrived.

Everyone, including Carolina, rose to their feet.

From an office behind the reception area, Fidel Castro made his entrance. Opening his arms in a gesture of camaraderie, he warmly greeted his colleague and dear friend, President Juan Ignacio Santos del Alba.

After a strong embrace, the two heads of state took their seats in another grouping of rattan couches similar to where Carolina was seated with her companions.

A couple of waiters approached them immediately, and Commander Castro ordered something that Carolina couldn't decipher from her vantage point.

Her gaze averted toward Colonel Treviño in a silent question, wondering if she was expected to be near the presidents during such an obviously social moment, but the Colonel shook his head.

A few minutes later, a line of waiters entered the lobby with trays of green drinks in crystal flutes, and wandered among the guests to serve them.

Commander in Chief Castro observed from his seat while the waiters served all the guests, and once all were served, he stood. All followed his lead.

Using the ring that he had used since the Revolution, he tapped his glass lightly.

All the guests turned toward him and waited in silence.

The First Secretary of the Central Committee of the Communist Party of Cuba and President of the Councils of State and Ministers, Fidel Castro Ruz smiled at the gathering, turning on his heels to include all his collaborators and guests before offering a toast that no one present would ever forget:

>>Mr. President, I was about to say esteemed or your excellence, but I believe that I shall just say dear Mr. President:

I plan to be brief even though I have nothing written (there was laughter in the crowd).

I shall not try to explain it now, I will try to explain it myself later, but the fact is that I believe we have many thing in common, a great deal of affection, a great affinity between Mexicans and Cubans, between the Mexican Revolution and the Cuban Revolution.

The first social revolution in this hemisphere was the Mexican Revolution. The first social revolution —as Mr. President himself has said many times— in this century. The first social revolution or the second social revolution, we call it the first socialist revolution in this hemisphere, the Cuban Revolution.

History does not occur unreasonably; events do not occur in vain.

We think that this common history, this experience, unites us. We have differences, but the difference is not in the legitimacy, nor in the purity or strength of our revolutions, the difference is in the historical moments, the conditions and the circumstances in which each occurred.

We have always been interested in the Mexican Revolution; we are interested today, and will be interested tomorrow, in its experience, its development, and its ideas. We cannot forget that this Mexican Revolution was always a source of inspiration for the Cuban revolutionaries and it still is a source of rich experience.

I have meditated, I have tried to think profoundly about your problems in this stage and I know they are difficult problems, I know that you do not have an easy task ahead. I have tried to understand, to follow the evolution of politics in Mexico during these years. I have followed the efforts of President Santos del Alba closely; I have read his speeches and perhaps because of this trip I will read far more. We have different styles. I talk a lot, he talks very little.

Sometimes I have thought that one of the tasks of a leader is to teach and we often, above all during the first years of the Revolution, tried to explain, to teach, to make others understand the problems. But I have been able to observe that Mr. President does the same: he tries to explain, to teach, to make people understand the problems, but he does it in a far briefer manner.

I remember one of his speeches in which he said that his professional diversion was a professorship, precisely because he had been a professor, but he has the right to say that because he was a professor; I have no right to say it, as I was only a student. And so when I go to Mexico, when I converse with President Santos del Alba, then I think that perhaps my professional diversion was to be a pupil, and my habit is to respect and admire my professors. But these are not just words of courtesy.

Perhaps we Cubans are capable of understanding the problems of

Mexico, because we have been facing similar problems for twenty years, facing problems of under-development, facing difficulties of all types, struggling to improve living conditions for our people, to develop our economy, to develop ourselves not only economically, but socially as well. And we understand each other, we understand these problems.

Throughout these years there are some ideas that we have defended insistently and we find that in Mexico we see Mr. President insisting on a number of ideas that greatly impress us. I will cite an example, which is his view on education. He says that education is the fundamental investment in the fundamental resource and that is exactly what we conceive in our country as the definition of education, and we can subscribe to his words: the fundamental investment in the fundamental resource.

He has expressed other ideas insistently that we also share completely: the idea that educating, capacitating is the way to make unequals equal, to create a true opportunity for the talent, intelligence, and the vocation of each human being. Juan Ignacio likes to cite poetry, I do not tend to be an addict of poetic comments, but I do remember, I believe it was Becquer, that classic of Spanish literature when he spoke of genius: that how many geniuses lay hidden, without being touched by the golden hand capable of awakening genius. I have always believed that there are many, many geniuses among the populace, but the road to developing those talents, those intellects, is the equality of opportunity in education.

This is the first time that I have truly read an idea like that. It is linked with another belief of President Santos del Alba's that cannot be found in the classical books on politics, but is nonetheless interesting when he says: that equal opportunity is not enough, but what is needed is equal security. He goes on to add —if I remember correctly— that it is an insult to history to speak of equal opportunities among the unequal. And that is a belief that I truly ascribe to in its entirety.

He has said many things. I also recall his basic beliefs, which are realistic and express the anguish of a statesman, the profound concern of a statesman facing the problems of today's world, and that is that peach is impracticable if the economic relations between States do not change.

Alongside these basic concepts of his policies we have been able to appreciate his concerns which are unobjectionable, from the point of view of Mexican interests and from the point of view of the interests of any populace, which is how to guarantee food for the Mexican people taking into account the shortage of food in the world, the crisis of 1973; to produce food, to supply food to the Mexican people; to use natural resources: oil, gas and other resources for the development of Mexico; to create jobs, to solve the problem of unemployment, to invest those resources to find a dignified job for each and every Mexican. It is impossible to not agree with these basic ideas.

This afternoon we express our trust in Mexico, our faith in Mexico. Some exceptional circumstances have been created around Mexico and I wonder: Is there a people more deserving than Mexico to have this opportunity? Is there any other country in Latin America that has suffered more wounds than Mexico in its past, that has sacrificed more than Mexico. Is there any other country that has struggled more than Mexico? Is there any other country that deserves a better destiny than Mexico, is there any other country that we Cubans should wish a better destiny than Mexico? I firmly believe that Mexico is facing an historical juncture and is on the threshold of a great historical opportunity.

Mexico had more natural resources than Italy, than France, than Spain, so why can't Mexico —which above and beyond those natural resources has one even more valuable resource: Mexicans—, why can't Mexico become an important industrial power in our world. I believe it, I am convinced, I am sure Mexico will become that power. It is not only a simple question of faith; it is also a result of the history of Mexico, of what you have been able to do up to now. And for us, you are a banner, a trench in Latin America, and we know what trenches mean, because we too are, or believe that we are, a modest trench among the countries of Latin America.

We always keep in mind what José Martí, that extraordinary man, wrote a few days before he died in combat: It had to be in silence and all that I have done to this day and all that I shall do with the independence of Cuba is to keep The United States from extending across our American countries.

We have modestly carried out this duty; history assigned us that task, just as Mexico is today assigned the task of being a trench. If we pass inspection on the rest of our America I believe there is no country with better conditions today, or with better aptitudes to defend that trench.

Today, in our conversations, in our meetings, in our exchange of ideas with our colleagues, we will have enriched our comprehension of this fact and this reality.

I have had many opportunities to converse with Mr. President, well, I believe we are friends (applause is heard from audience), frank, open, sincere and honest friends.

One can ready many books, speeches and documents, but there is nothing like dealing directly with a man. And that is how it will be. This contact will increase our feelings of affection, of friendship and of solidarity. I do not envy the President's task, perhaps I could tell him this: I envy the privilege of his enormous historic responsibility. His task is hard and difficult, but I am sure that he will succeed. It is our most fervent wish.

Mr. President will succeed. Mexico will succeed, which is said with our deepest conviction. For that, if in fact we must toast, I wish to toast President Juan Ignacio Santos del Alba, for his success, and for Mexico>>

All the guests applauded President Castro's words while the two heads of state embraced one another.

Carolina couldn't help but reflect on the seriousness of the meetings that she would be attending that day. Only three days earlier, she had attended the meeting in the White House in which the Mexican delegation was advised that the North American President had decided to cancel his participation in the Cozumel Summit if, in fact, President Castro were to attend.

This meeting between the presidents of Mexico and Cuba was the only concession that the North Americans had been willing to concede in their rejection of Castro. Mexico would become Cuba's exclusive and official spokesperson in the summit meeting to which Cuba had the same right to attend as the United States; not only by international law, but by multilateral treaties to which both countries were signatories.

Carolina was amazed by President Castro's great dignity in accepting such a rejection, as well as by the confidence the Cuban President was entrusting to Mexico. As she took a sip of the delicious Mojito she had been served, she asked God and all His Saints to make her worthy of her mission.

"Carolina, where are you, woman?"

Carolina turned in time to come face to face with Alejandro, her loyal companion in Washington, D.C.

"Alex! How great to see you. I didn't see you on the hydrofoil."

"I came straight here from Washington, on the advance trip."

"Excellent! So, maybe you can tell me what time the private meeting is to take place?"

"Yes, in about fifteen minutes. Treviño sent me to take you to the Kiosk."

"The Kiosk?" Carolina was perplexed because private conversations between heads of state were never carried out in the open because of the remote possibility of espionage by satellite.

The Major read her thoughts.

"Don't worry," he said, "it is covered, and furthermore, it is at the end of a thirty meter pier out over the bay. We've already sent divers down to check the bottom all around it, and there is nothing there. They will have absolute privacy."

"Absolute except for the obvious exception of yours truly who will be taking notes on the entire conversation, and in English just for grins and giggles." Carolina was more nervous with every minute that went by.

Alejandro took her by the arm, and he guided her across the terrace of the lobby toward the beach. As she stepped down to the beach to take her first steps, her shoes filled with sand, and she stopped.

"At least until I get to the pier, I am taking my shoes off," she told her companion. "They're full of sand, and I'd prefer to walk barefoot than suffer the pain of the damned sand scratching my feet with my shoes on."

"Hurry up, woman... they're here!"

But his warning came too late. The two heads of state were approaching and Carolina already had her shoes off. And to add insult to injury, she had them in her right hand; the one with which she should have saluted her Commander in Chief.

She tried to switch her shoes from one hand to the other, but one of the fell, and the point of the heel made a direct hit on her big toe. She stifled the yelp of pain that was fighting its way out of her mouth, but she couldn't hide the pained grimace from planting itself firmly on her face as she raised her right hand to her forehead.

As they passed in front of her, the two heads of state returned her military salute. Carolina was almost certain she'd detected an amused sparkle in President Castro's eyes, but she didn't move until they had advanced a few steps ahead.

"And this is where I'll have to leave you, *amiga*," Alejandro said. "They're early, and you were supposed to be waiting for them on the kiosk before they arrived. So I wish you all the luck in the world. See you!"

And Carolina felt terribly alone and frightened. She had translated many a private conversation between heads of state, but this was the first time she would meet Fidel Castro, and his mere presence had already knocked her out of emotional balance.

But she was, above all, professional, and she overcame her nervousness. She stood a moment thinking about her shoe dilemma, but then decided that she could walk much faster without them, at least until she reached the pier.

She took firm and decisive steps, looking down at the sand to avoid stepping on something that might run her stockings. When she finally saw the pier in front of her, she lifted her gaze.

The two heads of state were waiting for her on the platform, two steps above the beach, as any gentleman of their generation would have done. They were both smiling at her, and this time Carolina had no doubts whatsoever. They were very amused.

She decided to take the initiative.

"A thousand pardons, Mssrs. Presidents, but I found it impossible to walk in the sand with my uniform pumps, so I had to remove them. I am so sorry to have held you up for so long," she said as she set her shoes on the platform.

President Castro reached out his hand to help her up, and President Santos del Alba did the same. Both of them were laughing out loud now. Carolina was horribly embarrassed and certain that she was blushing, but she took the hands they'd offered her to step up. Once on the platform, she took two precise strides to step into her shoes, not able to even shake the sand from her stocking because the gentlemen hadn't let go of her hands.

President Santos del Alba took the opportunity to introduce the lieutenant to President Castro.

"*Don* Fidel, I think this would be a good moment to introduce one of my collaborators from the Presidential Staff's Office, Lieutenant Carolina Suarez, who will honor us with her companionship this afternoon."

"It is an honor to make your acquaintance, Mr. President." Carolina shook the Cuban Commander in Chief's hand, and noticed that his hand was smooth and warm.

"The honor is mine, Lieutenant," he responded, adding, "so you are the translator who will do us the honor of taking notes on the issues to be dealt with the northern giant, right?"

At that moment, Carolina felt strangely sad, but she didn't know why. But she returned his smile, and spoke with such humility that she surprised herself.

"Y-yes, Mr. President, if you wish, it will be an honor to carry out the task, although I am sorry to say that I am neither a diplomat nor a minister on the level that the task would require."

President Santos del Alba placed a hand on her shoulder in a paternal manner.

"That is precisely why you're here, Carolina, instead of a minister or diplomat. You have translated for me in hundreds of conversations, and you have a gift for never changing a comma or a period. You never edit, and you never offer an opinion. Your profession is an art, and you are truly a master of your art."

Carolina was beginning to understand. She would be preparing Fidel Castro's words so that they could be heard or read by the President of The United States, since he had been uninvited to the summit meeting. And now she understood the sadness she felt. The bearded *don* Fidel was a man who had dedicated his entire life to improving life for Cubans, and whatever his politics, she was no one to judge him.

But neither was anyone else. The foreign policy of Mexico, since the Revolution of 1910, had always been that of non-intervention in foreign affairs. And Mexico had always been a good friend to the people of Cuba. And now Cuba's friend, Mexico, would have to speak for Fidel Castro.

It was a very delicate situation and Carolina was terrified, but by the same token it made her mad and sad at the same time; for once again, Mexico was finding itself in the painful position of having to speak for the government of Cuba without really being able to defend its interests.

She lifted her gaze and realized that the two heads of state were gallantly waiting for her to go first and walk the entire length of the pier to the kiosk, in front of them.

She smiled at them both, and began to walk. The sand inside her stockings was scratching her feet painfully, but she walked straight, like a good military woman. When she got to the kiosk, she didn't know of the tears running down her cheeks were from the pain coming from her feet, or from the sadness she felt for this degrading situation in which the United States President had put the Cuban President.

She took the seat that had been set for her, evident only because of the notebook and pencils placed upon the small table with a secretarial chair less than a yard behind the round table set for the Presidents. To one side of the notebook, they had left a pitcher of iced tea, a cut crystal glass, and a plate with ham rolls, fresh cheese and some saltines. On another plate there was a nice selection of Cuban candy and cookies. The table for the heads of state had the same things, except for the beverage. Added to the pitcher of water and another of iced tea, the hotel had placed a number of bottles of cola, and a bottle of Havana Club Rum.

Carolina made a mental note to only eat a cookie or so, and not the selection of salty hors d'oeuvres to avoid being too thirsty. The iced tea had too many diuretic properties to drink it during a meeting that could last a few hours with no possibility of a break to run to the bathroom. Carolina had always been amazed by the enormous capacity that presidential bladders seemed to have. Didn't they ever have to pee?

She remained standing until the two presidents were seated, and then she took her place. She discreetly opened the notebook to take notes.

For the following two hours, she never lifted her eyes from her notebook. After serving President Santos del Alba a *Cuba Libre* of Rum and coke, President Castro served himself one, and after a short toast in which he courteously included Carolina, the two began their talk about the issued that *don* Fidel would have discussed in the summit meeting, if his participation had been accepted.

He never referred to the United States President by name, but as the Giant of the North, or the Capitalist, or in moments of true rage, with more despicable names, always apologizing to Carolina for his uttering.

And if truth be told, his language had at no time been foul or unpleasant. On the contrary. Carolina had always considered Santos del Alba as one of the finest orators in the world with a command of the Spanish language only surpassed by the King of Spain, but Fidel Castro's command of the King's language exceeded and surpassed any limits of intellect and vocabulary that Carolina had ever heard. Listening to him was like hearing an oral reading by one of the great masters of the Golden Age of Spanish Literature, and his manner of speaking was both charismatic and enigmatic.

Furthermore, she realized that he had a perfect command of the English language, because even though she was to one side and behind him, he realized it when she would momentarily stop writing in order to remember a term in English when they spoke of technical matters. Invariably, even before she could recall the exact term, Commander Castro would turn toward her and translate the term in question.

If someone were to ask her to describe this charismatic Cuban leader, Carolina decided that that one lovely, but unusual kindness he showed a simple foreign translator described his personality better than anything else she could possibly say.

When the meeting was over, Carolina closed the notebook and placed the pencil on the table. She was just about to get up when the Cuban President turned toward. She remained seated.

"And now, Carolina. I am going to give you a test," he said. His eyes veritably sparked with mischief.

"As you wish, Mr. President."

"Tell me about sugar, using your notes if necessary."

Carolina didn't need to review her notes.

"Yes, sir. In my report I shall limit my comments to mentioning Cuba's exporting sugar to Mexico as a supplementary subsidy for Mexican national consumption, which allows the Mexican production to be for export, which is calculated at 4.5 million tons of sugar annually for U.S. consumption."

She noticed an expression on both men's faces which seemed to show they were pleased, although somewhat concerned, so she hurriedly added:

"And at no time does Mexico export the Cuban product, but rather only the Mexican product which is duly documented with Certificates of Mexican Origin."

The heads of state exchanged glances indicating that Carolina's understanding of the issues discussed was not only clear, but that she had understood the possible political ramifications of the conversations.

Chapter 5

When she awoke the next morning, Carolina stretched her body to the full length of the sofa bed and yawned. She looked at her alarm clock and smiled. It was still early.

Between sleep and consciousness, her experience of the day before seemed but a dream. She had been so emotionally jolted by the image of President Castro surrounded by his closest collaborators on the dock at the Isle of Youth, waving farewell to the delegations of his friends from Mexico as the military band played *The Swallows,* that she had hardly slept all night.

She had finished the transcription of her notes in a sufficiently legible and comprehensive format just as the *Kometa* was docking in Cozumel, and then she had duly destroyed the typewriter ribbon along with her notebook, although she was perfectly certain that no one —besides her— would ever be able to decipher her shorthand. She had invented it herself, and it had no resemblance whatsoever to either of the two main schools. But just on the off-side chance, she had destroyed her original notes anyway.

On disembarking, she had immediately gone off in search of Colonel Treviño, and she had given him the singular document before climbing into the minibus that would take them back to the hotel.

On the way to the hotel, the Colonel had quickly reviewed the document. Carolina could imagine precisely which point of the document the Colonel was reading every time he arched his eyebrows or when his face showed a slight expression of a feeling that she was unable to interpret. Was it fear? Displeasure? She didn't know, but at that moment she was simply too exhausted to care very much.

Furthermore, she was starved for food, and for sleep. She had been working on the document from the moment the ferry had sailed until it had docked in Cozumel, while her travel companions had been dining and drinking. For fear of spilling something on the documents, she hadn't eaten a bite nor had she drunk a sip of anything, and now she was ravenously hungry, and just as thirsty.

However, when they arrived at the hotel, all the facilities were closed except for the bar where they only served sandwiches and snacks, and nothing sounded good to her. She'd finally decided that she was sleepier than she was hungry, and retired directly to her suite to find a little snack in the minibar before sleeping.

Now the bottle of mineral water that she had hardly touched was sitting on the coffee table, and the bag of peanuts that she had opened the night before was still full. If she had been hungry the night before, now she was famished.

She lifted the telephone and dialed room service. She ordered the Continental Breakfast with yogurt, cereal, fruit and a soft-boiled egg, and then ordered three croissants, toasted with butter and marmalade, and a carafe of coffee with three cups, in case her roommates wanted something before or instead of going down to the hotel restaurant.

Once she'd made the call which was the most important thing on her mental list of her day's activities, she stood and crossed the room to the bathroom. She thought a hot shower might do her a world of good, since between the hours she'd spent on that kiosk at the end of the pier and more than six hours on the hydrofoil ferry, she felt as if she had a thick layer of salt on her entire body.

Before going to bed the night before, she had tried to brush her hair, but it had been impossible because of the film of salt that had tangled it.

As she bathed, she heard someone knocking at the door. She had been about to cover herself with a towel to open it, when to her relief she heard women's voices. She finished her shower, grateful to her roommates for having opened the door for the room service waiter.

She stepped out of the shower and dried herself, wrapping her head with her towel like a turban. After slipping on one of the thick terry robes that the hotel provided for every guest, she stepped back into the suite for breakfast.

But there was no tray and no food.

She only heard some voices coming from the bedroom that her roommates were sharing, and other noises that definitely sounded like sobs.

Carolina gently tapped on her friends' door, and opened it a crack.

"May I?"

"Of course, Carolina. We were waiting for you. Please, come in." It was Susana's voice.

As she entered the room, Carolina found her roommates in pajamas and still in bed, and another girl seated on a chair near the window, crying. She had to get closer to see who it was because the strong morning sun blinded her momentarily.

"Monica! What is it, sweetheart?"

It was one of the youngest girls in the group of Presidential pages, Monica Valladares. She was the daughter of a general who was a close friend of General Porfirio's. She was only eighteen, and was like a daughter to all the older women of the Presidential Staff's Office.

Carolina approached the girl, and the young woman rose to her feet, collapsing into Carolina's arms, sobbing. She was a petite girl and quite pretty; with long, dark hair and enormous blue eyes, which at that moment were bloodshot and swollen from crying.

"It's all right, dear. There, there... please calm down and tell me what is wrong?"

Lorena was so mad she was sparking and about to spontaneously combust.

"That louse Santiago is what's wrong, Carolina. You and Alejo should have castrated him when you had the chance."

Carolina held the girl at arm's length, and stared at her intensely.

"General Santiago? Tell me exactly what happened, Monica." Her voice was trembling with rage, and frightened Monica.

"Don't worry, sweetheart. I'm not mad at you. I'm furious with Santiago for reasons that have absolutely nothing to do with you. Please, Monica, tell me what happened."

Monica took her seat again, and grabbed a tissue from a box on the table. Just at that moment, there was a knock at the door.

"That will probably be a waiter with coffee and croissants," Carolina said, and peered around the room. Her roommates were in pajamas and Monica's face would scare a ghost, so she was the only one who could possibly answer the door. "Monica, don't move. I'll be right back."

She went out to the door, and received the waiter with her trays of food and coffee. But the mere appearance of the young girl from the group of pages and interpreters under her command had managed to make her lose her appetite.

She signed the waiter's bill, and took the tray of coffee from him.

"Might you have another cup out there? It seems I'm short one," she told the waiter, deciding she should offer Monica some coffee, too.

The waiter nodded, and briefly disappeared into the hotel hallway. He returned a moment later with another cup.

"Thanks," Carolina said. "Have a nice day."

She didn't even wait until the waiter had left to return to the bedroom with the tray of coffee.

She laid the tray on the table next to Monica's chair, and began serving the coffee. She knew Lorena and Susana drank theirs the same as she did, without sugar or milk. She served them first, and they both sat up in bed to drink theirs, appreciatively.

"Do you take sugar or cream in your coffee, Monica?"

She had served the cup, but Monica made a gesture with her hand, refusing the drink.

"If I swallow anything, I'll vomit," she youngster said. "I have been hysterical all night, and vomiting."

Carolina put the cup down on the opposite side of the table from her, and sat down on the other chair.

"Now, I want you to tell me everything, Monica... and don't be embarrassed. We are all women."

She was imagining the very worst, and set her facial expression in a semi smile to try not to express any emotion while listening to the girl's narration of events.

Monica blew her nose once again, and took a deep breath.

"Well, here it goes. The problem is that if I tell my father, he'll kill me."

"Your father would never hurt you, Monica. But, please, tell me."

"Do you remember that gorgeous Brazilian guy that I met in Venezuela?"

"Of course I do. I was rather worried about you. I was beginning to think that you were going to run off with him."

"You're kidding! I would never do that, but I do like him really a lot. Anyway, the Brazilian delegation arrived yesterday, and Carlos came with them."

"I suppose I should jump for joy, but I don't understand what this has to do with General Santiago."

Monica squirmed in her chair, and then continued.

"Well, once my Brazilian was registered in the hotel, he came looking for me in the lobby of the Hotel Melia where we had set up the reception tables for the delegation staffs. As you can imagine, I was thrilled to see him, and I asked for permission to have lunch with him. Susana said I could, and we went to the hamburger shack on the beach to eat."

Carolina was about to interrupt again, when she noticed Susana gesturing toward her to be silent.

"And then," Monica continued, "after lunch, we went for a walk on the beach. When we got to a nice little private cove, we sat on the sand, and well, you know..."

"Monica! Don't tell me that..."

"No! Of course not. We didn't do anything wrong, and we were fully dressed and everything, but all of a sudden General Santiago appeared out of nowhere, and said that Susana had assigned me to do the advance trip to a beach near the Cozumeleño Hotel, where they were going to offer a welcome cocktail party for the staffs of the foreign delegations."

Carolina arched her eyebrows toward Susana, and Susana shook her head in a negative response. Furthermore, Carolina had received the entire itinerary of events from the day before, and she didn't remember having seen any welcoming cocktail party on a beach near the Cozumeleño Hotel. The whole purpose of carrying out all the events of the summit meeting at the Hotel Melia was for the security that this particular venue afforded. What Monica was saying made no sense, but Carolina continued to listen without interrupting her.

"Of course, I agreed to go, and I introduced him to Carlos.

Then Carlos told me that he would call me that night in my room, and he left. Then Santiago accompanied me to his car, and I got in. He got into the driver's seat, and then put his hand on my knee."

"Santiago was driving? Where was his driver? Or his aide?"

Monica shrugged her shoulders.

"It seemed weird to me too, but who am I to ask questions?"

"You are the person who is finding it most unpleasant to have the old goat's hand on your knee, to begin with," Lorena interrupted furiously.

"Yeah, yeah, I know," Monica said sadly, "but I just kept thinking that he was touching me sort of in a fatherly way. I mean, after all, he knows my father, for God's sake..."

"And I have a feeling that he is going to get to know him a lot better, too," Susana interjected.

Carolina hushed her roommates by shooting a look in their direction that said it all, and she prodded Monica to continue. "Pay no attention to our little friends' sick jokes," she said, forcing a smile, "and please, continue."

Monica was calmer now and instead of crying, she was beginning to get mad. This was an excellent sign, as far as Carolina was concerned, that Santiago hadn't harmed the young woman permanently.

"Well anyway, that's why I didn't say anything, but I did move closer to the car door to get his hand off me. He seemed to get the hint and put both of his hands on the steering wheel. But then we got to the beach. It was one of those on the other side of the hotel zone where you have to go through the tropical forest to get to the beach. It seemed like a weird place to hold a cocktail party, and I told him so."

"And what did he say?" Carolina felt her blood beginning to boil.

"He said that he agreed with me, but that it was a place that had been highly recommended to him, and as a courtesy, he had to take a look at it in order to at least know what he was rejecting."

"My God! How far can this guy go?" Carolina exclaimed.

"Anyway, I walked over to the beach with him, and he was all over me."

"He what? Oh, Monica, how dreadful!" Susana was on her feet now, pacing back and forth across the room. "Did he rape you?" She was practically yelling, but lowered herself down on the bed again.

"Almost..." Monica was crying again, and this time her face was twisted into such an expression of terror that the other three women assumed similar expressions. "He ripped my blouse, and when I tried to run, he grabbed me by the arm, here."

She showed them a large bruise on her arm, the size of a large hematoma and tinged in a dark purple, almost black. The three women gasped in horror.

"And then he threw me down on the sand and climbed on top of me, and he had his pants unzipped and down. I had our blue uniform skirt on, and he had it lifted up and was trying to rape me. But that isn't the worst part, Carolina. I think I killed him." The young woman burst into sobs.

Susana yelped out and jumped to her feet again. Carolina remained calm.

"How did that happen, Monica? I can assure you that if you killed him, it was nothing more than a random act of kindness on your part to exterminate an insect that doesn't deserve to breathe the air that the rest of humanity breathes."

"I was yelling with all my strength, but the cretin just kept pushing against me, and kept telling me that since I was going to give myself to the damned Brazilian kid, that I should give myself to a true man who knew how to satisfy a woman. He made me so nauseated that the hamburger I'd eaten came up and I started to drown in my own vomit. He pulled himself up a little; just enough so that I could turn my head to the side, and in that fraction of a second I saw a coconut and grabbed it. I hit him in the head as hard as I could, and he fell over unconscious. I tried to find a pulse, but I couldn't."

"And then what? Did you call someone?"

"No. I remembered that he had left the car keys in the ignition, and I ran just as fast as I could to the car. I got in and drove myself back to my hotel."

"Which one?" Carolina asked.

"I'm in the Cozumeleño, with Ivana."

"Who have you told about all this? Does anyone else know what happened to you?"

"No, Carolina. Ivana went out with her boyfriend last night. She is going with a guy from the Fourth Division, and he is staying at the Cozumeleño, too. I suppose she spent the night with him, because she never came back to the room."

Carolina hugged the girl.

"So you spent the entire night crying your heart out not knowing what to do, and you've only come to tell us now? Don't you know that in this kind of situation, you can call us any time of the day or night?" She hugged the girl tightly. "Poor little thing," she said maternally. "It's just not fair for something like this to happen to someone as sweet as you."

Over Monica's shoulder, Carolina stared intensely at Susana, and then averted her eyes toward the telephone. Susana understood perfectly, and lifted the receiver.

"Yes, Miss. Connect me to General Santiago's room, please."

After a few minutes, she hung up the phone. She sat pensively a moment, and then dialed the Command Center.

"Hi, who is this? Oh, Lieutenant. This is Susana Aragon. Is General Santiago down there?" There was a long pause. "You don't say! Is he badly hurt?" There was another pause. "Oh, that's good, but what a shame, anyway. Did they catch the suspects?" There was another, longer pause. "Yeah, well I suppose that's just the way it is with gangs, isn't it? Well, if you speak with him, please tell him that we're all thinking about him. Thanks, Lieutenant."

She hung up the phone, and burst into laughter. The others turned toward her, and she explained between guffaws: "Don't worry, Monica. You didn't kill him. But you did leave him with a bump on his head he'll never forget, and a headache that will make him think of you for a long time. But even though he dearly deserved to die, you didn't kill him. That is the good news. The bad news is that they sent him back to Mexico City for complete bed rest for a few days, and he won't be back."

"That's the bad news? I would call that the good news. At least we won't have to deal with him, and it gives us time to decide how to deal with the situation." Lorena was deeply relieved, thinking that the whole situation would end then and there.

Carolina didn't agree.

"So we're just going to let him fade into complete impunity?" She saw the horrified look on Monica's face and hastily assured her. "Have you both gone absolutely mad? No! After what he did to me in Washington, and now this... as far as I'm concerned, I will not rest until I see him rotting in military prison. And with just a little bit of luck, he will get a flamingly gay cell mate who will teach the son of a bitch what rape is all about!"

Monica laughed despite herself.

"Carolina, you are a riot. But I agree with you wholeheartedly. We have to figure out when and how to report him, and to whom, no?"

Carolina was still pensive, but not Susana.

"Look, *Chicas*," she mused, "I don't think this is the right time to do anything about it, directly. But even so, we should file an official complaint, with a report from the medical service confirming the hematoma on her arm, and they should examine her to substantiate any further bruises on her legs or genitals, too."

"Yes, I am bruised, but since he didn't penetrate me, it wasn't rape. Was it?"

"In military justice," Carolina responded, "intent is the same as completion. It is still "moral turpitude and abuse of power," and given that this happened when he was on duty, he can be degraded, sent to military prison for up to nine years, lose not only his commission, but his years of service, benefits and retirement pension; and above and beyond that, after serving his sentence within military justice, he can be prosecuted in civilian court, too."

"That's seems only barely enough," Monica said with a grimacing expression.

Carolina seemed lost in her thoughts, but suddenly turned to Susana.

"Susana, why don't you call the Command Center to see what physician is here from the medical service. I think that's a good place to start, whatever we decide to do with this later."

"You have no idea how embarrassed I would be..." Monica said. "It's just that no one has ever... well, you know."

The three women turned toward the youngest.

"No one has ever... what?" Lorena was about to laugh, but she contained herself.

Carolina understood immediately.

"You've never had a pelvic examination. Right, Monica?"

"No. It's because I'm still... well, you know..."

"A virgin," Carolina offered. "So there has never been any need for those things." She sat on her chair, getting angrier by the minute. "And that bastard tried to rape you," she said sadly. "I am beginning to think that military justice isn't enough punishment for the jerk." She stared directly into Monica's eyes and asked, "Are you willing to go through that type of examination?"

Monica hesitated, but finally answered firmly.

"No. The truth of the matter is that I feel very lucky because he didn't succeed in hurting me, and because I am still the same as before. Perhaps smarter and less naive, but that isn't such a bad thing. At least I know now that I can't trust absolutely anyone, right? But by the same token, I am uncomfortable with the idea of his going unpunished."

Now Lorena was the one to get up.

"With one call alone, I can assure you that he will be very punished, *amiga*, and he will know exactly why he is being punished, if you want me to make the call."

The young woman hesitated again.

"I believe I'll have to think a while on that one, but thanks for the offer."

Monica was very aware of the identity of the person that Lorena would be calling, as Lorena's affair with the Chief of Police in Mexico City was one of the most widespread secrets of the Presidential Staff's Office. He was known as an executioner for personal justice, and Monica wasn't sure she really wanted to bear that type of justice on her conscience. She firmly believed in karma, and was afraid of affecting her karma by bringing bodily harm to another human being, even if the human being in question wasn't worthy of respect as a member of the human race.

"I understand, but just say the word, okay? And that goes by carbon copy to all of you. You, too, Carolina, because what he did to you was nearly as bad."

"Yeah, but Alejandro taught him some manners. What seems

weird to me is that he would still be up to pulling something like this only three days after living through the worst embarrassment of his life for a similar crime. That's what is worrying me the most. If he gets away with this, who's to say he won't do it again?"

Monica was visibly shaken.

"What are you talking about? Did he do the same thing to you?"

"No, with me it was different. He simply went to the front desk and got a copy of the key to my room, and told me quite openly that he would be up in a while. He said it as if I had somehow invited him."

"And then?" Monica's eyes were wide with disbelief.

Carolina laughed.

"Well, when he sneaked into my room with a bottle of champagne a little later, he was greeted by Alejandro Davila, who was waiting for him in my bed."

"The horny little troll!" Monica couldn't control her giggles. "Then what did he do?"

Carolina giggled right along with Monica.

"Well he stopped, stuttered three times, and made a run for the door. What else could he do? And what is funnier yet is that on the plane on the way back to Mexico, he never lifted his eyes from the magazine that he was pretending to read. He was dying of embarrassment. But given that this all only happened three days ago, the guy really does worry me. In order to pull something like this so soon after the last episode, he really must be one very, but very, sick man."

"I agree with you completely on that point," Susana said, "and somehow, I think we have a moral obligation to stop this guy cold."

Lorena laughed. "Cold doesn't seem to be an option with this jerk. That is precisely the problem. He seems to be hot all the time. His dick runs his life. Just give me the word and I'll make that call!"

The three other women exchanged looks, and all three of them nodded to one another. Carolina was the one to speak for herself and for Monica, as they were the two victims.

"Lorena, why don't you call Arnulfo on behalf of *Las Chicas de Palacio*, and explain to him that this bastard has tried to rape two of us, and if he could please send him a little message from us all, that he had better start eating one hell of a lot of Salt Peter to calm his animal instincts, if he wants to continue life with all of his intimate parts fully intact?"

Lorena threw her head back and laughed.

"*Las Chicas de Palacio!* I love the name. It sounds something like a club for gutsy women, don't you think? And of course we can have Santiago punished. Arnulfo's men call this type of punishment a *chill*, and it may the the only way, other than turning him over to military justice, to chill him out. What do you think?"

"For the time being, I think it is necessary, and well deserved," Carolina said, and an involuntary and Machiavellian smile slowly formed on her lips.

"I, too, believe it is... well, necessary," Monica said with a certain air of mischief creeping into her tone of voice.

Susana was quiet, so the three others turned toward her.

"What about you?" Lorena said. "Do you think it would be an injustice, *Madame* barrister, for us to have a little justice carried out in a way that befits *Las Chicas de Palacio?*"

Susana laughed despite her concerns. She always preferred solving any problem in a purely legal way, and the idea of having General Santiago beaten, regardless of how badly he truly deserved it, was simply not the road she would have chosen. But on the other hand, she had to admit that under the circumstances, it might be the only choice they had to stop the repulsive military man from continuing to commit the atrocities that he committed with this young woman. She shivered at the thought of what could have happened if it hadn't been for that coconut that had been within Monica's reach, and she stood beside her colleagues.

"I agree, too. How could I not? I am a *Palace Chick*, too, aren't I? But listen up, Lorena. You shouldn't make the call from here, because all the phones in the hotel are tapped. I suppose we'll just have to wait until we get back to Mexico City for you to ask your boyfriend for this little favor. Right, Lorena?"

"Right," Lorena agreed in a conciliatory tone of voice, "but the minute we get back to Mexico City, I am going to make the call."

It wasn't until that moment that Carolina remembered the toasted croissants with marmalade, the yogurt and fruit that she had ordered hours earlier.

"Listen, it's almost eight o'clock and we haven't had breakfast. I ordered some croissants and a few other things if you'd like, although I imagine it's all cold. Why don't we hurry and get dressed, and go down for breakfast in the dining room? All the heads of state will be arriving this afternoon, and we probably won't have a chance to eat together until the *Up Wheels Party.*"

A half hour later, the four women were having breakfast together in the hotel restaurant, talking about anything and everything, without mentioning the recent events with General Santiago, other than to giggle like fools every time one of the colleagues came over to gossip about what had happened to the General. They would listen attentively to the stories about the gang members that had mugged the General, making the appropriate comments, and once their colleagues had left, would roll with laughter.

The last story had been the best, because the officer mentioned that they had found Santiago with his pants down, and the rumors were flying about his having been raped. That was the version of facts that Monica had liked the best.

With everything going on, Carolina had forgotten to ask Lorena about her mission with Tanya Monteblanco, and recalling it, she hesitated to ask about it in front of Monica. But thinking about it, why not? Monica was now sharing a much more important secret with them, and her sense of discretion was obvious. Carolina sincerely liked the girl. She was young, but very mature. Carolina felt great empathy toward her, perhaps because of what they had in common: The Rapist General.

"Hey, Lorena!" she said to Lorena who was thoroughly enjoying her cheese omelette. "Did you carry out that little mission I gave you?"

Lorena laughed.

"But of course, Lieutenant. How could I not? And I think you're right, because the woman is ready to turn herself into a veritable Mata Hari.

Carolina wriggled down in her seat, and rested her head against the back of the booth.

With that piece of news, and after what she had witnessed the day before, her hypothesis was being proved more and more every day. She decided that from that moment on, she would definitely have to pay very close attention to everything that went on around her during the summit meeting. She could have beaten her head against the restaurant table for not having done this throughout all the years of her career in the Presidential Staff's Office.

Or hadn't she? Now that she really thought about, it was obvious that she had witnessed everything there was to see in the summits of the past, during her many trips abroad and during the visits of so many foreign dignitaries to Mexico. On some level, she had to have witnessed many things that at the time had made no sense to her, but that in the long run, had awakened her consciousness to the concerns that had led her to the conclusion that the Presidential Chief of Staff was manipulating international politics to his heart's delight, using everything and everyone within his reach to achieve his goals.

She just had to recall every detail of every meeting; who had been present, what they had done, with whom, and what the results had been.

The motivations and ultimate goals were yet for her to discover, but Carolina was sure that everything she needed to know to find her way out of the political labyrinth in which she had lived for so many years was actually within her reach, if only she could put things in perspective from this new point of view.

But right now she didn't have time to think about anything other than the summit meeting. Within six short hours, they would be attending the cocktail party to welcome all of the heads of state, and she knew that sometime after the cocktail party, the private conversations would be held between President Santos del Alba and the President of the United States.

Treviño had told her to be ready to attend that meeting at any time, as its scheduling would be almost spontaneous.

Above and beyond mentally preparing herself for that meeting, she still had a lot to do. She needed to check the sound equipment between the translation booths and the summit conference room, and to supervise the reception process that the group of pages from the Presidential Staff's Office was managing in coordination with the pages from the Ministry of Foreign Relations.

They usually didn't get along very well, which wasn't surprising given the average age of the girls. They were young, and lacked the necessary experience to have enough confidence in themselves to get along, without feeling threatened by the girls from the other group.

It was Carolina who finally got up to wish the rest of the women a great day so that she could go up to their room and get her uniform on. It was time to go to work.

Chapter 6

As they entered the grand hall and adjacent terrace to attend the welcome cocktail party offered for the heads of state of the twenty three countries participating in the summit meeting, Carolina and Susana hesitated briefly on the staircase landing that led down to the hall. The room was appointed with simple elegance, and its austerity only made the distinguished guests stand out more.

The two women were also dressed with simple elegance. Susana wore a long, light blue silk skirt with a long tunic in different shades of light blue. Carolina wore a simple but modest long black dress, with a neckline just low enough for evening.

As they scanned the room visually, they both smiled. They never ceased to be amazed by the mere presence of so many of the world's most powerful leaders under one roof, amenably chatting and trying the beverages and hors d'oeuvres offered by the event's host country.

Each woman had her own mission: Susana, as the director of the presidential pages, would offer Mexico's greatest hospitality to all the heads of state in the hope that their stay would be as pleasant as possible. Carolina, as director of protocol and communication, would also offer the heads of state any assistance needed with simultaneous interpretation or written translation; their press releases, or to coordinate their private conversations when interpreters might be needed.

But Carolina had another mission to accomplish this particular evening. General Porfirio had asked her not only to meet the President of the United States, but to try to establish a rapport with him so that he would feel comfortable with her during his private conversation with President Santos del Alba that very evening after the formal state dinner.

Carolina had a plan, and to pull it off, she needed the help of General Todd Heinrich, whom she had met during the Chancellor's meeting a few months earlier.

At the bottom of the staircase, the two women separated and each went about their particular duties.

Susana was already chatting happily with Crown Price Fahd Al-Faisal when Carolina finally spotted General Heinrich. The General was alone, drinking a Margarita, so Carolina took advantage of the moment to approach him.

"Mr. Secretary," she greeted him, "how nice to see you again."

The U.S. Secretary of State turned toward her and smiled widely.

"Miss... uh," it was obvious that he recognized her, but didn't remember her name.

"Carolina Suarez, General," she responded quickly.

"Yes, of course," he responded as he offered her his hand. "I remember you perfectly from other summit meetings, but I must admit that I am terrible with names."

"Don't give it another thought, Mr. Secretary."

Carolina shook the General's hand, and he pulled her toward him to give her the customary air kiss next to each cheek. Carolina responded in kind.

After chatting about the usual nonsense and trivialities that people tend to chat about in official cocktail parties, Carolina decided to dare to ask him to introduce her to President Troyer.

"You see," she explained, "after dinner, I will be interpreting during the private conversations between your President and mine," she said with an air of confidentiality that she knew would win over the retired general's trust, "and it would help me a lot if I could hear his intonations and the way he expresses himself just so I don't have to go in there cold."

"I would have thought you had translated for them many times before," the Chancellor said.

"No, because this is the first official visit your President has made to Mexico. The times we have visited the United States, Lucy, from the White House, has done the interpreting. It's a matter of protocol, that's all. But now, it's my turn."

"Then say no more," the General responded, and then he took Carolina by the arm to take her to the President of the United States.

President Troyer was an imposing man, but at the same time, he seemed very sincere when the General introduced him to Carolina.

"I am very pleased to meet you, Miss Suarez. So you will be our translator tonight? I couldn't be happier, because I see that you speak English perfectly. Where did you learn it?"

"From my mother, Mr. President. She is American, and besides always speaking it at home, she also sent me to schools abroad."

"Ah, that's why! But how nice, really."

And now, Carolina decided, it was time to put her plan into action. She had planned it with her mother a few months earlier. Clearing her throat, she hesitated again, then spoke.

"Mr. President," she said with a humble tone of voice, "there is something that I have always wanted to ask you. May I?"

The President stared at her tenderly, and in a fatherly way said, "Of course, young lady."

Carolina fixed the most serious expression she could muster, and let the bomb drop. "Whatever happened to your mother's turtle?"

President Troyer stared at her in disbelief, and then threw his head back and howled in laughter.

"My God! How the Hell do you know about my mother's turtle?"

Carolina flashed him her most innocent of smiles, and then she winked at him.

"That is a state secret, Mr. President."

At that precise moment, the Prime Minister of England approached, and after a warm greeting, Carolina excused herself to greet other heads of state she'd had the pleasure of meeting during past summit meetings. Tears were brimming from her eyes from her controlled laughter.

General Heinrich caught up with her.

"Hey, Devil-woman, you set me up!"

His words landed on Carolina like a bucket of ice water.

"Oh, Mr. Secretary. Please forgive me..."

But the General was doubling over in laughter, so she didn't continue her apology.

"I haven't seen him laugh like that in ages, Carolina. Thank you for that. But you must tell me about his mother's turtle. I have to admit I have never heard the story."

Carolina flashed him the same innocent smile she'd given the President.

"If I told you, I'd have to kill you," she said with a giggle, "but I am very glad you like my little joke."

At that very moment the General's boss was calling him over, and Carolina left the cocktail party to check on the special diets she'd ordered in the hotel kitchen.

The story about Troyer's mother was one her mother had told her. It seems that during Carolina's mother's brief acting career, Troyer's mother had been her next door neighbor in Hollywood.

Carolina's older sister and Troyer's daughter had played together often during their infancy when Mrs. Troyer had her granddaughter with her.

According to the story, Mrs. Troyer was already quite senile, and just a bit senile, so she tended to fret terribly over things that were of little to no consequence. And she had a giant tortoise as a pet. The poor woman would become hysterical every time the tortoise would withdraw into its shell, and would go running to Carolina's mother to ask for help, "because something terrible had happened to her turtle!"

She had often called her son Gerald out of important meetings to rush to her side because of these turtle tragedies, but the future President of the United States had always treated her with affection and respect, explaining over and again that the tortoise would, in fact, come out of its shell after its nap.

And he had always and sincerely thanked Carolina's mother for the kindness she showed his mother, for had it not been for her, he would have had to make many more emergency visits to his mother's home.

For Carolina, entering a hotel kitchen was like recharging her batteries. She had always been fascinated by professional kitchens, and she always swore she would have her own restaurant someday.

The Executive Chef greeted her cordially. "Good evening, *Madame*. How may I help you?"

"Good evening, Chef Gaston. I just came down to be sure you had ordered rice for the Crown Prince of Saudi Arabia. Is it ready?"

The Chef's eyes opened widely, and this confirmed Carolina's fears.

"Don't worry because you still have ten minutes before dinner is to be served. But it must be rice with only green vegetables, no carrots nor garlic, and it must be completely vegan, with no chicken brother whatsoever."

"Yes, Madame, I'll prepare it personally," the Chef assured her, and he almost ran to his prep station, shouting out orders to the rest of the chefs to bring him a pressure cooker, immediately.

Carolina discreetly wandered around the whole kitchen, without disturbing anyone except to comment on the elegant presentation of the entrees, or to taste a bit of something one or another chef offered her. Whether she liked it or not, she congratulated each chef sincerely.

It was already too late to change anything, other than to be sure that the Crown Prince was served his rice exactly the way he liked it.

Carolina made a mental note to mention this error to Abdul-Al-Horny, because if the truth were to be known, it was precisely Abdul's responsibility to see that this had been done. She rather relished in the idea of scolding a Saudi Arabian Sheik.

Once satisfied with the delicious meals for that evening, Carolina headed for the formal dining room to see that all the heads of state were to be seated in the places she had assigned them. If it hadn't been for her trip to Cuba, she would have supervised all of these details personally, but it hadn't been possible. She had delegated the responsibility of supervising these tasks to her right-hand man, a young officer who was truly a jewel, and who was becoming more indispensable to her every day.

She walked around the entire dining room, and other than removing the yellow flowers from the table where the First Lady of Mexico would be seated, she found everything to be in order. She had no doubts whatsoever. Gerardo was a genius.

Doña Gloria Romero de Santos del Alba had arrived unexpectedly that afternoon, and had upset the entire Presidential Staff's Office. She was the only first lady attending, which caused protocolary problems for Carolina. She had gone to greet the First Lady immediately upon hearing about her arrival, and was very pleased to learn that she would only be attending this dinner. She would be returning to Mexico City that very night.

However, and regardless of the fact that the First Lady of Mexico would be there for a very short time, it was important not to displease her in any way.

And *doña* Gloria detested the color yellow, more than anything else in the world.

Carolina realized that the rest of the tables had floral arrangements with a smattering of yellow, and she prayed to God that *doña* Gloria wouldn't cause a scene. She had made scenes over far lesser things in the past, but Carolina trusted that not even Gloria Romero would throw a tantrum in front of twenty three heads of state.

On the other end of the dining hall, she spotted her loyal assistant, Gerardo.

"Gerardo! Great job!" she raised her voice so the young man could hear.

Gerardo noticed that Carolina had one of the flower arrangements in her hand, and stopped what he was doing to rush to her side.

"Are the flowers terrible? he asked with a fearful tone.

"No, Gerardo, not at all. On the contrary. They're beautiful. The problem is that *doña* Gloria is in town, and you know what that means."

"She hates anything yellow," Gerardo finished Carolinas statement for her.

The young man snapped his fingers and an enlisted man ran to his side. Gerardo handed the flower arrangement to the young man.

"Look, Sergeant. You'll need to remove everything that is yellow. If you could put a red or pink rose or carnation in its place, that would be great, but nothing yellow. Okay?"

"Yes, Lieutenant, as you order, Sir," the young man said. Then he asked permission to be dismissed, and ran to carry out Gerardo's orders.

"I was just heading for the kitchen, if you think everything else looks okay here," Gerardo said. His voice was showing his fatigue.

"Don't worry. I just checked everything. Everything is in order, but as usual, Abdul-Al-Horny forgot to order the rice."

"Holy Mother! Did you order it?"

"Yes, and Chef Gaston is preparing it personally."

Gerardo Vaneek's face showed his relief.

At that moment the sergeant returned with the new flower arrangement, and after thanking him, Gerardo placed it just in front of the place setting where the First Lady of the nation would be seated.

"How does it look from there?" he asked Carolina.

"It's perfect. And now, I don't know about you, but since we have nothing to do for a little while, why don't we sit in the lounge? They can find us there if they need us for anything, don't you think?"

Gerardo pretended to collapse.

"God, yes, girlfriend. I am about to collapse from exhaustion. But, don't you have to attend the dinner? I just know I put a place card with your name on it right next to Abdul-Al-Horny at one of the staff tables."

"Oh, no! There is no way! Gerardo, please be a love and take my place card away. I have no desire to dine nor do I want to waste any time by sitting at one of the tables. I would far prefer staying here with you to rest a while because I have to translate for the private meeting between Santos del Alba and Troyer later on tonight."

But Gerardo was already running to the dining hall to remove the place card and table setting for Carolina. He hesitated, as if paralyzed, at the door. The delegations were already filing into the room, searching for their tables. He turned on his heel and ran back to Carolina.

"You're going to kill me, but it was too late. All the staff people are already taking their seats, and the heads of state will be there in about five minutes. What do you want me to do?"

Carolina couldn't help but laugh at the terrorized expression on her subordinate's face.

"Nothing, and don't worry about it. I'll go sit for a while, until they've served, say... the entree. I'll pick at it for a minute, and then you'll come in to whisper a terribly important message in my ear. I'll make a properly concerned expression, and will excuse myself with my table companions to take care of an extremely important matter. What do you think?"

"I think we're both in the wrong field. As actors, we'd be superstars!"

"Just make good and sure that all the entrees are served and then give me two or three minutes before rescuing me, but way before the speeches begin, because if I have to listen to even one speech, I swear that I will degrade you. Agreed?"

"Agreed."

"You're a love, Gerardo. Thank you."

The only thing Carolina hadn't figured into the equation was Abdul-al-Horny.

As she entered the banquet room, Abdul was already standing beside the table, and his facial expression clearly showed he was pleased to have been seated next to Carolina. He was looking around the room, probably searching for her. When their eyes met, they both smiled.

As she approached, she held both arms out, and took both of Abdul's hands. They greeted each other with a light kiss on both cheeks, and then Abdul held Carolina's chair for her.

Once seated, she greeted all the rest of her dinner companions, introducing herself to those she did not know.

By the time the first course was served, a delicious *ceviche* made with scallops and shrimp accompanied by a good dry white wine, Carolina had begun to relax a little. She was chatting with all her table companions, and she was finding their company very pleasant. And as always when he was with her, Abdul was behaving like a complete gentleman.

"By the way, Carolina, I forgot to tell you that we need to coordinate the private conversations between the Crown Prince, Troyer and Santos del Alba," he said in a low voice just as they were serving the soup course.

"What conversations? I have no documentation on any such meeting," she responded through clenched teeth, struggling to keep a perma-smile on her face, as her subordinates called it.

"Nor will you," Abdul spewed back without changing his very own perma-smile. "But if I am notifying you, you can be certain that it has been duly programmed only for the people involved; as in: for the three heads of state, for me, and now for you."

Abdul's tone had bothered Carolina, and she had to make an effort not to retort in the same manner. She tried a bit of the soup, and made an almost unperceivable face, but Abdul noticed it, and laughed.

"I didn't like it either. What is it?"

"It's something that the First Lady ordered this very afternoon," Carolina answered, and she lifted the menu card that had been printed just minutes before the dinner to make that precise change ordered by the First Lady. The card read:

State Dinner

Coastal Ceviche

Cream of beets and peanuts

Carolina didn't bother to read the rest, and turned to her colleague.

"Cream of beets and peanuts?" she said, struggling not to change the expression on her face, especially in view of the fact that a number of guests seemed to be enjoying the dish thoroughly.

Abdul smiled courteously and put his spoon down.

"Not in this life, at least," he said in a very low tone, and then he looked toward Carolina with his signature sparkle from deep within his eyes. He was a very handsome guy, even with his white tunic and "monk's veil," as Carolina always called the Arab turban.

"Anyway," Abdul continued, "when can we get together to talk? The private conversation will take place tomorrow immediately after the first round of conversations in the summit. Could I invite you for a cordial after dinner?"

Carolina hesitated because she couldn't divulge anything about the private conversation that for which she would be translating after dinner. She thought about it for a minute, and then smiled at Abdul.

"Thanks, Abdul, but I have a staff meeting tonight. So, why don't we have breakfast early tomorrow morning? If you'd like, why don't you be my guest in the restaurant, at about six-thirty?"

I'd like that, but not in the restaurant, because what we have to discuss is too confidential. Why don't you come to my suite?"

Just because of Abdul's nickname, Carolina shook her head.

"No, because the rumors would fly with the speed of a cyclone. That would not be a good place to talk."

"Then, how about your suite?"

"Worse, yet. Aren't we supposed to be very discreet?" Carolina had definitely detected an even more unprofessional sparkle in the Arab's eyes than usual.

"Then, how would you feel about having breakfast on the beach between this hotel and mine? That way no one will even notice us, and we can chat with absolutely no chance of any hidden microphones or cameras."

"That sounds fine. So, about six-thirty?"

"We had better make it a little earlier, before the swimmers come down for their morning exercise. Does six sound all right?"

"Fine. As a matter of fact, I'm going to go down to swim at five thirty, and I'll swim toward your hotel until I see you."

Abdul laughed, amused by the idea of their clandestine date.

At that very moment, Gerardo approached just as they had agreed he would. He leaned over and whispered into Carolina's ear. "I am here to rescue you from Sir Horny."

Carolina stifled her laughter, and turned to look toward her assistant with a very worried expression on her face.

"Thank you, Gerardo. I'll be right there."

Then she stood, and addressed all of her table companions. "Gentlemen, I beg your pardon, but duty calls. If I don't return quickly, it will be because they will have found something with which to occupy me the rest of the afternoon. I do hope you have a lovely evening."

Then, after bidding each of them farewell by name, she left the dining hall.

It was barely sunrise when Carolina went down to the beach. The light of dawn tinted the clouds in a rosy yellow hue, and the bay was so calm that it appeared before her like a bright turquoise mirror. The air was brisk, so much so that she shivered when she removed the caftan that covered her bikini. She would have preferred a more modest bathing suit given her date's reputation, but this was the only one that she had brought in her luggage.

As she tested the water with her big toe, she was pleased to find it quite warm, and after tucking her security badge into the top of her bikini, she dove into the water.

The water revived her physically as well as mentally, and she floated on her back to thoroughly enjoy the sunrise.

She thought about everything that had occurred in the private meeting between the presidents of her country and the Giant of the North, and she smiled. It had truly been very interesting. The two main points under discussion had been a tremendous success for the bearded enigma of the Cuban island republic, to Carolina's amazement. However, she couldn't help but wonder how many battles the Cuban government had won over the years with the same tactic. It was obvious that upon being uninvited to summit meetings in order for the American President in turn to attend, in a strange way, Castro had a definite advantage in any negotiation with that country through his unofficial Mexican spokesman. Natural diplomacy and human nature would, more or less, dictate a favorable result. It had never occurred to Carolina that this was precisely Castro's rather ingenious strategy, but above and beyond human rights issues and world politics, she had to admit that Fidel Castro deserved great respect, if for no other reason than his genius for getting his own way.

It was at that very moment that she realized what the private meeting between the three heads of state would be about that very afternoon: oil and sugar.

She turned over in the water, and began swimming toward the next beach. She had to swim further from the beach in order to skirt a sandbar that separated the private beach at the Melia Hotel from the wider beach that ran the entire length of the hotel zone on the island.

Suddenly, as she turned her head to breathe, she was so astonished that she swallowed water. She stood in the water, and fortunately could touch the sandy bottom. There, on the point of sandbar that separated the two beaches, a huge black and white tent had been set up, with three sides closed and only the side that faced the open sea. There was a table in the middle, and along the entire back wall were long tables filled with fruit, hot dishes, milk products and a large coffee pot. The smell of coffee made her mouth water.

Directly in the entrance to the tent was Abdul-Al-Horny, wearing bathing trunks, with an open robe on top. Carolina couldn't help admitting to herself that he had to be one of the more beautiful examples of the male gender that she had ever seen.

But this was a work session, nothing more, but Carolina had to repeat the warning to herself a number of times to arm herself with enough valor to force herself out of the water.

As soon as he saw Carolina, Abdul took a towel from a table next to the entrance, and approached her to cover her.

"Good morning," he said cheerfully. "You're very punctual," he greeted Carolina as he wrapped her in the towel.

"Good morning." Carolina took a step backward to dry herself, and then followed Abdul toward the tent. When he reached the table from which he had taken the towel, Abdul picked up a soft terry cloth robe and offered it to Carolina.

Carolina accepted it gratefully, because she felt absolutely naked in the lascivious gaze of her Arab counterpart. She opted for joking about it; her usual cover in uncomfortable situations. As she put the robe around her shoulders, it caught on the chain of her security badge, so she took the badge off and placed it to one side of the towel she'd left on the table, making a mental note not to forget it before returning to her hotel. That badge was irreplaceable, and no one could enter the summit conference without one.

"Your great discretion is most impressive," she said laughing.

"Building something like this right on the beach will surely fool everyone, won't it? They'll never know we're here. Right?"

Abdul smiled at her.

"I decided on this exaggeration in shamelessness for a very good reason," he explained as he motioned for Carolina to take her seat at the table. "It turns out that by the time I got back to my hotel, two different people made comments about my clandestine date with the chief of protocol from the Mexican delegation."

"How could that be?" The only person to whom Carolina had mentioned the breakfast was her assistant, Gerardo, for reasons of duty and not because of any particular trust. "But no one, not even my roommates, knew about this visit."

"Obviously someone at our table heard us during dinner, but it doesn't matter. I made the only decision that seemed reasonable, which was to make an ovation of obvious seduction to the young woman that everyone thinks I am courting anyway. I hope you don't mind."

"Oh, how nice! So now, instead of calling me *Mara Hari,* they're going to call me *Madame.*"

But she couldn't keep a straight face, and had to concede the point. Reputations and fame aside, the main responsibility for both of them was to keep the afternoon's meeting in the strictest of confidence, at least until the meeting took place. Afterward, it would be common knowledge.

Carolina stood up from her chair, and served two cups of the rich Arabian coffee. She carried them to the table, but Abdul had already gone to the buffet to serve them both plates of fruit and yogurt. She sat down anyway, and sipped a bit of her coffee. It was stronger than Mexican coffee, but less bitter than Turkish coffee.

Abdul returned to the table with the two plates, and Carolina thanked him.

"The coffee is exquisite. It's better than Turkish coffee; not so bitter."

"The coffee is Colombian," Abdul told her, "but roasted and ground in Saudi Arabia. And the sugar is Mexican, so thank you for the compliment, but these are two of the products that we do not have in Saudi Arabia."

It wasn't until that moment that Carolina realized, for the first time, how dependent Saudi Arabia was on imports, even for the most basic needs of their people.

"Well, yes, I suppose there wouldn't be a great deal of land where you could cultivate coffee in Saudi Arabia, but at any rate, your roasting method and grind is excellent."

"Well, the truth of the matter is that there is practically nothing cultivated in Saudi Arabia, with the exception of oil, if you can consider the petrochemical industry as cultivation."

"Hmmm," Carolina mused, "and petroleum products are not exactly edible... but it does bring in a lot of cash."

"Yes, money. And with that money we buy the things we need from the rest of the world. We are one of the most dependent countries in the world," Abdul said decidedly. "And that is precisely what the meeting is about this afternoon, just like the one you attended in Cuba."

Carolina didn't change the expression on her face. How much did this guy know about her trip to Cuba? As much as he tried to act like a great friend; as much as he alluded to his desire to establish a relationship with her; the fact was that her experience in the field of international politics was firm and ubiquitous. She was apt to be the one person in the world less likely to fall into even the most elaborate of traps. On the other hand, if he really did know the details and purposes of the Cuban trip with the approval of, and under orders from the Mexican government, then it would be ludicrous on her part to deny it. She opted for an answer similar to those she tended to give the press, hoping not to offend him.

"Well, if there was, in fact, such a trip, you will understand that I am not at liberty to discuss it."

Abdul nodded his head, and ate a bit of his fruit. She did the same, but could hardly taste anything due to an uncomfortable nervousness that seemed to be taking control of the situation.

Abdul noticed that his guest was uncomfortable, and quickly changed the subject.

"I understand perfectly, so don't give it another thought. But anyway, the meeting will be around five-thirty this afternoon, aboard the warship "Cuauhtemoc" which is anchored in the bay."

"Listen, Abdul, I'm afraid we had better cut this conversation short." Carolina had not received any orders regarding the ship, nor the meeting, and the conversation was making her very uncomfortable. "I have no orders to this effect, and in case you've forgotten, I am a military officer."

Abdul stood from his chair and crossed the room to a table, upon which there was a briefcase. He opened it and removed an envelope, which he took to Carolina.

Carolina opened the envelope quickly, and found a document on the official Army stationery. It was a written order which stated that she should consider the instructions given her by the Saudi Arabian Secretary of Protocol as orders, and that she was to coordinate a meeting that afternoon. It also said that she should treat all matters regarding the meeting with the utmost discretion. There was a warning in the document that she had never seen before during her five years in the army: *You will not discuss the content of this document with absolutely no one, with the sole exception of the person indicated herein and the undersigned."* The document was signed by the Commander in Chief of the Mexican Armed Forces, Juan Ignacio Santos del Alba.

Carolina gulped, and turned her face toward Abdul, who was smiling at her sweetly.

"Carolina, we have known each other for a number of years, and I believe that during the time we have known each other, other than to try to seduce you a couple of times, I have never deceived you in any way. Why would I do so now when we are finally enjoying a romantic date together in front of Allah and the whole world?"

Carolina laughed despite herself.

"I'm sorry, Abdul. The truth is that I behaved very badly, but so did you. If you had given my orders from the beginning, I wouldn't have distrusted you for a minute. But you need to understand that first I am a military officer, and then a woman."

Abdul shuddered at the thought of a military woman. The idea simply did not mesh with his culture or his personality.

Carolina duly noted his reaction.

"And that, my dear friend Abdul, is the reason why we could never be a couple. We are just too different, in all ways. We are from two totally different cultures, and although we are sincerely attracted to each other, we would never work as a couple. However, that doesn't mean that we can't be the very best of friends..."

She held her hand out and placed it over Abdul's hand, and he squeezed it tightly.

"I accept your friendship, but it pleases me greatly to hear you admit that you find me attractive, because I am very attracted to you, too."

Carolina patted his hand as she withdrew hers, and smiled at him.

"And that will be our little secret, but as friends. Now, back to work. What do I need to do to prepare for this afternoon's meeting?"

An hour later, once she had bathed and was beginning to dress to go to work on the first day of the general summit, Carolina was suddenly overcome with horror. She had left her security badge in Abdul's tent!

She was momentarily overwhelmed with panic, but swiftly reacted and ran to the telephone. She felt she shouldn't even confide in her roommates, but she knew she could trust Gerardo. Furthermore, he would never consider her breakfast other than a prelude to a brief affair, and it didn't even matter if he spread the rumor. By this hour of the day, half of the world would have heard about the mad affair between the two chiefs of protocol.

She dialed the Gerardo's room number. Fortunately he hadn't left his room yet and he answered.

"Gerardo, please come to my room."

"I'm on my way."

She hung up the phone, and immediately opened the door to look out into the hallway. She didn't even want her roommates to hear her. Gerardo was on the far end of the hall in a room set up for four people, and Carolina was impatient.

She finally saw her young assistant running down the hall, fixing his tie as he ran. His hair was still wet and his tie was crooked when he halted before her.

Carolina followed her motherly instincts, and immediately began straightening his tie as she spoke in a low voice.

"Gerardo, I need you to go to the Hotel Cozumeleño very discreetly, and go up to Abdul-Al-Horny's room." She noticed Gerardo's eyes stretching wide as a sly smile formed slowly on his lips, but she ignored him. "He should still be in his room, but if he's not, you'll have to search until you find him. It seems that I left my security badge on the beach when I had breakfast with him, and I need you to bring it to me just as fast as possible. Understood?"

"Yes, boss-of-mine. I'll be back in a jiffy!"

And without another word, the young man turned on his heels and ran down the corridor. Carolina went back into her room, and after closing the door behind her, she head a giggle coming from the hall, a short distance away. She left the door unlocked so that Gerardo could enter discreetly as soon as he returned with the badge.

The room was still perfectly silent. It was barely seven, and the first activities of the day were to begin at nine, so her roommates probably wouldn't be getting up until eight.

Thankful for the peaceful moment, she returned to the bathroom to dry her hair, put a little makeup on and dress in the official uniform of the day. Just as she'd finished dressing, the phone rang and she ran to answer it lest it awaken her colleagues.

"What's wrong?" she answered furiously because Gerardo had no business calling her on this matter over a tapped phone line, but fearing at the same time that he probably hadn't been able to find Abdul.

It wasn't Gerardo. It was the unmistakable voice of General Porfirio.

"I don't know, Lieutenant. What's wrong with you? I'll see you in my suite in thirty seconds."

"Yes, General."

And now? What the hell am I going to do? Carolina couldn't even walk through the halls without the damned badge, and she had to go up two floors to the General's suite. *Well,* she thought, *what if I go up the stairs?* But thinking about it, she knew there would be guards at the door on each floor. There was only one way, and it meant she would have to take one of her roommates into her confidence.

She crept into her colleagues' room, and awakened Susana.

"Susana, I'm sorry to wake you, but I need your help," she

whispered.

Susana stretched and sat on the edge of the bed.

"What's wrong, *amiga*? You're white as a ghost."

"I have to ask you for a favor, but I can't tell you why."

Susana laughed.

"If it has something to do with your romantic breakfast with the Sheik, then I'm sorry to inform you that it is the most divulged secret in the Chief of Staff's office, my dear."

"Something like that... but Susana, General Porfirio just ordered me to his suite. Would you loan me your security badge? I promise I'll get it back to you before you're even dressed."

Susana hesitated a half of a second, and then broke out laughing.

"So you left it in the other hotel? *Ay amiga,* that was really, but really stupid."

"Susana... I told you that I can't explain anything. But Gerardo will be back any minute with my badge, and we'll exchange them back just as soon as I get back from seeing the General."

Susana couldn't stop laughing, but she opened the drawer in her night stand and took out the coveted security badge.

"Here you go, *amiga*, and if you don't get back before breakfast, just look for me in the dining room. I'll put your badge on backwards, and we can exchange them there."

Carolina took the badge and placed it around her neck, making sure that it was turned around when it fell.

"*Gracias, amiga,* I owe you one!"

"One? What, a court martial? I'd say you owe me a hell of a lot more than that!"

Carolina threw her a kiss as she ran out the door toward the hallway.

Chapter 7

When she entered General Porfirio's suite, Carolina found her Commanding Officer with a cup of coffee in his hand, standing on the terrace, gazing out at the beach. He had a deeply worried expression on her face.

"Good morning, General," she greeted him formally.

The General turned toward her.

"Serve yourself a cup of coffee and come out here with me," he said, "because I have a nit to pick with you."

Carolina tried to serve herself some coffee, but her hands were trembling so that she realized that she wouldn't be able to hold a cup in her hand without spilling its contents. She decided to go out to the terrace without the coffee that would probably have choked her, anyway.

The General was wearing a sweat shirt, and his appearance screamed of the exercise he had just done. He was leaning over the balcony railing.

"Sit down, Carolina. Don't you want any coffee? There are also some toasted croissants with marmalade, if you'd like some."

"Thank you, General, but I've already had breakfast."

The General flashed her a Machiavellian smile.

"Yes, I know. And quite deliciously, I would say."

Carolina felt a wave of heat rising from her feet right up to the top of her head, and she couldn't find a word to say.

"Y-yes, General."

The General continued without taking his eyes off the beach.

"Did you see who's swimming?" he asked Carolina.

She rose to her feet and advanced toward the General. She looked down at the beach and saw General Heinrich swimming with President Troyer. About three hundred yards from the beach there were two Mexican warships forming a sort of arch that covered the deep water channel dug into the coral reef for boats to pass. She knew from the military notifications she received every day that the warships were there to hold the shark nets that the Americans had brought. Far beyond the warships she spotted the magnificent tall sailing ship, the "Cuauhtemoc."

"I suppose they're perfectly safe from sharks thanks to the nets that we have over the deep water channel. Right?"

The General smiled, never averting his eyes from the beach.

"Yes, I suppose so, but it's not the sharks that worry me."

"No? Then, what?"

The General's thick lips began to form an even more Machiavellian smile.

"Barracuda."

Carolina shuddered. She knew that the barracuda was a much more aggressive fish than the shark, at all times.

"Do you mean to say that there are barracudas in the bay?"

"Pretty often, and big ones, too."

"And don't the nets help to keep them out?"

"No, the weave is too wide. The barracuda can swim in and out just as if they weren't there."

"And may I ask why you didn't tell the Americans to bring a net with a tighter weave?"

The General laughed.

"Because they didn't ask. In fact, they didn't even consult me. They are the experts, aren't they?"

Carolina had to stifle the burst of laughter that was struggling to get out.

"I see, General," she said. She continued to gaze at the beach, and noticed that the American President had left the water, followed by his Secretary of State.

The General turned and entered his suite. He sat on the sofa, and patted the cushion next to him.

"Sit down, Carolina."

She obeyed, and waited for a brow-beating. It was more than obvious that the General knew all about her breakfast, and he probably thought that she was having a mad romance with the Sheik, just like everyone else thought. She was not in the least bit happy about not being able to talk about her orders or her activities with the General, but her orders had been very precise, and she wasn't about to disobey them. If that meant that she would have to put up with an unwarranted reprimand from the General, then that's what she would have to do.

The General was smiling.

"Carolina, to begin with, don't ever doubt that I am intensely aware of everything that goes on in this country, if not in the entire world."

"I have never doubted that, General. But I should tell you that..."

"You should tell me nothing. Your orders forbid it."

Her head spun around so quickly to look at him that her neck hurt. She raised her hand to rub her neck, and her badge turned around. She discreetly turned it around again.

"Look, Carolina... or should I call you Susana? There are simply things we do not mention in this business. It's better that way."

"Yes, General."

Carolina had absolutely no idea what he was talking about, but she felt far more comfortable, and she had stopped trembling. She really needed a cup of coffee.

"May I serve myself some coffee? I really could use one, after all."

Without waiting for an answer, she rose from her seat and served herself. She returned to the sofa and sat down next to the General again.

"How yummy!" she exclaimed after tasting the coffee.

"Yes, it's less bitter than Turkish coffee, and not quite as strong as Arabian coffee," General Porfirio said with a sardonic smile. "But drink it quickly so you can get back to your suite before Susana violates military law."

He picked up an envelope from the coffee table, and handed it to Carolina.

Carolina felt the shape of her security badge inside the envelope, or better said, the *nit* that the General had alluded to picking when she'd entered his room.

"General, I don't know how I could have left it there..."

The general flashed her a half-smile.

"Let's just say, for the time being, that you lost it in the throes of passion, or at least that's your cover."

"Yes, General." She stood up to leave, but now she was trembling again as she walked toward the door that led to the hallway.

"Don't let it happen again, Carolina. I hope you deserve the trust that we are bestowing on you."

"I promise I won't let you down, General."

Closing the door behind her, Carolina was very relieved, but by the same token, she was more confused than she had ever been before.

Who was in charge? Or rather, who was whose puppet?

At that moment, she was beginning to think that everyone was a simple puppet for one, sole omnipotent force out there, and the ramifications of such a great and powerful force not only inspired a strange respect in her, but a terrible fear on a level so deep that not even she could fathom it.

At summit meetings, only the heads of state are allowed inside the venue; neither vice presidents nor secretaries of state are allowed in. Only the presidential entourages at the highest security level are even allowed into the waiting room, but even they cannot go any further than there.

The venues are insulated with highly technological soundproofing materials so that no sound whatsoever can be heard outside the venue. Neither security guards nor chiefs of staff are allowed in.

The venue used for a summit meeting affords the heads of state a sacred privacy that allows them to feel completely at ease to speak freely and however they want, with no protocol or titles to deal with.

At least, that is the image projected worldwide regarding summit meetings.

And it would be true, if it were not for the need and existence of interpreters. The interpreters are privy to each and every one of the issues discussed in summit meetings.

Each hosting country is responsible for every interpreter, and after carefully examining a candidate's past to be considered as a summit interpreter, all of the security information is shared by the host country with all of the rest of the participating countries. Any country can reject any candidate without stating a reason, so the security requirements are very strict and the investigation is thorough. In Mexico's case, even the private telephone of each interpreter is tapped electronically to assure the greatest security possible around a summit meeting. If even the most minor detail in the interpreter's life is detected that could raise the least suspicion that the person could be a security risk, the interpreter is eliminated immediately.

Interpreters tend to have impeccable moral standards, a comfortable financial status, and above all, they are people with a very strong sense of patriotism. Their work is very well paid, and they are paid the international scale from the moment they leave their homes until they return after a summit meeting.

The three official languages at summit meetings are French, English and Spanish, but in the interpreters' booths the native languages of all the heads of state are covered; however, everything that a head of state says in his native tongue is simultaneously translated only to French, English and Spanish. The other heads of state may switch between languages and listen to the topic of the moment in whatever language in which he or she is most comfortable, or in the original language if he or she understands it.

Personally, Carolina spoke five languages, although for purposes of simultaneous translation, she was only certified in three: French, English and Spanish. Through her years on the job, she had made her best effort in contracting the very best linguists of Mexico. Among her professional team consisting of seventeen interpreters, she could cover the translation needs in twenty-four languages.

Her interpreters were exemplary, both personally and professionally, and she had been proud to submit the teams' security reports to all of the heads of protocol in the participating countries. She had been thrilled, but not surprised, that not one of her interpreters had been rejected.

Sitting on a sofa in the loneliest corner of the waiting room, Carolina had spent over an hour with her cordless headset connected to the electronic center that controlled the interpreting booths. She listened to one, then another translation channel, carefully trying to detect any change of topic that might require an interpreter with a higher security clearance, or worse yet, a sign of fatigue in one of her interpreters. Fatigue is the worst and most feared enemy of interpreters, because it invariably causes mistakes. A simple error in translation during a summit meeting can change the course of history for humanity.

Suddenly, she realized that the woman who was translating from French to English had just made a small error that she would normally never do. Without hesitation, Carolina picked up her radio and called the interpreters' lounge.

"Sixty-six Owl, are you there?" she asked in the code used by the Presidential Staff's Office to avoid any potential espionage through radio frequencies.

"Yes, boss-lady." It was Gerardo's voice.

"Send me a British soda, would you?"

"Sure, Seagull, coming up! How do you want it?"

"Frappé, if you would."

She turned off the radio and rose from the sofa. She headed directly for the door to the booths, and ran her badge through the digital reader. The door opened.

She walked to Cabin Three, and opened the door silently. On the desk was an extra headphone, and she picked it up. She placed it on her head, and sat down on the interpreter's bench. The interpreter looked grateful, but never stopped translating.

Carolina listened for a few moments; her finger raised in the air. The girl continued to translate without missing a word. Once there was a pause, Carolina lowered her finger, and from that point on, she continued to translate in the girl's place, not missing one word.

The interpreter removed her headset in silence, and exited the booth without making a sound. Through the large glass window that on the heads of state's side was a simple mirror as if it were part of the decoration in the venue, she took a visual tour of each leader's face. No one seemed to have noticed the switch.

A few short seconds later, the substitute interpreter entered silently. Since it was a man, and the change of voices would be obvious, Carolina continued to interpret until the French President had finished his discourse. Meanwhile, the new interpreter adjusted the head phone and took his place next to Carolina. Once the Prime Minister of Great Britain had begun her discourse in reply, which was being interpreted by the translator in the next booth, Carolina stood up and followed the new interpreter's finger. As soon as he lowered his finger, she disconnected her headset and left the room in silence.

As she came through the door into the waiting room, the girl who had been removed was waiting for her.

"Did I make a mistake?" she asked her boss.

"Nothing important, Julia, so don't worry about it. Go and rest for a while, and I'll put you back in later. I'll bet you haven't eaten anything."

The girl was embarrassed. "No, you're right. It's just that I always get really nervous the first day and I'm afraid to eat."

Carolina draped her arm around the girl's shoulder, and squeezed her gently.

"Well, we're going full force now, so there's no excuse or pretext not to eat. Please go eat something, watch television for a while, and clear your mind. I promise you'll feel better."

"Thanks, Carolina, and I am really, really, sorry."

"Don't be. No harm done."

Carolina was already listening to the different channels again, and she returned to her corner, but not before serving herself a cup of coffee.

As she sat down, she noticed that General Porfirio was watching her. His face showed no expression whatsoever, as always in public.

An hour later, the General approached her, and sat down next to her. She had already switched out two interpreters for substitutes with higher security clearances, and had pulled it off transparently. At this point every booth had an interpreter with the proper security clearance, and none of them seemed to be fatigued.

She turned her head toward the General and arched her eyebrows in a questioning manner. She never spoke to anyone, not even her Commanding Officer, while on this duty. No one, with the exception of her calls to Gerardo to replace interpreters as need. And even those calls were extremely short and precise.

The General handed her a small piece of paper, and she read it. It had only two words, and they were the two words that Carolina detested the most: Joint Communique.

She nodded her head and picked up the pencil that she had left on the coffee table, but she continued to listen intently.

She quickly scribbled a note on the same piece of paper that the General had given her, regarding the three main topics of the afternoon:

Mexico to OPEC - NO

Independence of Belize - YES (Guatemala to desist in territorial claims)

Mexico to GATT - Discussed but not decided.

She handed the piece of paper to the General, and smiled at him as she dropped the pencil onto the table again. As she did so, her eyes averted to a full scan of the room, and as always when the General pulled this, they were alone.

As an attorney with her doctorate in international law, Carolina was perfectly conscious of the fact that what she had just done was in violation of all international codes of professional ethics. Actually, it could be considered an act of high espionage meriting a trial in the International Court of The Hague. However, her

Commanding Officer had been doing this for a number of years in all the summit meetings that took place in Mexico. He had tried to get her into the booths a number of times at summits in foreign countries too, but that is where Carolina had drawn the line. As a military officer traveling on an official passport, she didn't even have diplomatic immunity. The General always insisted that an official passport actually commanded more privileges than a diplomatic passport, but she hadn't studied international law in vain. In practice, it was true, to a certain extent, at least in governmental circles in host countries. However, when it came to matters of summit meetings that fall under the provisions of the Geneva and Hague Conventions, she was simply not about to risk her own skin for anything or anyone.

General Porfirio had accepted her decision on the matter rather sullenly, but he hadn't insisted again.

After another thirty minutes, Carolina realized that the meeting was about to end. She rose from the couch and walked to the door, still listening to the last jokes that the President of the Philippines was telling. In the hallway between the waiting room and the interpreters' lounge, she cracked up. She couldn't believe her own ears: The President of the Philippines was singing the farewell song from Sesame Street, and all the heads of state were laughing hilariously.

As she entered the lounge, she threw her arms up in the air in a triumphal gesture, catching her headset at the same time.

"It's over!" The entire team, including the pages, applauded. "The interpreters may now attack the beer or anything else you may want as long as you don't have private conversations to translate, but the pages will have to wait for Susana's orders." She smiled at Susana, who was at the other end of the room, with bare feet propped up on a cushion. She looked as tired as Carolina felt, but smiled sadly. "My thanks to each and every one of you. You have done a stupendous job, and I truly appreciate you all. We'll see you at ten-thirty tomorrow morning, folks."

A few of them got up and went to the bar, and others said their good-byes to retire to their rooms or the pool; all of them to their own version of rest. Carolina had learned from the start that it was counterproductive to organize anything formal for the interpreters. They were a very different species of humans, and did their best work if they were just left alone.

Gerardo was waiting for her next to the electronic cabinet. She crossed over to him to give him her transmission equipment and radio. Without saying a word, her assistant put them away in the console and locked it. He started to turn the key over to Carolina, but she stopped.

"I'm still on duty, Gerardo, and I have to go out to the *Cuauhtemoc*. You'd better keep the key."

Gerardo reached out and turned over the security badge that hung around Carolina's neck. His facial expression changed from worried to relieved.

Carolina understood.

"I'll tell you later," she said.

"It's not necessary." Gerardo flashed her a smile from ear to ear. "I'm glad, that's all. I have been on pins and needles all day long, but I knew you couldn't say anything about it," he whispered.

"Thanks, Gerardo, you're a love." Carolina gave her trusted assistant a hug. "But I'm off and running."

She made a hand gesture toward Susana and Lorena to let them know she would see them later, and ran out to search for the launch that would be carrying her out to the tall ship *Cuauhtemoc.*

The majestic naval training ship *Cuauhtemoc* always awed Carolina, and this time wouldn't be the exception. From the sea, the beautiful sailing ship looked even bigger and more beautiful than it did when it was docked. As the pilot launch approached, the officer sounded one long blast on the air whistle, which the *Cuauhtemoc* answered with two shorter blasts.

To Carolina's relief, they were lowering a stairway with a platform to the calm sea. She had imagined herself climbing a rope ladder or something just as bad, and the image hadn't pleased her in the least.

However, the pilot boat dropped its speed to avoid causing any wake at all, and she was able to step off the launch easily. She had no problem climbing the stairs even with her straight uniform skirt, and stepped down to the upper deck with one short jump. The ship's captain was waiting for her at the foot of the stairs.

"Welcome to the *Cuauhtemoc*, Lieutenant Suarez. It is an honor to have you aboard," he said as he offered his hand. Carolina took his hand with the same informality as he had shown her.

From the other direction, a young cadet approached her with a pair of moccasins with rubber soles. Carolina accepted them gratefully.

"The decks are highly waxed and polished, Lieutenant, and I'm afraid your heels might be a bit dangerous, so I took the liberty of finding you some safer shoes."

"And much more comfortable ones, I assure you, Captain."

She removed her pumps, and placed them on a shelf just next to the stairs. She put on the shoes that the young cadet had offered her, and felt surprisingly relieved. Her feet had swollen during the day, and the sudden comfort made her realize it. She stood up straight again, smiling.

"If you'll just show me where you want me, Captain, I imagine the participants in the private conversations will be arriving any minute."

"Of course, Lieutenant. Captain Alvarado will take you to the private dining room, where we have everything set up for the meeting. I trust you'll find everything you need, but if you need anything at all, or are hungry for something we haven't served, our chef is entirely at your service."

"Thank you very much, Captain, for your hospitality." Carolina was astonished by the Captain's consideration, and couldn't even imagine how he would treat the heads of state in view of how he was making her feel like a veritable queen.

"On the contrary, Lieutenant. This is your home. The *Cuauhtemoc* belongs to all Mexicans, and it is an honor for us to welcome you here."

Carolina followed Captain Alvarado across the deck, and then through a labyrinth of hallways until they reached the luxurious private dining room that the ship's commander had mentioned.

She nearly gasped when she entered the room. It was much larger than what she had imagined, and much more luxurious. There was a buffet set up with shellfish delicacies, salads, cold cuts, enchiladas, tostadas with *nopales*, little rolled tacos with different fillings, and even a table set with both Mexican and international desserts: flan, chocolate cake, a few fruit desserts, and Mexican fruit paste with cheese. It was all making her mouth water, which pleased the Captain.

"I take it the cook made a good selection?"

"You have no idea! But, what a spread! I don't believe I have ever seen anything in my life that looked so good, but you must realize that I am the one who eats the least on these occasions, Captain."

The Captain looked crushed. "Why is that?"

"It's just that I am the interpreter, so I never stop talking. Just the nature of the beast, in my job."

The Captain laughed, and took a few steps forward to the buffet. He picked up a plate, and turned to Carolina.

"Then, I must insist that you try some before the presidents arrive."

She hesitated, not really wanting them to walk in on her as she ate. The Captain understood her hesitation intuitively, and insisted again. "Don't worry, because first we'll hear the whistles, and then it will take them another ten minutes, at least, before they get here. And If you're worried about your breath after eating, I have some mints, and there is a bathroom in the hallway so that you can freshen up before they get here."

That was all it took for him to convince her. She hadn't eaten a thing since her breakfast with Abdul, and she had eaten very little even then, so she was famished.

"Then, by all means. Thank you, Captain. But if there is still a little time, I notice that there is one dish missing from the buffet. The Crown Prince is a vegetarian, and he will eat nothing if there is no rice. Do you suppose there would be time enough to have a bit of rice prepared with a green vegetable?"

The Captain's face displayed a horrified grimace and he called the waiter who was waiting at attention on the other side of the door that led to the ship's galley. He quickly explained what they needed to make quickly, and the waiter ran to the kitchen, but not before being warned by Carolina that they not add any carrots or garlic to the rice.

The Captain wasn't only grateful, but relieved.

"Thank you for the tip, Lieutenant. No one had mentioned the rice."

Carolina made but another mental not to chide Abdul-Al-Horny.

She served herself a little bit of everything to avoid disarranging the beautiful trays of food, and sat down next to the Captain, who had also served himself a plate.

As they ate, Carolina asked him all kinds of questions about the ship, and the Captain answered gladly. The ship was the pride and joy of the Mexican Navy, and there wasn't an officer aboard that wouldn't enjoy talking about the majestic old training ship.

They had finished their plates and a waiter had cleared everything but their water glasses when they heard the pilot boat's first long whistle blow.

Carolina stood immediately, and excused herself with the Captain to freshen up in the bathroom, but not before accepting a couple of mints before leaving the dining room.

She freshened up quickly, then as she opened the door to the hallway, she found the Captain waiting for her.

"Would you like to watch how we do a reception for three presidents?"

"Oh, yes, Captain. I would love to!"

"Follow me, then, Lieutenant."

Carolina followed him up a spiral staircase, and they soon emerged on the navigation bridge, where the compass and ship's wheel were located.

"We can see everything from here," the Captain said.

"Yes, Captain," Carolina said, surprised at her own excitement over seeing the presidents' official reception. It wasn't the first time she had witnessed presidential receptions all over the world. But she just knew this one would be very special.

The ship had already answered with the two, short whistle blasts, and before long they saw the first president's head; which of course was the host's, President Santos del Alba. He saluted the Captain of the Ship and all the sailors, and took his place next to the Captain while the future Saudi Arabian Head of State —although internationally recognized as the president *de facto*— was received first by President Santos del Alba and then by the Captain. Finally, the President of the United States came aboard, and he was received in the same manner.

The three presidents took their places on the red carpet behind gold cords in the center of the deck, and a long whistle blast was sounded.

The Navy Band of Mexico played the Royal Anthem of Saudi Arabia. The Crown Price placed his hand over his heart, and was visibly pleased. Then they played the National Anthem of the United States, and that President also put his hand over his heart. After playing the two official anthems of the two countries, the band paused.

There were three long whistle blasts, and all the sailors, officers and troops stood firm in a military salute, including Captain Alvarado and Lieutenant Suarez, from their perch on the bridge.

The band the Mexican National Anthem, and they all sang in sweet homage to their country. After the anthem, they all waited for their Commander in Chief to close the salute, and as he did, there was such a massive movement of arms being lowered that it was audible in the silence of the calm day.

Carolina had to swipe at a fleeting tear as she turned back to Captain Alvarado, and she wasn't surprised to see that he was as moved as she was.

"Thank you, Captain," she said as she followed him down the stairway, "I wouldn't have missed that for anything in the world."

"It's impressive, isn't it?"

"Impacting, Captain."

Upon reaching the deck again, the presidents were approaching, guided by the Captain, Juan Alarcon. They stood firm again, and the Captain saluted his President and Commander in Chief, who returned the salute.

As the last head of state passed, the Captain took his leave, bidding Carolina a good day. She responded warmly, and followed the presidents to the elegant dining room.

Captain Alarcon stayed outside the door, and as Carolina passed by him, he quickly explained to her that only she would enter the room with the presidents, but that he would personally stand guard at the door during their stay for whatever they might need.

Carolina was nervous, but there was no turning back.

She mustered all the courage she could find, and entered the dining room. The three distinguished gentlemen were serving themselves from the buffet, with gusto. Carolina approached them to explain the ingredients in English. President Troyer served himself a taste of all the Mexican dishes just like President Santos del Alba. The Crown Prince was hesitant. Carolina assured him quickly:

"Your Highness, the rice is prepared to your liking, with no chicken broth, and only green vegetables," she explained, and the Arabian prince smiled gratefully. "And your Highness, there are a number of other completely vegetarian dishes with nothing prohibitive; especially the *nopales*, which are a Mexican delicacy that I imagine you would like."

The Prince served himself a *tostada* with *nopales*, and the Mexican President laughed.

"Carolina, what are you serving my guest? Did you explain that he's eating cactus?"

The word cactus is the same in both languages, and the Prince looked at her strangely.

"Yes, your Highness, *nopales* are a type of cactus, but I assure you that they are delicious."

The Prince shrugged his shoulders, and served himself another along with a hefty serving of rice.

The main table was round, and set for four. Carolina served herself a large glass of ice water, and sat at the only unoccupied place. The three men began to rise to their feet in a gentlemanly manner.

"Please, gentlemen. That is not necessary," she said, embarrassed.

The Crown Prince glanced over at her and realized that she hadn't served herself.

"Aren't you going to join us?" he asked kindly.

"Thank you, your Highness, but I ate before you boarded," she said, adding: "I was starving and I couldn't resist trying the buffet."

"Well done!" the Prince said, "because everything is wonderful, especially the cactus. You will have to give me the recipe for the *nopales*, as we can surely cultivate the same type of cactus in my homeland."

"I would be honored, your Highness. I will be sure to give the recipe to your staff, but actually, you already have this type of cactus. It's the common round, spiny type that grows the cactus apples, and I have read that the nomadic tribes in your deserts use the cactus apple as a source of water just like our ancestors did."

"It's the same? The spiny cactus?"

"Yes, your Highness, but of course it is peeled and the spines are removed."

"Excellent. Truly excellent," the prince repeated as he slowly ate the *nopales,* enjoying every bite. "Who would even have thought that cactus could be eaten like this?"

"Before you leave, I will see that you receive some cactus apple cheese, too, your Highness."

"Cactus cheese?" The Crown Prince laughed, incredulous.

"Well, it's called cheese, but it is more like a rich, sweet candy. I will see that you get the recipe, also."

Carolina noticed that President Santos del Alba was enjoying the conversation.

"Now that you mention it, Carolina, if I remember correctly, you're from Guanajuato, aren't you?" the Mexican President interjected. "They make a lot of cactus apple cheese there, and *cajeta*, too."

"Yes, Mr. President, in my homeland we enjoy a lot of goat milk products as well as cactus, precisely because of how arid so much of our state is."

The Prince seemed more interested by the minute in the subject.

"From what I see," he said, "Mexicans are very resourceful people and make do with whatever is available."

The Mexican President laughed.

"They say that necessity is the mother of invention, and our ancestors had a definite knack for living off whatever the land gave them. If there wasn't enough fodder for a cow, they would simply raise goats that can eat anything and still give milk. But yes, we Mexicans tend to be quite resourceful."

President Troyer had remained silent during the conversation, slowly enjoying his meal. Carolina noticed that he hadn't tried the cactus at all.

"We learn something new every day in this life, and very interesting things," the Crown Prince added.

And from the discussion about cactus, the three presidents began their conference on the subjects previously discussed; first by the Cuban and Mexican presidents, then by the Mexican and United States President, and now with the Saudi Arabian Crown Prince.

Upon comprehending Mexico's firm position regarding its supplying Cuba with oil at pre-established prices, the Prince's expected outburst came:

"But what lunacy!"

Carolina hesitated before translating his words, but then she realized that President Santos del Alba had understood perfectly. President Troyer was about to respond, but the Mexican President asked for the floor.

"Your Highness, as *don* Fidel isn't present for this meeting on President Troyer's request, I feel obligated to respond to your heartfelt indignation regarding the fixed price on the oil supply to Cuba. Mexico is not a member of OPEC, and it will probably be a very long time before we can develop our production enough to have any impact on OPEC. But I do understand your concern about such a low price on Mexican crude exported to Cuba. However, you must understand the enormous demand for Cuban sugar in Mexico."

"I don't see the connection between the two products," the Prince said.

"Neither do I," the United States President said.

President Santos del Alba smiled at them both, and explained.

"It is a very complicated connection. By the end of the century, Mexico will be exporting approximately fifty thousand tons of sugar every year to the United States, and another approximately eighty thousand tons of sugar to Saudi Arabia. We export a total of more than one million tons of sugar a year. Your two countries have promised to raise your import quotas even more in order to increase the market for Mexican sugar."

"Which will happen immediately upon our signing the North American Free Trade Agreement," the U.S. President interjected.

"Possibly, but we are a long way from agreeing on a balanced treaty, and that is a matter we will discuss at another time. Mexico's sugar production is approximately five million tons a year, and we have a national consumption of approximately four million, five hundred thousand tons. Regardless of your point of view, and however this is calculated, in order to meet the demand for sugar for export, we have a deficit of a half a million tons of sugar annually just for national consumption."

"I still don't understand what this has to do with oil prices," the Prince was not satisfied.

"It is very simple. Mexico needs the international currency from our exports, just like any other country in the Third World. However, if our Mexican sugar exports that we need for our currency baskets is leaving us a deficit for our domestic demand, then we need to import sugar," he said, duly noting the rising anger in the U.S. President, so he quickly gave in to a political concession by adding: "despite its inferior quality, for national consumption. Cuba is offering us the sugar that we need at a very low price as long as we sustain the agreed price of Mexican crude, which is approximately twenty percent lower than the price in the Free Market of Amsterdam, and which covers the difference in the price of sugar that we agreed upon, and the world market prices."

"But that doesn't make any sense, and it doesn't even seem to be in Mexico's best interest," the Crown Prince said, and the United States President nodded his head in agreement.

"Actually, it does work for us, if you realize that they are buying crude, only. In Mexico we lack the refineries to handle even our own production, so we have a surplus of crude."

This time, the United States President joined the conversation, laughing.

"I must ask, then. Where does that barbarian think he is going to refine it? Cuba has no refineries."

"Ah, but that is where you are wrong, my friend." It was as if Santos del Alba had hoarded a nuclear bomb for the end of the conversations. "Actually, he does have a refinery. It's in Cienfuegos, and it was built with Russian capital many years ago. It will be necessary to modernize and update it, but there is a very important financial group in Northern Mexico, the Beta Group, that is financing this update for the refinery. It will be ready for production within six weeks. And that investment by one of the strongest financial groups in my country is also in Mexico's best interest. This will create a very important source of employment which will improve the living conditions of many thousands of families in the northern part of my country."

Both Santos del Alba and Carolina realized that neither of the foreign heads of state was convinced. Santos del Alba stood up and stretched, and then he walked over to the dessert tray. He served himself a bit of flan, and returned to the conference table.

Carolina had come to know her Commander in Chief very well over the years, and she couldn't help but smile. She knew exactly what he was about to say: nothing.

"Don't you want any dessert?" he asked after tasting the first bite of the sweet dessert. "I can assure you that this is, by far, the best flan I have ever eaten."

Carolina stood immediately, and served two plates of flan in a ceremonious manner. Then she presented the plates to Mexico's two guests, with great pride.

The two guests tried the flan, and it was patently clear that they loved it.

The three presidents enjoyed their flan to the very last bite, and Carolina offered them all a cup of coffee, which they graciously accepted.

As she served the coffee, she asked, "President Troyer, you drink yours with two lumps of sugar, don't you? And your Highness, you take yours with three lumps. Right?"

Without waiting for a response, she served their coffee as she knew they drank it, and then took her seat again.

As they drank their coffee, she watched as the two guest presidents slowly began to react. Their eyes were sparkling. The message had been very clear: it was a barter that worked in the best interest of four countries. If, in fact, the world could live without Mexican crude if necessary, life itself would not be as rich or sweet without sugar. The consumption of sugar *per capita* in Saudi Arabia, as well as in the United States, was over thirty kilograms a year.

Once reaching an agreement on the subjects discussed, the Mexican and United States Presidents decided to toast with a snifter of brandy. The Crown Prince was known worldwide as being a non-drinker by religious conviction, but he decided to make the important occasion an exception to his steadfast rule.

The Mexican President served four snifters, and presented them almost ceremoniously. Carolina accepted the snifter, feeling honored to have been included.

They all stood to honor President Santos del Alba's toast.

"Gentlemen, I offer you Mexico's deepest affection, the warmth of our people, and the sweet gifts of our land."

The two guests smiled, and they all took a sip of the brandy. Carolina noticed that the Crown Prince barely touched the lip of the snifter to his lips, but the effect was the same.

As the three presidents prepared to leave, Carolina stuck her head out the door where Captain Alcaraz was waiting.

"Captain, the presidents have finished their meeting, and are ready to take their leave," she said through the partially open door.

She saw the Captain make a gesture toward someone out on the deck, and then she opened the door. The Captain entered, and explained to President Santos del Alba that they would return to port exactly as they had come.

"But there is no reason to make two trips," the President said. "Lieutenant Suarez will be traveling with us."

She made a point of remaining at a discreet distance during the departure ceremony, and soon found herself aboard the pilot launch again, heading for the hotel.

When they reached the hotel dock, she disembarked first on the insistence of the dignitaries. Their impeccable manners embarrassed her terribly, but who was she to argue the point with such distinguished companions?

She waited at the foot of the dock while they disembarked, and then bid them a good night. The three of them thanked her for her assistance, and they all congratulated her on her excellent job in translating.

She followed the three heads of state down the long pier, and once on firm land again, they were received by their respective security teams. President Santos del Alba was received by General Porfirio. Before accompanying the President to his suite, the General glanced over in Carolina's direction. She didn't change the expression on her face, but when their eyes met, it was as if they had held a conversation. The General smiled, knowing that everything had gone well in the private conversations, and he turned on his heel toward the hotel with the President.

Carolina turned toward the swimming pool. It was nine o'clock in the evening, and she hoped to find a friend or colleague from the Presidential Staff's Office with whom she could enjoy a drink and some light conversation. It had been a very heavy day.

As she entered the gardens where the bar and swimming pool were located, there was a lot of activity. The staffs of all the delegations were taking their free time very seriously. Some were swimming, some were playing beach volleyball, and others were thoroughly enjoying a full spectrum of tropical drinks while they chatted and joked.

She spotted Gerardo in a lonely corner of the garden, sitting alone on a bench, peering through a thick tropical plant. Intrigued, Carolina approached him.

"*Hola, hola,*" she chimed happily, and the young man turned toward her as he placed his index finger over his lips to hush her. With his other hand, he patted the bench next to him for her to sit down. She quickly did so, and gave him a curious, but funny look.

Gerardo pointed in the direction of the plant, and she peeked through to see what was holding his attention so.

There was Tanya, with the Canadian Prime Minister. Carolina couldn't understand more than a couple of words from their conversation, but it was obvious that Tanya was in full seduction mode.

"*Órale!*" she whispered to her assistant. "I see Tanya is making her move!"

"You're not going to believe what I have to tell you, *amiga*," Gerardo whispered. His eyes were sparkling like a child who had just discovered his big sister making out with her boyfriend.

A few minutes went by, and the Prime Minister took his leave, bidding a formal farewell to Tanya. He walked toward the hotel with firm, quick steps.

Tanya sat on the closest chair, and lit a cigarette. She smoked it slowly, glancing at her watch every two or three minutes. After about five minutes, she put out the cigarette on the ground, and stood, yawning and stretching as if she were very sleepy.

Then she followed the Prime Minister.

Once she was out of hearing range, Gerardo laughed and picked up his radio.

"66-Owl to J-Major," he said to the radio.

There was a second of static, and then General Porfirio's voice was heard.

"What's up? How's it going?"

"X-Maple is at position 16, with his blanket."

"Good. Very good. Hey, have you seen 66-Seagull?"

"Affirmative."

"Tell her she did a great job and to get some rest until our breakfast at seven tomorrow morning."

Carolina nodded her head.

"Affirmative, Sir."

Gerardo turned the radio off, and burst out laughing.

"I feel like the matchmaker of the Chief of Staff's office, I really do."

"Oh, Gerardo, at this point in the game, are you actually shocked by anything that goes on in the Presidential Staff's Office?"

Carolina had propped her feet up on the other chair, and had called a waiter over. He was standing before them, and she order for them both.

"Could you bring us a couple of Bulls?"

"Yes, Miss, with pleasure."

Gerardo looked surprised.

"*Bulls*? Are you trying to get me drunk?"

"Why not? At this particular moment, I can't think of anyone with whom I would prefer having a good, stiff drink and some good conversation. Do you find the idea distasteful?"

"Of course not, but I have to tell you this: you are not my type!"

They both laughed, united in their private secret. Gerardo was a gay man, and Carolina was the only person in the entire Presidential Staff's Office to whom he had admitted it. A few may have suspected it, but they would never dare to ask. He was a highly cultured and knowledgeable man, and very respected throughout the Presidency.

Carolina felt very fortunate to have him on her team, and she never tired of telling him so.

They worked together in a different manner from the rest of the military staff. Since they had both been civilians before being contracted by the presidency, and only then drafted as officers in the Mexican Army, they both shared the stigma of being *cardboard* military, as the career officers derogatorily liked to call any officer that hadn't graduated from the Academy.

It was not only a pejorative term, but it was unfair. At any given time, the so-called cardboard military officers tended to be even more subordinate than career military, and they excelled more in their tasks because of being made to feel so inferior by all the teasing that they took from the so-called real military.

That night, Carolina took her friend and assistant into her complete confidence. She told him all about the meeting with Sheik Abdul, the trip to Cuba, and about her suspicions regarding the manipulation at the highest levels of world power. Finally, she told him what to do if, someday, she didn't return from a mission.

Gerardo listened and added a few anecdotes to the conversation to lighten things when the conversation became too serious, and they drank a lot of *Bulls*.

Suddenly Carolina looked at her watch, and jumped.

"Do you realize that it's almost midnight? We'd better get some sleep, or neither one of us will get up for duty tomorrow morning!"

"Damn! I hadn't noticed the hour," Gerardo said. "Let me call for the check and we'll leave," he said.

"I already signed it to my room," Carolina said, conscious of the fact that her room had higher food and beverage privileges than Gerardo's. "That's the least I can do."

They stood, and Gerardo left a few bills on the table to cover the waiter's tip, and the two companions walked slowly back to the hotel.

As they entered the lobby, they found two French men arguing with the night clerk. They approached to see if they could help.

"*Que puis-je faire pour vous?*" Gerardo said to the younger one of the two, and the young man turned toward him.

"*Quelque chose,*" the young man said in a very seductive tone.

Carolina had to stifle a giggle, and decided to go up to her room, but before she could reach the elevator, Gerardo had caught up to her.

"Carolina, there is a problem with the French delegation. It seems that they don't have an adaptor to plug in their word processor, and ours don't work because they don't have their letters nor accents."

Carolina was exhausted, but she didn't push the button to call the elevator.

"I cannot believe that there isn't one current adaptor in this whole hotel. Did you ask?"

"Yes, but they had looked all over, even in the Command Center, but the officer on duty insists that we don't have any adaptors that would work."

Carolina thought a minute, and then an idea occurred to her.

"I imagine that they have the damned adaptors in the stores down in the Free Zone, don't they?"

"Yes, but all the stores are closed, and the work they have to do can't wait until tomorrow."

"Yes, but I imagine that there is an emergency telephone number on the doors at the stores, don't you think?"

"Yes, if you could define this as an emergency."

Carolina smiled.

"Well, for the French, it is, so it is for us, too. Get us a car, Gerardo, and let's go."

Fifteen minutes later, the two Mexicans and the two French men were walking on the sidewalk through the center of the town, searching for an emergency number to call the proprietor of one of the stores to have one opened for them.

But there wasn't a number anywhere, and all the stores were closed.

Carolina caught up to Gerardo, who was chatting in a most friendly manner with the young French man, and she pulled him aside discreetly.

"Look, Gerardo," she said, "this is ridiculous. Catch up with the men, and don't let them turn around to see me for about two or three minutes... then I'll call you."

"What in God's name are you about to do?" Gerardo knew from experience that Carolina would do whatever was necessary. "Are you going to break a window?"

"No, I'm going to do something I learned a long time ago. I am going to open a door."

"With what?"

Carolina took off her military cap, and removed the two long pins that held her long hair up.

"With these!" she said in a triumphal tone.

Gerardo shrugged his shoulders, and did as Carolina had asked.

In less than two minutes, Carolina called out to them. "Look!" she said in French. "This door is open. Come on!"

The four of them entered the store that to Carolina and Gerardo's relief, had no security system to be tripped by their presence.

In a blink of an eye, they found the coveted current adaptor, and the French took it. By their reaction, one would have thought that they'd found a million francs, and not just a simple current adaptor.

They searched all over the packaging until they found the price, and the younger French man took out a bill that more than doubled the price. He left it next to the cash register, and they all left the store.

Carolina was able to turn the disk in the door knob to lock the door from the inside, but was unable to lock the dead bolt from the outside.

"Oh, well," she said to them all, "at least the door knob is locked, even though I can't lock the dead bolt. I just hope that no burglars break in before the owner opens tomorrow morning and we end up getting blamed."

As she went to bed that night, Carolina finally fell into a deep sleep and didn't awaken until after 6:00 A.M. She had to hurry if she was going to be on time for the breakfast meeting with General Porfirio at 7:00 A.M.

There was only one short meeting left of the summit that meeting, and then all the participants would be leaving for home.

Chapter 8

"*Salud!*"

Carolina raised her champagne flute and clicked it lightly against her two companions' flutes. They had all arrived at the "Up Wheels Party" at almost the same time; approximately ten minutes after President Santos del Alba's plane had taken off.

The summit had come to an end with no problems, but this time General Porfirio hadn't asked Carolina for any information for the joint press release. During breakfast that morning the General had given it to Carolina —three hours before the summit was to begin— so that she could translate it to English and French. That press release gave Carolina her third piece of evidence regarding her theory, and she would have considered her hypothesis a thesis, if it had not been for one doubt: she had always been amazed by General Porfirio's solipsism —which bordered on narcissism— about everything that happened around him. If her theory was correct, then the General either was, or considered himself to be the Puppet Master of the World. This was the worst case scenario. At best, he was such an incredibly talented international chess player that by simply moving his pawns appropriately, he was truly causing a chain reaction of actions, reactions and decisions, on the highest levels, worldwide.

Through it all, she had discovered one undeniable piece of evidence, clearly shown on this last joint press release. General Porfirio could not possibly have known about it before the last meeting of the summit, if it had not been for his indirect and puppet intervention, through Tanya, with the Prime Minister of Canada: Canada had voted with Mexico against the resolution proposed by the United Stated regarding the North American Free Trade Agreement.

Sunday morning had begun a bit cloudy, but fortunately it hadn't rained during the departure ceremony in the hotel gardens. Everything had turned out perfectly, and after the ceremony, the heads of state had begun their withdrawals. Those who were taking off in jumbo jets were flown to the international airport in Cancun by helicopters provided by the Presidential Staff's Office, and the rest were going, one group after another, to the airport in Cozumel.

The President of the United States had been the first to leave, but in his own helicopter. This had always bothered Carolina, deep down inside and without ever showing it. The Secret Service were always openly distrustful of the security teams in other countries, and she wondered if taxpayers in the United States had any idea what each little luxury White House security insisted on having was costing them. Above and beyond the Presidential jumbo jet and a number of other planes to transport the entourage, they always took a C130 Hercules to carry the presidential bullet proof limousine. Furthermore, they always had a helicopter carrier, if not a full carrier group, close to shore and not too far from any summit meeting to be sure that the President only flew in helicopters belonging to his own country.

But by the grace of God, they had already received the notification that Air Force One had left the International Airport of Cancun.

The second entourage to leave was the Saudi Arabian delegation, and the Crown Prince had left on a helicopter for Cancun only with his brother, the Oil Minister. The delegation, including

Abdul, had left on the hydroplane an hour earlier. Carolina had seen Abdul briefly before he'd left, and had promised to see him during the following summit meeting that would be taking place after the first of the year, in India.

Lorena and Susana were scheduled to leave on Monday night on the last military flight, so for them, that evening was purely for rest and recreation. Carolina was off duty also, but she still had one last mission for the next day before returning to Mexico City. The Prime Minister of India, Indira Gandhi, had shown great interest in visiting the archaeological zone of Monte Alban, and General Porfirio had assigned Carolina to accompany her in a Puma jet helicopter. From the State of Oaxaca, they would fly in the same helicopter to the Presidential Hangar in Mexico City, where the Prime Minister's plane would be waiting for her flight home.

Gerardo had already returned to Mexico City on the first military transport, and Carolina had sent her luggage with him. She had only kept one briefcase with only essential items for that last day: a clean blouse to use with the same uniform she had used for a couple of hours that morning, a night shirt and a change of underwear.

She had put on her bathing suit below her blouse and shorts, which was perfectly acceptable attire for these informal parties.

Tanya's absence was noticeable, and Carolina asked Lorena about her. "What about Tanya? Isn't she going to join us?"

"Yes, *amiga*, but she said that she would catch up with us in a while because she wanted to say goodbye to someone." Susana laughed wickedly, and Lorena threw her a silencing look. Yes, Susana, she went to say goodbye to her *galán.*"

"Her what?" Carolina asked innocently, as if she didn't know exactly of whom they were speaking.

"Yes," Susana answered, before Lorena could, "and man! Did

she catch herself a nice little fish!"

"X-Maple?" Carolina asked in a low tone of voice.

Susana smiled at her, but at that very moment the door opened and Tanya walked in. She looked beautiful, wearing a black bikini with a flowing, open caftan over it.

A group of military officers on the other side of the room stood and saluted the actress with great respect, and she saluted them back with a gesture of her hand.

"Please don't get up, gentlemen," she told them as she flashed them a huge smile. "I'm glad to see you all, but please, remain seated." She walked directly toward the women who were seated at the dining room table, and they all got up to receive her.

"*Hola Chicas,*" she greeted them all, and then kissed the air next to each woman's cheek. "What are you drinking? It looks good."

Lorena handed her a glass.

"It's the *Santos del Alba* version of a Mai Tai," she said, "which is actually a *conga* mixture of fruit juices and some Havana Club Rum."

Tanya took a sip. "Wow," she exclaimed, "that really is good. I had always figured Mr. President as a man who had a very refined taste for the good things in life. Guess I was right?"

She sat at the table with the women, and picked at a few cold cuts and cheeses that they had found in the refrigerator in the suite, without speaking. She looked tired and as if she hadn't slept very well. Also, she hadn't put any makeup on.

"You should go out like that all the time," Susana told her, "because you look fresh, young and beautiful, Tanya."

Tanya laughed and there was a note of sarcasm in her voice.

"Thanks, *amiga,* but the exaggerated makeup goes with my personality. Today I dared to come out this way because I figured that everybody here could be trusted, and even if they couldn't be, I really don't fucking care!"

Carolina looked at her understandingly, and for a brief moment their eyes met. Tanya understood perfectly that which Carolina couldn't say, and smiled at her.

"And now," she said in a happier tone of voice, "I would like to offer a toast for a job well done. To all of us!"

Carolina clicked her glass with the rest, and added: "To *Las Chicas de Palacio!* Watch out world, because united, girls rule!"

Tanya laughed with the other women, but deep inside her, she felt only a profound sadness. She always felt the same way whenever she had to complete a mission for General Porfirio.

If she had met the Prime Minister under other circumstances, she probably would have found him charming and interesting. But because of how she had to meet him, strike up a conversation and seduce him made her a veritable prostitute in her own eyes, and she hadn't liked the reflection staring back at her in the mirror that morning. She hadn't made up because she didn't even want to look like herself.

Carolina was determined to lift the actress' spirits.

"Hay Tanya, did you hear what happened to General Santiago?" her facial expression showed her wicked pleasure in being able to tell someone new the anecdote.

"I heard something about him being mugged, or something like that."

Susana and Lorena burst into a fit of the giggles, but Carolina contained her laughter, and told Tanya everything that had happened, in a very low voice.

After she finished the story, Tanya was laughing as hard as her colleagues, and between the anecdote and the three Mai Tais that they had drunk, her feelings of culpability had become but a vague memory.

"*Ay, Chicas*, you'll never know how much good it's doing me to be with you, today," she told them sincerely. "You guys have a definite knack for turning even the most unpleasant things into something hilarious."

Lorena gave her a smile that only barely masked her profound understanding.

"Look, Tanya," she said in her lowest tone, "we are living in the dirtiest business in the world: politics." She finished her Mai Tai and handed her glass to Carolina. "Make it stronger this time, would you?" She turned back in Tanya's direction. "If you don't keep your sense of humor, then sadness, or what's worse yet, depression, can take over. That's why we always get together in these little parties so that we can forget our sorrows for a little while."

"Or better said, *drown* our sorrows," Susana said, "in alcohol!"

Tanya sat comfortably in her chair, and observed the three women. She liked them all, each in a different way, but she realized that she really didn't know them very well. With the confidence that their words had inspired in her, mixed with the drinks she'd consumed, she finally dared to ask them about themselves.

"Know what? I just realized that I really know very little about all of you. Carolina, I know you're an attorney, also a widow and that you have two children, but that's all I know. Susana, I know you got divorced at the beginning of this term and that you have two teenagers, but that's it. And Lorena, although I know you better than anyone else in the group, I really know very little about you other than the few conversations we had as a group when Salvador Arzate Bachi and I have gone to dinner with you and Arnulfo. I would really like to get to know you all better."

For the following half hour and three drinks, the three women told Tanya a little about their lives, and a number of details came out regarding each woman that the others hadn't known before.

Lorena explained that she had met Arnulfo Mendoza, the Chief of Police, during a parent-teacher conference. She had been his son's teacher. From the moment he met her, the Police Chief had begun courting her in a way that the provincial teacher had only dreamed could be possible. Finally, she'd agreed to have dinner with him, and their relationship had gone on for over three years. Mendoza was still married, but she had divorced the man she'd been married to at the time. With Mendoza's help, Lorena had no problem whatsoever keeping full custody of her little son. Arnulfo Mendoza had been the perfect paramour. Lorena had never wanted for anything, nor had her son, and thanks to the infamous cop, she now had a financial security which she would never have been able to achieve as a school teacher.

Susana told her the story of her difficult marriage which had ended in divorce, but described some details that Carolina had never known. After Lorena's story, Tanya couldn't help but ask if there had been another man in Susana's life, too. She knew Susana's ex-husband, and he'd always seemed to be a great guy, and handsome, too.

"Yes," Susana answered. "How intuitive of you!"

Carolina looked at Susana with an incredulous expression because she would never have thought Susana to be the type of woman who would be unfaithful to her husband, so Susana's answer shocked her.

"It turns out that he had been running around with this guy long before he met me."

Carolina turned with a shocked look on her face, while Lorena and Tanya exchanged confused looks.

"So your husband was... is..." Carolina was stammering, but she couldn't help it.

"I think the word you're looking for is *gay*," Lorena interjected.

Susana laughed over her friends' reactions.

"Yes. Call him gay, queer, homosexual or the queen of fairy land, but the fact is that I lacked the necessary equipment to give him everything he needed in a relationship, so he left me for his business partner, and they have just celebrated their twentieth anniversary of eternal love. How divine, no?"

"But if he was in love with a guy, why did he marry you?" Lorena couldn't grasp the concept.

"It's very simple, *amiga*," Susana said with a sad tone of voice. "He is from a very important political Mexican family, and he had his own political agenda. So I was the perfect fit. But after living with him for twelve years, after bringing two little angels into the world that are now adolescents that need a father more than ever, the man decided out of the blue that he could no longer live a lie. So he came out of the closet, forgot about his political agenda and his family, to boot."

Tanya's mouth was hanging open, as were Lorena's and Carolina's.

"I can't think of a thing to say," Lorena said, and Carolina nodded her head in agreement.

Susana laughed and drank what was left of her cocktail. She handed her glass to Lorena, and asked her for another as she turned toward Carolina.

"Now it's your turn, *amiga*. Are we finally going to hear the mysteries of your life?"

"Mysteries?" The idea made her laugh. "I have no mysteries in my life. On the contrary. My life is an open book, and a rather boring book, at that. I married my commercial law professor and had two kids. I was widowed at thirty, and here I am just trying to earn a living and support my kids with dignity."

"Hah!" Lorena said sarcastically. "And you travel around the world doing one of the most luxurious jobs in the universe. You rub elbows with the most powerful political figures in the world, and from what I understand, you're dating a colonel that adores you. If that's what you consider a boring life, then you are absolutely out of your mind."

Carolina smiled lovingly at her friend, and realized that her words had sounded ridiculous.

"You're right, Lorena," she said. "Anyone would be happy with my life, that is, unless they had to live it. In the first place, I do travel a lot. But other than some little side trips I've taken with a friend or two on weekends, all I know about the world could fit in the town square in Mexico City. I mean, I know government offices in seventeen countries, the best hotels near those government offices, and of course, the airports. It's no different from living and working in Mexico City. When was the last time one of you went to the National Museum of History and Anthropology? Or the San Carlos Museum? Or even to Chapultepec Park?"

The three other women shook their heads.

"That's the way it is when I travel," Carolina continued. "If I fly commercial, they only buy me first class tickets because they think I can sleep on the flight and be ready to go straight to work when I get there. I don't have any 'down' time. They give me hotel suites so I have room for my computers, file boxes, etc. They all go out to party at night while I stay in, writing the reports we have to fax to the presidency before the general gets there in the mornings. If I occasionally go out with some friend from my youth and get back to the hotel late, and I'll just find a pile of papers that my colleagues have left for me to review and process. So, believe it or not, the trips are not exactly fun. Then, add the fact that I am away from my children approximately six months out of every year, and just see which of you would like to trade places with me."

Susana stretched her arm out and caressed Carolina's hand, and Carolina continued:

"As for the colonel, well, he is a good man. He is loving and understanding, and he treats me very well, but we don't see each other very often. With all my traveling, I try to spend as much time as possible with my children when I'm in Mexico City, and he is constantly complaining because I never want to go anywhere for a weekend without the kids. Furthermore, about two weeks ago he gave me an ultimatum: either I marry him, or we're through."

Tanya took Carolina's glass from her hand and fixed her another drink.

"Here, girlfriend... I think you need this. Why is the colonel pressuring you? What's the hurry?"

"Thanks, Tanya." She lifted her glass in the air as if she were toasting, and took a long drink of the sweet beverage before placing her glass on the table. "Well —and this is to remain between us, please— it turns out that they are sending him to Washington D.C. as the Military Attaché at the embassy. He is leaving within the month, and wants us to get married so I can go live with him there."

"And what about your kids? Do they want to live in the United States?" Susana asked.

"I'm not even sure I want to live in the United States," Carolina answered, forcing a smile. "And that's why I'm plagued with doubts about it all. I feel like if I truly loved him, it wouldn't matter in the least where we lived, don't you think?" She didn't wait for an answer. "But if I haven't even discussed the possibility with my children, it must be because I already have enough doubts about my true feelings for him."

"Then I would say you have already made your decision."

Susana was right. Up to that moment, Carolina hadn't even admitted it to herself.

"Yes, I suppose I have. The problem is that I have no idea how to tell him."

Lorena laughed.

"A 'no, thank you' would seem more than enough for me, don't you think? Furthermore, *amiga*, too many words just get in the way in these cases. If things were reversed and you were the one who wanted to get married, I can assure you that Arturo wouldn't think twice about telling you no, and I bet he wouldn't give you any deep explanations about his decision, either."

Carolina was quiet and pensive, and then took another long drink from her glass.

"No, I don't suppose he would. I just don't know..."

Tanya looked at her sympathetically.

"Listen to me carefully, *amiga*, because this is something my grandmother told me a long time ago: Deciding not to decide is also a decision. Don't pressure yourself. If Arturo brings it up again, just tell him that you have decided not to decide anything quite yet."

Carolina burst out laughing. "You don't know him," she said between peals of laughter. "He is the most... well the most..."

"beautifully frustrating man in the world." Tanya finished her sentence. "And yes, dear friend, I know him. I know him very well."

The emphasis on her last two words hit Carolina like a ton of bricks.

"What? You mean that..."

"Yes, Carolina, I used to date him too, a number of times during my travels with the Presidential Staff's Office. So if you need an excuse to break things off with him, I just gave you one."

Carolina began to twist her face into a grimace, but then she cracked up again.

"I don't need any excuses," she said in a voice so loud that the officers that were drinking in a corner on the opposite side of the room turned around to look at her. "But I can tell you this much... the son of a bitch is going to pay for this one! I have always been faithful to him!"

Lorena turned her head with a knowing look, and Carolina laughed. "Well, with that one little exception, Lorena. However, that was a few years ago, and during one of those *if you can't be with the one you love, then love the one you're with* kinds of evenings. It never went any further and no one was ever the wise to it. Not only that, but it was in Brussels, so it doesn't count."

"What do you mean by: it doesn't count?" Lorena had her usual mischievous look on her face.

"It doesn't count," Carolina insisted, "because it was just one of those really romantic moments in life that no one can ever resist, and that the next morning just becomes part of your emotional data base as if it had been some sort of erotic dream, and nothing more."

"Whoa! You really know how to justify things, don't you?" Lorena sat thinking a minute, then added, "But I like the concept. I like it a lot."

"Don't even think about it, Lorena," Susana said quickly. "Arnulfo would not only be capable of killing you over an infidelity, but he would very likely kill your lover, too!"

"Not the lover I have in mind," Lorena said with a Machiavellian expression on her face.

The three women turned in their chairs to face her inquisitively.

"Do you mean to tell me that not one of you has ever even thought about making it with Santos del Alba?"

There was no response. All three of the women's eyes got as big as saucers. Lorena shrugged her shoulders, and laughed. "Don't worry, *Chicas,* because he's never even given me the time of day. He's far too involved with his Labor Secretary."

The romance between Santos del Alba and the Secretary of Labor was another rather poorly kept secret in the Presidential Staff's Office. Doctor Lilia Lumiere was a woman who had weaseled her way into the presidential campaign as a volunteer, and somehow managed (and probably not in a very honorable way) to end up not only with a post in the President's cabinet, but also in the President's bed. The Presidential Staff's Office had a constant duty of hiding her any time the First Lady happened to arrive anywhere by surprise and, as degrading as it was for them, the entire Presidential Staff's Office staff had, at one time or another, been part of the plot to cover the clandestine lovers from the beginning of Santos del Alba's term. Everyone thought that as soon as his term was over, Santos del Alba would divorce the First Lady to marry the love of his life.

"Don't kid yourself," Tanya said with an air of confidentiality. "Santos del Alba is just like any other man, and he would probably be the easiest man in the nation to seduce."

"Why?" Carolina didn't agree. To Carolina, Santos del Alba was like a father figure, and she respected him tremendously.

"Because he is a man who is completely protected and isolated from the world," Tanya insisted, "just like all heads of state. They live in a surrealistic world, where everyone adulates them. But they really have no social life nor personal life, above and beyond what their security people allow them. It isn't the real world."

"And that makes them more susceptible to seduction?" Carolina didn't get it.

"Yes, if it is true, and sincere. Just think about it. They are constantly surrounded by people who are just there to see what they can get out of them. If you want to want to unravel a head of state completely, a little bit of sincerity mixed with a bit of subtle seduction will always give results. If you get right down to it," she said with a facial expression that reminded Carolina of her Siamese cat when she was in heat, "I'll bet you all a weekend in Paris that I can seduce him."

Her three companions burst into laughter, but they stopped as soon as they realized that Tanya was perfectly serious. Lorena reached out her hand toward Tanya's.

"You've got a bet, wild woman!" she said.

Tanya shook her hand, and then she shook the other two hands reaching out to her by the somewhat catatonic other women.

Carolina looked at Tanya, amazed by her intrepid friend. What the woman had said regarding the isolation of presidents affirmed her theory that in most cases, it was precisely the Joint Chiefs of Staff who truly manipulated and molded world politics. She really wanted to tell her friends about all the manipulation she had witnessed over the preceding five years, but she was afraid that her desire to share was coming from the liquor, and not her common sense.

However, this woman had just made a bet with them that she would end up in bed with the President of Mexico, so what the hell? Her theory was probably not even as scandalous as that, although if it was true, it could have far more reaching ramifications than just a one-night stand with a president.

She glanced around the suite, and fortunately, the four women were alone. Their male companions had left, and were probably visiting the other *Up Wheels* parties that other foreign delegations were throwing.

"Okay, *Chicas*," she stammered, "if the afternoon is going to be about challenges and confessions, then I have a big one for you."

Lorena, Susana and Tanya turned toward her, and prodded her to continue.

"Look, what I am about to tell you is just a theory, but it's a hypothesis that I have been able to prove many, many times over the last few years, and based on my findings, I believe that the four of us, from this very moment on, could easily become the four most powerful women in the world."

"And you have just had your last drink!" Lorena said as she grabbed Carolina's glass from her.

Carolina snatched the glass away from Lorena, and finished it off in one long gulp.

"On the contrary. I need another."

She handed her glass to Lorena, who shrugged her shoulders and served her friend another drink. If she had counted correctly, Carolina had had four, and this would make five. She poured less rum into it this time, just in case, and gave the glass back to Carolina.

"Thanks, *amiga*... and thanks for making it weaker. Now, I am not kidding around. I'm going to tell you what I have seen over the last few years. But first, we have to make a secret pact. Nothing of what we're talking about today can ever leave these four walls. Agreed?"

They all brought their hands together at the middle of the table, and Lorena said, "*Chicas de Palacio!* United we prevail!"

"United!" they all said in unison, and clapped their hands together again.

Then, Susana stood up.

"If you're serious about the manipulating, then we are not exactly in the most secure spot on earth, are we? I would suggest that we grab a few little bottles, a bag of ice and some hors d'oeuvres, and take a picnic down to the beach where nobody can hear us... neither electronically nor personally."

The three agreed, and they got up to pack their picnic. They found a backpack that was a perfect size for their food and drinks, and a few minutes later they had managed to push a table and some chairs right up to the shore break at the ocean.

From a terrace on the fifth floor of the hotel, a young officer called *Los Pinos,* the official residence of the President.

"Give me the Presidential Joint Chief of Staff's Aide's office, please."

After a long pause, someone answered.

"Lieutenant, this is Major Alburto calling from Cancun. Has General Caballero Castillo come upstairs from the residence yet?"

When General Porfirio answered, the major reported what he was observing on the beach at the Hotel Melia.

The General smiled as if entertained when he hung up the phone.

Four women picnicking on the beach was nothing to worry about.

The following morning, Carolina bid her companions a fond farewell before heading for the jet helicopter that would be taking her off with the Prime Minister of India, since she probably wouldn't see them again until the President's State of the Nation report a few months later in Mexico City.

She was a little late, and was still adjusting her uniform as she walked out of the elevator to the lobby. Mrs. Gandhi's aides were in the vestibule, and Carolina approached to greet them.

"Good morning," she greeted them. "I'm Lieutenant Suarez, and I have been sent to accompany Mrs. Prime Minister to Monte Alban," she explained.

"Yes, Lieutenant, we were expecting you," the chief aide said, shaking Carolina's hand. "Mrs. Prime Minister will be right down, and the helicopter is ready for boarding in the heliport. The escort helicopter is circling the hotel.

At that moment, the elevator doors opened, and a tiny woman in black pants and a long tunic came out. She had tennis shoes on, and a baseball cap. Carolina had to look twice to realize that it was the Prime Minister.

Before Carolina could even step forward to greet her, the Prime Minister came up to her and offered her hand and Carolina took it in hers immediately.

"Mrs. Gandhi, it is an honor to meet you," she said nervously.

"The pleasure is mine," the woman answered. "So you are Lieutenant Carolina that is going to join me in my visit to the archeological site."

It wasn't a question. Carolina was momentarily overwhelmed and couldn't think of a word to say to one of her all-time idols, but she overcame her nerves.

"That's right, Mrs. Gandhi. They have conferred that honor on me."

The Prime Minister linked her arm through Carolina's, and guided her toward the lobby.

"And we are going to have a wonderful time, young lady, so please just relax!"

From that moment on, Carolina felt as if she were on an outing with a good friend, because of Mrs. Gandhi's mild manner and informal demeanor.

They climbed aboard the Puma Helicopter, and Carolina started to enter the rear staff cabin, but the Prime Minister stopped her.

"Carolina," she said, "please sit with me. It is a fairly long trip, and I don't like having breakfast alone. They've made a wonderful breakfast for us. Won't you join me?"

"Of course," Carolina said with a big smile. "Besides, I'm starving."

She sat at the other side of the table in front of Mrs. Gandhi, and soon their plates were served. There was yogurt, fruit and hard rolls with a nice selection of cheeses. The two women chatted amenably on many subject as they had their breakfast, and Carolina couldn't help but wonder where all the food could possible fit into the slender little woman. Mrs. Gandhi was probably wondering the same thing about Carolina, who because of the slight hangover she had after her night of cocktails with the *Chicas de Palacio*, was eating far more than she usually ate and was thoroughly enjoying every bite.

After breakfast, Mrs. Gandhi asked for a cup of tea, and Carolina asked for a strong cup of coffee. Just as they were finishing their drinks, the pilot announced that they were about to land at Monte Alban's Archaeological Zone.

Mrs. Gandhi turned in her seat toward the window, and gasped when she saw the enormity of the place.

"But how absolutely beautiful it is!" she exclaimed. "Is this the first time you've been here?"

"No, Ma'am, I was here once as a child. But this is the first time I've visited as an adult, and I can assure you that I am just as excited as you are. It is marvelous, isn't it?"

The helicopter was bare landing when Mrs. Gandhi had unbuckled her seat belt. She was on her feet and waiting in front of the door before her aides and the flight attendants could get there to open the doors.

Once on the ground, everyone stood still in the silence, upon the silent orders of the Prime Minister's aides.

She knelt, and kissed the ground.

Carolina didn't know what to do, because she normally would have followed any gesture from a head of state by imitation... but in this case she didn't know if the gesture was out of emotion or for religious reasons.

She chided herself for not having researched Hindu customs enough before making this trip with such an important person, and she felt ashamed of herself.

As if the Prime Minister had read every thought that had crossed her mind, she turned toward Carolina after she rose to her feet.

"Pay no attention to me, Carolina. I am extremely sentimental, and I feel I should render homage to your gods just as I would in my country when stepping into a sacred place."

Carolina was moved by the woman's sentiments, and she smiled at her.

"And now," the Prime Minister said, "let's explore this wonderful spot!"

For the following two hours, the two women climbed every temple they found, and they explored places that Carolina had never seen on her trips to the archaeological zone as a child.

Finally, they reached the very top of the hill from which the entire valley could be seen.

Carolina was amazed at the energy Mrs. Gandhi seemed to have. Carolina was out of breath because of the altitude and the climb, but Mrs. Gandhi, who was at least twenty years older than Carolina, was as fresh as a cucumber.

When the Prime Minister sat down, Carolina was grateful for the chance to rest for a moment. Mrs. Gandhi patted the rock next to where she was seated, inviting Carolina to join her.

Carolina obeyed gratefully.

For several minutes, the two women gazed upon the valley below in silence, marveling at the majestic structures built thousands of years before.

Finally, Mrs. Gandhi spoke.

"Do you meditate, Carolina?"

"Yes, Ma'am, I believe I do. I practice Integral Yoga, and am Roman Catholic by religion, so I suppose I do, in my own way."

"That's good. In a place like this, it is good to put your mind in a blank state to listen to your ancestors. They can tell you so much, if you are one of their chosen."

Carolina was fascinated by the idea and closed her eyes, trying to put her mind in a blank.

Mrs. Gandhi laughed.

"No, not like that. We are not praying," she explained. "To put your mind in a blank, you must focus on one special point, preferably at a distance."

Carolina fixed her gaze on a rock at the other end of the valley.

"Good. Now, don't think about anything. Just focus all of your being and mental strength on that point, and don't think about anything. It is far more difficult than it sounds, but you can do it. I promise you that, but I'm not going to talk anymore. Relax, because we have all the time in the world."

Carolina continued to concentrate on the rock, and little by little, she found her mind clearing itself of all thought. She had no idea how long it took, but she suddenly felt an inner peace that she had seldom felt before. She breathed deeply, enjoying the sensation, but suddenly her mind's eye began to see images and ideas that broke her meditation.

When she turned toward Mrs. Gandhi, the woman was standing, and smiling down at her.

"It worked, didn't it?

"I don't know. I truly don't know. I felt very serene, as if I were floating in the air, and then I starting thinking about a thousand things and lots of images went through my mind."

"And you didn't listen to the messages and didn't watch the images carefully?"

"No. They broke my meditation."

"The next time, you must listen to what they are saying, and you need to study the images carefully. You will learn a lot from them. I can assure you that you will."

"The next time I come here it will probably be in another twenty years, if I'm lucky," Carolina said laughing.

"That is where you are wrong, Lieutenant."

Carolina looked at her with a confused expression on her face.

"If you close your eyes right now, I can assure you that you will be able to visualize the point that you were looking at in your meditation. Isn't that right?"

Carolina closed her eyes briefly, and indeed, she could visualize the rock.

"Yes, Ma'am. I can," she told Mrs. Gandhi.

"Then, it will be very easy for you to return to this very spot in meditation, any time you want. You will feel the same serenity, and you will see the same images and have the same thoughts. But the next time, you must listen to them. You will learn a lot from this type of meditation."

They were now climbing down from their perch, where the helicopter was waiting for them.

"I'll do that, Mrs. Prime Minister. I'll definitely try."

"A sincere attempt is the goal. You must not give up, because you will receive the messages when you need them, and not before."

"Did you receive a message during your meditation?" Carolina was immediately sorry for asking, because this type of question was prohibited by all international rules of protocol on all levels.

Mrs. Gandhi laughed.

"Don't worry, Lieutenant, because I don't mind your asking. And yes, I received many messages, and they all affirm the same messages I have been receiving for quite some time, now. They say I must be prepared for the end of one cycle and the beginning of another."

Carolina didn't understand the meaning of her words, but she dared not ask another question.

After the farewell ceremony to Mrs. Gandhi at the Presidential Hangar in Mexico City, Carolina felt a profound sadness as she watched her plane leave.

That enigmatic and charismatic woman had reached the very core of her soul, and she wished her Godspeed. She had wished the same for so many people over the years that she had lost count, but with Mrs. Gandhi, she wished it from the bottom of her heart.

The meditation class she had received would be a gift that would last her for the rest of her life, and in a way, Carolina's life changed that very day. She wouldn't realize it for a long time, but the change in her spirit began that day with the Prime Minister of India.

Chapter 9

"Madame, Attorney Santos is here, and he would like to see you."

Tanya Monteblanco de Santos looked up toward her friend and servant and arched an eyebrow, intrigued by the unexpected visit from her attorney and brother-in-law. He was President Juan Ignacio Santos del Alba's brother, and they had just buried her husband, former president Juan Ignacio Santos del Alba, in the military cemetery just a few days earlier.

His visit couldn't possibly have anything to do with a court decision on litigation over her deceased husband's estate, since probate matters took a number of years to sort out, and probably many more years when dealing with an estate so enormous that it could only be calculated in figures rounded to the closest tens of millions of pesos.

"Did he give you any indication of what he wants? He usually calls before just dropping in... How did he seem?"

Griselda recognized her friend and boss' anxiousness over the jurist's visit, and would have done anything in the world to ward off anything unpleasant for her. Tanya's life had been reduced, of late, to a series of unpleasant events of all types, and the expression on Guillermo Santos del Alba' face had definitely reflected his state of mind. Griselda hesitated for a moment, which was a sure sign to Tanya that the intruder was not bearing good news. She sat up on her satin chaise lounge in the luxurious bedroom where she had spent most of the day reading.

Tanya looked out at her garden sadly before getting up from her chair, and then she turned to look at herself in the mirror above her bureau. She made a face, unhappy with how she looked in general, and in particular because she hadn't combed her hair and didn't have a drop of makeup on. Of course she couldn't —even in the luxury of her most graphic of dreams— pass for the same movie star that she once had been. Although she had always thought of herself as a great actress, the national press had tended to refer to her youthful artistic career in much more disparaging terms... like "vedette" or "soft-porn star," despite the fact that she was the widow of the ex-president who, in her humble opinion, had done more for the country than any other president of Mexico.

"Show him into the library, Griselda, and I'll be down in a minute."

"Yes, Ma'am."

The tiny woman vanished in silence, and Tanya crossed the enormous suite toward her dressing room. She stopped before entering, though, and snapped on the indirect lighting to gaze at her luxurious wardrobe. Days earlier, she had told Griselda not to let any of the maids in to clean it. She had decided to organize her clothes by herself, because she still had things she hadn't used in over twenty years, and that she would never use again. They were only taking up room in her wardrobe, and she was determined to clean out everything that she didn't need.

Her mother had always told her that one must throw out everything old to make room for the new. She had not only been referring to clothes, but to life in general.

Tanya remembered her mother's words, and her eyes filled with tears. She turned off the light, and turned toward her bedroom again.

Enough of your emotional outbursts! she said to herself. If her attorney could show up without notice, then he would just have to be received by a simple housewife; in her sweats and with her hair uncombed. It wasn't worth making him wait just to see her all fixed up.

She walked to the hallway, and stopped in the door to breathe deeply. She squared her shoulders, and walked the few short steps to the great staircase that her husband had built as a replica of the great staircase at the National Palace. The national flag was no longer hanging from the mezzanine banister, and Tanya couldn't help but think about the moment when that same presidential flag had been placed on her husband's casket during the funeral, and then how they had handed it to her ceremoniously at moment of his burial.

She shuddered, and then adjusted her posture to enter the library where her attorney was waiting for her. He stood when she entered.

"Tanya, I am so sorry for coming without an appointment," he said when he realized his client wasn't dressed nor made up, "but I felt it was urgent to notify you of an... an event."

"An event?" Tanya arched her eyebrows in the manner that had made her famous in Mexican cinema. "But you said that there would be no probate decisions for at least eight months."

"Y-yes," Attorney Santos stammered, "that's right, but I never counted on a civil suit filed by the citizens of Mexico, and that is what has happened. The people of Mexico have sued us!"

Tanya felt like someone had thrown a bucket of ice water on her. She had to sit down; feeling like the room was spinning around her.

"I understand your words," she said in a weak voice, "but I don't understand what that means. How can *the people* of Mexico sue me?"

Attorney Santos del Alba sat down next to the actress with no invitation to do so, and sighed.

"If you had asked me the same thing three days ago, I would have told you that it was ridiculous to even contemplate the possibility," he said in a solemn voice that bordered on fury, "but now, I just don't know. I don't understand anything anymore. Times have definitely changed. There is no respect anymore, even for the most sacred matters! Twenty years ago it would have been unthinkable to sue the estate of an ex-president."

"But, what is the basis of their suit?"

"It's based on the fact that they say they can prove that even this home was built with public funds."

Tanya's face returned to its natural color again, and she stiffened. She stood up and yelled for her housekeeper.

"Griselda!"

The petite woman appeared immediately, and by the terrorized expression on her face, Tanya realized that she had been eavesdropping on her conversation with her brother-in-law. Although she would never admit it, she liked the idea of not having to explain anything to her servant.

"Griselda, please get General Porfirio on the phone." She turned toward her attorney again. "We'll get to the bottom of this mockery right now."

The attorney seemed uncomfortable, and Tanya remarked on it. "Is there something else?" she asked, raising her hand to stop Griselda from leaving. "Do you have any more good news?"

The attorney nodded his head.

"I don't think it has anything to do with the suit, but there is another matter we should discuss, and it would be better to tell you before talking with the General."

"Hold on, Griselda," she told her housekeeper, and then turned to her attorney again. "What is it?"

"I have some bad news."

Her brother-in-law's stammering was getting on her nerves.

"Worse than the news you just gave me? I doubt that very seriously."

"It's Carolina Suarez, Tanya. She died last week, in Spain."

Tanya collapsed on the couch in front of Guillermo Santos.

"But, how? She's younger than I am. Was she in an accident?" Tanya hadn't seen Carolina in several years, but the news moved her to tears, and she had to muster all her willpower not to break down.

"From what I understand, it was a heart attack. Her attorney called me this morning with the news."

"Why you, Guillermo?"

"Because I am the one who prepared her original will, and he had very precise instructions to notify me in case of her death."

"But what was she doing in Spain? I haven't heard anything about her in at least ten years."

"Nobody has known anything about her since January of 1994. General Porfirio spoke to her that month to wish her a happy new year, and she disappeared a few days later. I even teased the General about her disappearance, because as far as I knew, she had been living as a total recluse with her husband in *provincia*."

"So she finally got married? To someone from Guanajuato?"

"No, he's from Mexico City; someone she met in her final years with the Presidential Staff's Office, and from what I understand, it was partly for him that she asked for her release from the army. As soon as she was able, she disappeared to *provincia*. She was using a different name, but she was registered with the bar association with her professional registry number, so she was fairly easy to find."

"So she left Mexico after the General's phone call? Wow! That must have been some new year's wish! What did he do? Kick her out of the country?"

"No, of course not. Remember how she was... stubborn as a mule. If she really wanted to live *en cognito,* then the General's call would have been more than enough to inspire her to move."

"But, to Spain?"

"Who knows? It wasn't until today when I spoke with her attorney in Madrid, that I learned that her biological father was a Spaniard, and she still has some distant relatives there. I imagine it was just another refuge for her, like the cabin in Guanajuato up on the top of that mountain which was practically inaccessible. It looks like the only thing she and her husband wanted was to be left alone."

Tanya became immersed in her thoughts, remembering her gregarious and cheerful friend. The image that the attorney was describing of her friend during her last years of her life just didn't gel.

"But, what was she hiding from? I don't understand it, because she wasn't like that. She was cheerful and got along with everybody."

The attorney smiled at Tanya.

"She wasn't hiding *from* anything, but from what I have found out about her, she was hiding out *for* something: she had become an author, and hid out in very private places in order to write in peace."

The attorney pulled a number of books from his briefcase, and placed them on the coffee table. There were different genres of literature, but they all had the same author: Perla Dosamantes. Tanya knew her work well; she had read two of the four books on the table.

"You mean she was Perla Dosamantes? But I love her books!"

She picked up one of the books that she hadn't read, and gazed at it sadly.

"*Ay amiga,*" she said, thinking out loud, "you never lost contact with me, after all."

The attorney frowned. "I didn't know you were such close friends. At least from the time you married my brother, I never saw her here."

"I distanced myself from most of my friends after I was married, Guillermo, but Carolina was one of my closest friends. Actually, in a strange way, I could say that all the happiness that I had with Juan Ignacio during the last almost fifteen years are thanks to her."

Her own words brought out the grief that she had been holding in, and she melted into a sea of tears.

"I'm sorry, Guillermo," she said as she dabbed at her eyes with a handkerchief, "but I let my emotions out."

Good! the attorney thought, *because you have been as stoic as a statue, woman!* He reached out his hand to caress his sister-in-law's shoulder.

"It was about time for you to cry, woman... you have held it together all too well, especially since Juan Ignacio's funeral."

Tanya sat up in her set and took a deep breath to control herself.

"Well," she said after drying the last tears from her face, "where is the funeral going to be? Here in Mexico, or in Spain? Of course, I will want to attend."

"Of course, Tanya, but apparently, there will be no funeral, or at least I don't know if there will be one. Nevertheless, she has left you some very precise instructions, according to what her attorney in Spain has told me." He took a letter out of his briefcase. "He has sent me this fax this morning, and the rest will arrive tonight, at the airport."

The attorney handed the letter to Tanya. It was in Carolina's handwriting, and Tanya read it aloud in a trembling voice:

Hi Tanya,

By the time you get this, my body will be in ashes!

But don't worry, because the damned thing was pretty damaged and decrepit, as the years have not gone by in vain.

I guess I won't be making it to the last meeting of "Las Chicas de Palacio," but I have sent you my ashes with a very special legacy for you, and for Lorena and Susana. A package will arrive by Aeroméxico tonight, and if it isn't too much of a bother, I would appreciate it if you would pick up the package personally, since I don't trust anyone like I trust you, dear friend.

And tomorrow, or as soon as possible, I want you to hold the last meeting of "Las Chicas de Palacio" in your home, with my ashes there to represent me. Then I want you to drink some Santos Albanist Mai-Tais, after which you can open the package I have sent to you all.

This is my legacy which I leave to you three, my most beloved friends, and I promise you that with this legacy, we will all have achieved the goals that we pledged so many years ago in Cozumel.

I send each and every one of you a kiss and a hug, and to you, dear friend, a promise that when I get to the afterlife, I will look up our beloved Juan Ignacio to drink that Mai-Tai with you three. I'll take very good care of him until you join us. I promise you that.

Carolina

P.S. After your meeting, feel free to dispose of my ashes anywhere you want. They are only ashes, after all. They're not important.

The loving words from her friend moved Tanya, but they intrigued her just as much. She raised her eyes to the attorney's, and lifted her eyebrows questioningly.

"What do you think of that? What do you suppose the so-called legacy is all about?"

"I have absolutely no idea, Tanya. I only know that it will be arriving on the seven P.M. flight today, and that the package is coming in your name."

Tanya looked at her watch, and it was already ten minutes before six. She barely had time to bathe and dress if she was going to get to the airport on time.

She stood up, and when the attorney did the same, she hugged him.

"Thank you, Guillermo, for your visit and for this visit with my old friend."

"But how do you want me to proceed with the lawsuit?" The attorney realized that Tanya was practically throwing him out.

"We'll see about that after the meeting with my friends, Guillermo. But this is more important, and I have to get ready and call the girls before going to the airport." She turned on her heels and called out to Griselda. "Gris! Tell the driver to bring the Jag, because we're going to pick up my girlfriend! And get ready, because I want you to go with me. And tell my secretary to start locating Lorena Araujo and Susana Aragon to have them come here to the house tomorrow afternoon. Have her tell them that it is of utmost importance and that it has something to do with *Las Chicas de Palacio!*"

Attorney Guillermo Santos del Alba was showing himself out in silence, with a sardonic smile on his face.

Chicas? Girls? he was saying to himself. *Crazy old ladies of the Palace would be a better description!*

The entrance to Mexico City's international airport was packed with travelers because of the hour. Most of the international flights that arrived in the city landed between five and eight in the evening.

When the car slid into the lane which would take them to the arrival area of the airport, Tanya leaned forward to give instructions to her driver. "Thomas, please take us directly to the door for Aeroméxico, and wait for me there, please, while Griselda and I go to pick up a package."

"Yes, Ma'am," the chauffeur responded as he picked up a radio to transmit the instructions to Tanya's security car. "66-Taurus, we'll be making a 22 at the entrance to Aeroméxico. Clear the space, please."

"Right away," the voice answered, and Tanya could hear the same order transmitting to the lead car that was in front of them.

A few seconds later, she could see that they had placed a red light on the roof of the lead car and she heard the vehicle's siren opening a path in the traffic that was bottlenecked at the entrance to the airport.

Thomas followed the lead car, maneuvering the car perfectly without sideswiping any of the cars they passed.

Finally they arrived at the entrance to Aeroméxico.

Tanya looked at her watch, and it was 7:20 P.M.

"The flight landed twenty minutes ago," she told Griselda, "so I imagine the package will already be at Aeroméxico's counter."

Griselda nodded her head, and took her boss by the arm.

"Are you all right to walk through the crowds? Do you feel well?"

"Yes, thank you, Griselda. But stay close to me, will you? I don't want to make a fool of myself if I get an attack of agoraphobia."

She tried to force herself to laugh, but couldn't.

Griselda got out on the chauffeur's side of the car, and ran to Tanya's door. She noticed that some men with cameras were approaching, so she stopped. She gave a hand signal in the direction of Tanya's aides, and they quickly opened a path by forming a human barricade on both sides so Tanya wouldn't be swamped by the crowds.

Once satisfied that her boss would be safe from any disrespectful reporter that might accost the ex-president's widow, she opened the car door and held out her hand to help Tanya out.

Tanya took her friend's hand, and got out of the car with her usual elegance. Despite the fact that it was almost dark, she was wearing her sun glasses because they helped her to feel more protected from crowds in public places.

"Thank you, Griselda," she said as she linked her arm with the tiny women's, "and let's go, because I don't want to keep my friend waiting."

With the help of Tanya's security team, the two women made it to the Aeroméxico counter quickly. There was an employee there who greeted them with a wide smile.

"Mrs. Santos de Alba, it is an honor," the employee said. "How may I help you?"

Tanya flashed her one of her more elegant smiles.

"I have come to pick up a package that should have arrived on the flight from Madrid at 7:00 P.M. I understand that the flight landed about twenty minutes ago, so may I have my package?"

"Of course, Ma'am," the employee said. "Do you know how many pieces are in the delivery?"

Tanya had to stifle her laughter.

"I imagine it contains millions of pieces," she said with no expression whatsoever, and Griselda busted out laughing.

The airline employee looked confused, but disappeared through a door that led to the interior part of the airport.

"Ay, Tanya," Griselda said, "there's no stopping your macabre sense of humor."

"The same thing always happens to me at really solemn moments," Tanya said. "Haven't you ever noticed?"

The two women laughed again.

When the woman reappeared a few minutes later, she was carrying a square box about eighteen inches high by eighteen inches wide. Tanya thought it seemed small, given its content.

"Are you sure this is the only box?"

The employee looked over the manifest, and nodded her head. "Yes, Ma'am. It's just this package, but it is very heavy."

One of the aides stepped up to the counter and started to take the box from the employee's hands, but Tanya stopped him.

"Thank you, but I need to carry it myself."

The aide stepped back, and the employee placed the box on the counter.

"Mrs. Santos, could I bother you with a signature on the manifest? It's just a receipt."

The girl paced a document on the counter, and handed a pen to Tanya.

Tanya took the pen, and signed the document. Then she picked up the box, and thanked the young woman for her help before turning and walking somberly out of the airport.

Chapter 10

"This has got to be the most degrading and shameful moment of my life, Arnulfo!"

"Oh, Lorena," the young man said soothingly, "I am so sorry..."

Arnulfo Mendoza's son looked a lot like his father around the time when Lorena had met him.

"I just cannot believe those sons of bitches actually searched my underwear. Who the hell do they think they are? Worse yet, who do they think I am? A common criminal? Do they think I'm smuggling arms or drugs into Mexico in my underwear?"

"No, Lorena, I'm sure they don't. They didn't undress you; they only searched you electronically, and it has nothing to do with suspecting you of smuggling. It's just a general order. I can assure you that it had nothing to do with you, personally."

Normally, her plane just zipped into the private hangar in the General Aviation area of Benito Juarez International Airport, but occasionally customs and immigration agents would show up to check documents and cargo. Today had been one of those occasions, and his stepmother was furious.

He was riding with his former secondary school teacher, now his father's widow around the beltway toward Lorena's home in San Jerónimo Lídice. Arnulfo had gone to the airport to pick her up a few minutes after the Sabre liner had landed. It had once been his father's private plane, but from about the time of President Santos del Alba's last State of the Nation report, it had been transferred to Lorena's name.

Arnulfo had been only fifteen at the time, but even now every time he went to the hangar where his deceased father's plane had always been housed, he was overcome with the same fear he had lived as that adolescent trapped in that same plane on a runway with a bunch of strangers, including another child that he had never met before.

"I still remember the day that I was locked in that plane with your son," he told Lorena, as if he were thinking aloud.

Lorena smiled at him.

"Believe me, it was worse for me than it was for you guys," she said, and then became engrossed in her own thoughts.

That day had been like any other day when the State of the Nation was to be delivered. The entire presidential staff, both civilian and military, had to be in the legislative palace by seven A.M.

Her little son Franco hadn't had school that day, so she hadn't even poked her head in to say goodbye to him before leaving the house; a decision for which she had been very sorry a few hours later.

Fifteen years had gone by since that day which for Lorena had been the end of the happiest period of her life. She still shuddered just recalling it.

When she had arrived at the legislative palace, she had gone to look for Susana and Carolina. She found them having breakfast in the officer's dining room, and Lorena had gone in with a cheerful greeting only to be received with a silencing gesture by Susana, who then immediately told her to sit down.

Once sitting at the table, Carolina had said, "Thank God you're here Lorena. In about a half an hour, this place is going to be like a fortress, and they won't be letting anyone in but special guests that have their security badges."

Carolina's somber demeanor seemed strange to Lorena.

"Just like always, no?" she asked.

"Not like always, Lorena, but like never before," Susana said.

"Why? What's going on?" The hair was standing up straight on Lorena's arm, which was always a sign that something was very wrong. "Was there an assassination attempt?"

"No, but I have the distinct impression that there may be one," Carolina said, "because I have never seen the entire Fifth Division as worried and mysterious as they are right now."

The three women were speaking almost in whispers, but their words weren't unnoticed by the security officers surrounding them on all sides. Carolina felt as if her forehead was burning, and when she lifted her eyes, she saw an officer staring at her in a way that made her tremble.

"I don't know what is going on," she told the others, "but I suggest that we make light and happy conversation, because they are watching us in a way that makes me very nervous."

"Well, then," Lorena said. She sat up in her chair and looked for a waiter to call over to their table. "My dear Corporal, a cup of coffee, please," she said, and then turned to her companions again. "You'll never guess where I've been!"

Carolina sat up too, and raised her voice from a whisper to normal.

"In Acapulco, where you inaugurated the "Roman Palace."

Lorena looked at her astonished.

"How did you know?" Her voice complemented the pout that was forming on her lips.

"Because I receive all the day's activity reports in *Los Pinos*. You took off in the Sabre with Arnulfo on Friday night, you stayed at the Presidente Hotel, and early Saturday morning Arnulfo picked you to go to the house you just built up on the hill. You had a house-warming party with a bunch of people that nobody knows but who spoke at least six different languages and who came from nine different countries, each representing a law enforcement agency in their respective countries.

Lorena couldn't hold back her peals of laughter.

"There's no doubt in my mind, my dear Sherlock, that you don't miss a thing. Do you by any chance know what I had for dinner, or what we did in bed a little later?"

"No, but I can imagine."

To continue giving the appearance of light, social conversation in front of the curious and suspicious eyes of the security team, Carolina turned to Susana.

"Don't you want to hear all about your weekend's activities?"

"They wouldn't be very interesting," Susana said, "because I stayed at home relaxing with my kids."

"Ahah! But you were relaxing after a fabulous week in Paris with Alejandro Sansores, right?"

Susana smiled at her with her feline eyes.

"Yes, *amiga*, I had a wonderful time in Paris with Alejandro."

"Has anything come up about what we discussed?"

Carolina was an incorrigible meddler in the lives of her friends, but always in the spirit of the pact that they had made a few months earlier in Cozumel. Each woman had her mission, and every time they got together, she wanted a formal report on the progress of each woman.

Susana laughed. "A little something, indeed, but the plan hasn't fully matured yet. Don't worry; I'll let you know the minute something really good happens. Meanwhile, I am having a marvelous time. But what about you? You haven't told us a thing."

Carolina leaned over the table again and waved her hand for the other women to come in closer. She noticed that one of the officers was getting ready to eavesdrop on their conversation again, so she turned to him, saying, "Is it absolutely necessary for you to listen to every detail of a slight gynecological problem? If you would like to, you are welcome to sit with us so that you can take notes!"

The officer blushed and stepped away.

"Well," she told the girls confidentially, "it seems that I'm getting married."

"You're what?" Susana, said while Lorena spit out her coffee. "What's going on? I thought you had broken up with Arturo when he left for Washington."

"And I did, but he hasn't left me alone for a minute. He calls at all hours of the day and night. He sends me flowers. If I'm not at home, he talks to one of the kids to win them over."

"So then what?" Lorena had recuperated from her coughing fit, and her eyes were shining.

"Then he came for a visit two weeks ago and formally asked me to marry him."

"Just like that?" Lorena was giggling like a little girl.

"Just like that. So I asked General Porfirio for my release, and it is being processed at the Department of Defense as we speak. As soon as the paper work is finished, I'm leaving for Washington with the children."

"In other words, you accepted?" Susana had some serious doubts about it. "Even though you knew he's been unfaithful to you?"

"Oh, are you referring to the Tanya thing?" Susana nodded her head. "I have my doubts about that, but who am I to judge him? I had my own little crazy night out, didn't I?"

Lorena was thrilled over her friend's news, but Susana only shook her head.

"I just don't know, *amiga*. There's nothing in the world I want more than to see you happy, but there is something about that guy that just doesn't sit well with me. As presidential as he may be someday, I just have a feeling that he's going to end up hurting you."

Carolina looked at her grimly.

"Thanks for your good wishes, *amiga*," she said in a tone so expressionless that her displeasure was more than noticeable.

Susana sat up and made her greatest effort to look happy over Carolina's upcoming marriage.

"They really are my best wishes, Carolina. I mean it from the bottom of my heart."

By then, a uniformed officer from the Capital Police Department had approached them, and was standing next to their table.

"Miss Lorena, may I speak to you for a moment?" he said, leaning down toward Lorena.

Lorena turned toward him, annoyed by the interruption.

"Can't it wait? I'm having breakfast with my colleagues."

"No, Miss, it's urgent."

Lorena stood, visibly annoyed, and followed the police officer to a corner away from the rest of the presidential staff.

Susana and Carolina observed from afar, but all they could hear was an exclamation from Lorena after listening to what the officer had to say.

A few moments later, Lorena returned to the table and sat down. She was pale and livid at the same time, and she looked like she was about to cry.

"What's going on?" Susana asked her, and Carolina responded by taking Lorena's hand in hers.

"Nothing is going on," Lorena told them, but she couldn't stop the tears from flowing.

Carolina stood up and pulled at Lorena's hand. She looked around the room and realized that the officer had left.

"Let's go to the restroom," she said to her friend. "We can talk there. And look happy so nobody suspects anything."

First Lorena and Carolina started for the restroom, chatting as if nothing had happened, and then Susana followed, pretending to be swiping at a stain on the sleeve of her uniform.

Once all three of them were in the restroom, Carolina checked all the stalls and around the sinks to be sure that no one else was present, neither physically nor electronically.

"We seem to be alone," she announced, "but who knows for how long. So tell us, Lorena. What's going on?"

Lorena had let the tears gush by this point, and she was now sobbing uncontrollably.

"They have my son!"

"What?" the two girls wailed in unison, alarmed. "Who? How?"

"Arnulfo... the son of a bitch!" she answered between sobs.

"I don't understand anything," Carolina said. "I thought everything was going great between you two."

"And it is," Lorena said, trying to control her nerves. "I don't know exactly what is going to happen, but apparently Santos del Alba is about to drop a bomb in the State of the Nation report that is going to piss off a lot of very important people."

"So that's why all the officers are acting so mysterious." Susana was getting madder by the minute.

"Yes," Lorena continued, "but Sanchez wouldn't tell me what type of "bomb." However, he did say that it is something really, really big, and that they think there may be an assassination attempt."

"By whom?" Carolina had been present during at least ten assassination attempts during her years in the President's service, so the concept in itself didn't frighten her, but rather where the assassination attempt might be coming from.

"Sanchez didn't tell me that, either," Lorena said, "but the fact is that Arnulfo has my son, with his, in the Sabre liner on the runway at the airport. The minute the shit hits the fan, Sanchez has orders to take me to the airport. They have my passport and my son's, and Arnulfo is supposedly going to meet us on the plane."

"That's ridiculous!" Susana sputtered. "Arnulfo would never abandon President Santos del Alba, no matter what. They have been friends since their infancy."

"I know," Lorena said. "None of this makes any sense."

Carolina stopped suddenly, with her hand in the air.

"Wait a minute!" she said, remembering a report that had been on her desk that morning. She hadn't paid any attention to it, but now it was beginning to make sense. "When you got back from Acapulco, which hangar did you use? The Police Department's? Which one?"

"The Presidential Hangar," Lorena explained. "Arnulfo said that in honor of a sweet *Chica de Palacio*, they were going to take me straight home."

"And now, *amiga*," Carolina continued, "I want you to recall things very carefully. Did you see something different in the hangar?"

"What do you mean by different? I don't understand."

"Anything out of the ordinary. You know. You've been in that hangar twenty thousand times. Did the plane go clear into the hangar?"

"Yes."

"Did they close the door behind the plane?"

"Yes."

"The lights were on when you deboarded the plane, weren't they?"

"Yes."

Carolina closed her eyes to recall the layout exactly.

"Close your eyes, and listen. Remember, *amiga*." Lorena closed her eyes obediently. "On your right," Carolina continued, "there are shelves with a bunch of electronic devices. To your right, is the door. Right?"

"Right."

"Just in front of you is the TP01, the Jumbo. Right?"

"No. It wasn't there. The Sabre was the only plane in the hangar."

Carolina nodded her head.

"And where the 01 is usually parked, what was there?"

Lorena opened her eyes wide.

"Some boxes."

"What type of boxes?"

Carolina already imagined which boxes, because of another report that had passed through her desk that morning, but she wanted to be sure.

"They were like the boxes they always take to the room when we're traveling."

"File boxes?"

"Yes."

"About how many were there?"

"I-I don't know... probably about twenty boxes. Why?"

Carolina had opened her eyes and was smiling at them all.

"Because that means that Arnulfo is not abandoning his friend, Lorena. He is helping him."

Susana and Lorena didn't understand her at all.

"But if that's the case, why all the mystery?"

"That's what we'll be finding out in the State of the Nation Report," Carolina said, and linked her arms with her two friends. "Don't worry about your son, Lorena. He is in good hands. I promise you that."

That night, in Arnulfo's arms, Lorena had cried her heart out, despite Carolina's consoling words that had helped her to get through that horrible day without showing the hysteria that had overcome her since Sanchez's news during breakfast.

The so-called bomb dropped by President Santos del Alba had gone off at about the midpoint of his speech, when to the astonishment of the entire world; he had nationalized all financial institutions in the country. He had referred to the highest echelon of the world of finances in the country as traitors to the nation, and in similar terms referring to any citizen of the country who had participated in the flow of capitals from the country.

A number of congressmen, senators and invited guests from the financial world had gotten up and left without waiting for the end of the speech, furious over the President's decree. However, President Santos del Alba stood firm on his decision, determined to put an immediate halt on the flow of capital from the country.

Fortunately, there were no incidents nor breaches of security during the State of the Nation Report, and everything went well during the reception in the National Palace, too. The entire Presidential staff was alerted to detect any movement whatsoever that wasn't entirely typical, but there had been no problem.

The reception where the people of Mexico are invited into National Palace to comment on the speech also came off without a hitch. On the contrary, their congratulatory comments seemed more sincere than ever before. Other than the palpable absence of all the members of the opposition party and all the major financiers in the country, the day went as well as any other State of the Nation report in the past.

The minute the President had left the National Palace, Lorena had run to find Sanchez, who took her home. Arnulfo was waiting for her there, with her son.

But that day was the beginning of the end of Gordo Mendoza's golden reign. Once President Santos del Alba had finished the term, the following president had accused Arnulfo of Abusive Mismanagement of Public Funds and Corruption, and the ex-chief of the metropolitan police had to flee the country as a fugitive from justice.

Before fleeing, he had transferred all of his assets to Lorena's name, except for the home in the Southern part of the city where his legitimate wife and son lived. His bank accounts and foreign investments were also transferred to Lorena's name, and only Lorena would know from then on, where to wire the money that Arnulfo needed in his new life.

The responsibility had weighed heavily on Lorena. She had administrated all the assets that had been entrusted to her very well over three years that her paramour had been jumping from country to country, using different passports and identities in each one.

However, during the fourth year of the new six-year term, Arnulfo had been picked up by Interpol in New York City as he was boarding a plane for Costa Rica.

He was extradited to Mexico, and had spent nearly five years in a federal penitentiary. Lorena had visited him once every week, and had been faithful to him even in thought. It had been during his years in prison that his wife had died, and Lorena had even had to take care of her funeral arrangements.

It had been during those long years, and especially after the death of Arnulfo's wife, that Arnulfo Junior and Lorena had become such good friends. After all, Lorena had been his teacher, and had always been very fond of him. Arnulfo Junior had become Lorena's son Franco's mentor and friend, and somehow, they had all formed their own —albeit strange— family.

After *El Gordo* Mendoza was released from prison, Lorena had agreed to marry him, and they lived Arnulfo's final years of life as social and political pariahs in Mexico. Because of his conviction, most of the former chief of police's assets had been frozen, but until the full investigation into the provenance of each asset was completed, they'd been able to use the homes, at least.

However, after Arnulfo's death, the Attorney General's office had seized all of his assets, with the sole exception of Lorena's home, which had never been in Arnulfo's name. There had never even been an investigation into the provenance of the funds for its construction.

Lorena's attorneys had assured her again and again, throughout the series of lawsuits and trials, that all the assets would eventually be released, but after all the years and a never-ending succession of postponements, the only assets that had been released had been for direct payment of attorney fees.

When she arrived home, the maid was waiting with an urgent message: that she call Tanya. Arnulfo Junior looked at her with a strange expression on his face.

"Do you mean that you know Tanya Monteblanco?"

"Yes, Son. We're old friends from the Presidential Staff's Office. I saw her for just a couple of minutes at Santos del Alba's funeral, but it was like a circus with all the press and mourners, so we barely had a chance to talk. I imagine that everything has calmed down now, so I hope I can see her in the next few days."

"Good, Lorena. Well, I guess I'd better go. I'm supposed to pick my wife up at Franco's house."

I'm glad, Son... please tell him that I'll call him tomorrow. What is Cristina doing over there?" She tried to think, but didn't recall any grandchildren's birthdays that would get them all together at her son's house.

"Just visiting, that's all," her stepson answered. "Laura and Cristina get along really well, and little Arnie really loves playing with the girls.

Lorena made a terrified face just thinking about her two granddaughters playing with Arnie. The twins were six now, and tended to play with the tiny two year old as if he were a little doll that they could dress up and make up; whose hair they could style, and whose little body they could through into the far corner of their bedroom if he dared to complain.

"God help him!" she exclaimed. "Do you realize that playing with the twins borders on torture for your child?"

"Yes, but he likes it. I sure as hell can't deny him," he said laughing. "We are so much alike it's uncanny. His mother has been torturing me for ten years, and I still love it!"

"Well, son... thanks for picking me up at the airport. It wasn't necessary, but I loved spending a little time with you."

"You're welcome, Lorena. Franco would have come personally, but he was with some clients from France, and he couldn't get rid of them in time."

After saying goodbye to her stepson, Lorena headed for her studio, and closed the door behind her, removing the shoes that were killing her feet because they had swollen during her flight.

She crossed the room to her desk, and flipped through the envelopes that her secretary had left in little piles, scribbled with notes that cataloged the contents of each one as urgent or not.

She pushed them toward the side of her desk so that she could open her address book, and looked for Tanya's private number. Tanya answered on the first ring, with a sleepy voice.

"Tanya? Did I wake you? It's Lorena."

"No, *amiga*, I was just reading. I called you yesterday, but the maid told me that you were in Europe. How was your trip?"

"Fine, Tanya, but exhausting. I'm not exactly the Third Musketeer that I was twenty years ago."

There was a silence, and then Tanya spoke in a sad tone."

"And that is precisely what my call was about, Lorena. Indeed, there are truly only Three Musketeers left. One of the *Chicas de Palacio* has died."

Lorena sat up in her chair, preparing herself for the bad news.

"How? What happened? Who?"

"It's Carolina, Lorena. She died in Spain ten days ago."

"But, how? She was the youngest of us all! Did she have an accident?" she was crying now, and didn't even try to hide her tears. She took a tissue from her desk drawer and waited for an explanation while she wiped her eyes.

"Nothing is very clear, but we'll know soon, *amiga.* I believe she had a heart attack, but the fact is that she left instructions to have her ashes sent to us, and a package that contains, according to a letter she left, her legacy to us."

"A legacy? What's in the box? I don't understand."

"Neither do I, Lorena, because I haven't opened the box. I'm not going to open it until the three of us are together. That's what Carolina asked me to do in her letter."

"Have you notified Susana?"

"I've left her two messages, but she hasn't called me back yet. Her secretary told me that she's in New York City in who knows what conference at the United Nations, and from New York, she'll becoming straight to Mexico. She said that Susana has my message and that she'll call me as soon as she arrives in Mexico. She should be here tomorrow."

Lorena was still confused. "Listen, Tanya. I'm not understanding any of this. I thought that she was married. How does her husband fit in the equation? Wouldn't it be more logical for her husband to dispose of her ashes? Why us?"

"I don't know, *amiga.* All I know is that the woman never did anything without covering all her bases. She must have had a reason, and I believe we should respect her wishes. Don't you agree?"

"Of course, but I still don't understand it all."

"I don't either, but it doesn't matter. I'm going to trying to get Susana to come the day after tomorrow, if you can make it. Why don't we get together here at my house on Tuesday, after lunch, say, at about five in the afternoon?"

"If Susana can make it, I'm all for it. What should I bring?"

"Nothing, Lorena. Even that is in the letter. I'll have everything here."

"So will you call me to confirm, just in case Susana can't make it? Who knows if Mrs. Ambassador has any free time..."

"I can assure you that she'll make time, *amiga*. She loved Carolina as much as we did. I'll let you know if she can't make it for any reason, but if I don't call you, then we'll see you here at the house the day after tomorrow, at five. Okay?"

"Okay. And Tanya..."

"Yes?"

"I've missed you guys."

"Me, too, *amiga*. But Carolina's death is a lesson to us. We have to get together more often. Who would have thought... well, that something like this could happen?"

"I know. Well, kisses and hugs, and I'll see you Tuesday."

After hanging up the phone, Lorena got up and crossed the room to her book shelf. She pulled up a photo album, and opened it, but she didn't look at it until she served herself a snifter of brandy.

She spent the rest of the afternoon alone on the sofa, looking at each photograph that she had of the four friends together during different presidential events during those years past that now seemed but only a dream.

Chapter 11

Susana gazed out the plane window as the craft flew near the Popocatepetl Volcano, and in the darkness of night, she could clearly see the glow that was coming from the crater.

She sat up in her seat, anxious to see the spectacle that always overwhelmed her when flying home: the magnificent aerial view of Mexico City at night.

Once, a Mexican Air Force colonel in the president's service had made a comment that had impressed her. He'd said that despite all the beautiful cities of the world where he had landed —and he had landed in almost all the world's capitals, given his duties as the president's pilot— there wasn't a view in the world that could hold a candle to the view from a plane when flying over Mexico City before landing in at the international airport.

And Susana couldn't have agreed more.

Once the plane had touched down, Susana pulled her cell phone from her purse, and waited for the Captain to give his last announcement to the passengers before calling Tanya. She knew intuitively that something was very wrong, and she wanted to get in touch with her friend just as soon as possible.

She had wanted to call her from New York, but after the conference she had attended, she had gone out for dinner with some colleagues from the Mexican delegation, and hadn't returned to the hotel until it was too late to call Mexico.

She finally heard the Captain's announcement, and as soon as the plane was ready to dock, she dialed Tanya's number. It was nearly ten o'clock at night, and she was afraid she might be waking her, but she didn't want to wait until the next morning to call.

Tanya's private number answered on the first ring.

"Hello?"

"Tanya? It's Susana. How are you, *amiga*? You have no idea how sorry I am that I couldn't come to Juan Ignacio's funeral. As hard as I tried, I just couldn't get away."

"That's all right, Susana. I understood perfectly, but I received your messages and the flowers, and my children and I all appreciated the gesture. It meant a lot to us. I hear a lot of background noise. Where are you?"

I'm still on the plane, but I didn't want to wait any longer to call you, for fear of waking you. They said you had something very important to tell me. What's up?"

Tanya hesitated for a moment, trying to decide if she should give Susana the news by phone, or if it would be better to ask her to go to the house the next day to give her the news then. But she thought again, and decided that it wouldn't be fair not to tell her.

"Susana, I have some bad news. It's Carolina."

"Carolina? What's wrong?" Susana felt really guilty then, because she hadn't answered Carolina's last letter that was in her last Christmas card. "I haven't answered the letter she sent me last Christmas with her card, but she was traveling in Spain with her husband at the time, and..."

"Yes, Susana, but she's gone. She died the week before last, in Madrid."

"Oh, Tanya, I'm so sorry. I really am."

Susana felt like crying, but she had to control herself. It would be unacceptable for the Mexican Ambassador to the United States to get off the plane in tears. There could be any number of reporters waiting for her, and if it hadn't been for the fact that she hadn't notified them of her flight number and arrival, her sons would have been there to receive her, too.

"Susana, are you there?"

"Yes, Tanya, I'm sorry, but the news just hit me like a bomb."

"Look, I don't want to keep you because I know you have to deplane and go through immigration and customs, but I need to ask you a favor, on Carolina's behalf."

"Anything, Tanya. You can't count on me."

"I need you to come to my house tomorrow at five o'clock in the afternoon. Can you? It is very important, Susana, or I wouldn't ask you."

"Of course. I'll be there." At that moment they opened the plane's door, and the rest of the passengers were deboarding. "Look, *amiga*, you can explain it all to me tomorrow afternoon. I have to hang up. And Tanya?"

"Yes?"

"Thank you, Tanya. I love you."

"Me, too, Susana. I'll see you tomorrow."

After going through immigration and customs, Susana exited through the main lobby of the airport, visually searching for her driver. Finally, in the back of the lobby, she spotted him. He was holding up a sign with her name on it, and was smiling from ear to ear. Susana felt pangs of guilt, realizing that at the rather advanced age of her chauffeur, he was still working the same hours per week that he had worked when he'd been half his age.

"*Don* Memo," she greeted the old man, "I'm so glad to see you! How are you?"

"Fine, thanks to the good Lord, Ma'am," The old man stepped up to take Susana's bags, and she allowed him to, despite the apparent frailty of her loyal servant, so as not to offend him. "You look very thriving, Ma'am," he added.

"Thank you, *don* Memo," Susana said through clenched teeth.

That means that I look really fat, she thought to herself. Any time someone told her she looked "prosperous" or "thriving," she knew that it meant she was overweight.

She had fought obesity her entire life, but the older she became, the harder it was to keep the slim figure of her youth.

She followed the old man out of the airport, and except for a couple of photographers that snapped pictures of her, nobody bothered her.

Have I gotten so fat that no one recognizes me? she thought, but she put those and all other negative thoughts aside when she reached the car, because her oldest son was waiting for her there. The man was holding his index finger against his lips in a silent warning for her not to make noise.

After hugging her son, David, she peeked into the backseat of the limousine. There, she found her eight-year-old grandson, holding her newborn granddaughter in her arms. She couldn't stifle a gasp of excitement, and the baby moved violently as if she were waking up.

Susana climbed into the car, and sat next to her grandson, who handed her the baby girl.

"Hi, Grandma," David Jr. said as he kissed her on the cheek. "I brought you a little present."

"Hello, my darling," she said as she returned her cherished grandson's kiss, and then she held the tiny baby against her chest as she watched her son climb into the car. "She is precious, David. Why didn't you tell me that she was born? I should be furious at you, but I can't, because you have brought me the most beautiful little creature in the world!"

David smiled at her.

"Oh, Ma, it didn't make sense to tell you because you would only have come running for nothing. Nicole is perfectly fine, and as you can see for yourself, your granddaughter is perfectly fine, too. You couldn't have done anything if you had come. So you're just meeting her three days old instead of three minutes old. Believe me, it's all the same. I promise you that she hasn't changed."

Susana gazed lovingly at her tiny granddaughter; the first girl after five grandsons. She was absolutely beautiful, and Susana's heart filled with love for her.

"What's her name?" she asked David.

"Susana, after her grandmother."

Susana couldn't hold back the happy tears, but once they had started, all the tears she'd held inside during her conversation with Tanya on the plane started to flow too, and she finally had to hand her tiny granddaughter back to her father to avoid getting her wet.

The baby was still sleeping, and didn't seem to feel the change in loving arms.

"Gee, Ma, you're pretty emotional, aren't you?" David was worried.

"Yes, son... I'm sorry. It's just that I was just given some very sad news."

"What happened? Can I help in any way?"

"No, son, thank you. It's about an old friend of mine; someone I cared very much for. I just got the news that she died. Maybe you remember her from my years at the presidency. Do you remember Carolina?"

"Of course! She was a beautiful woman, as I recall, and she had a really cute daughter, didn't she?"

"Boy, you'll never change! Yes, she had a daughter about four or five years younger than you. The last I heard anything about her, she was married and living in the United States."

"See? All the good ones marry *gringos*. That's why we Mexican men have to import products from abroad."

He was referring to his wife, Nicole, who was French.

Susana laughed.

David leaned forward toward *don* Memo, and asked him to drive them to his home in *Las Lomas*, and Susana sat back in her seat to chat with her son and grandson during the ride to her son's house, not without noting all the changes in the city. As they veered from the *Viaducto* to the *Periférico*, she was amazed to see the beltway had two levels now.

"But, what in the world is that?" she asked David.

"It's the beltway's second story, and it actually seems to be achieving its goal of reducing the traffic in the city."

"Maybe so," Susana replied, "but you'll not get me up there even if you pay me."

As they cross the Third Section of Chapultepec to get to David's home in *Lomas Virreyes*, Susana made a face as if something smelled rotten. "When are they going to stop giving permits for new construction in Chapultepec Park?" she asked no one in particular without expecting an answer. "It's a crime against nature to cut the very lungs out of the city to build these monuments to bad taste."

David just smiled, but didn't say anything. He knew that the first two or three days back in the Capital, his mother would complain about everything and everybody. Then, she would become just as apathetic as the rest of the city dwellers.

A few minutes later, they arrived at David's house, and he started to get out of the car. Susana didn't move.

"Ma, aren't you coming?" David's voice sounded hurt, and David Junior was pulling at his grandmother's arm. Susana pulled him toward her, and gave him a kiss.

"No, David. You go. I am very tired, and I have a thousand things to do before my meetings with Mr. President tomorrow. Furthermore, Nicole is just recuperating and we need to respect her quarantine, at least." She noted the disillusionment in David's expression and smiled at him. "I'll come in a couple of days when Nicole is feeling better, and we'll talk then, son." She pulled at his hand. "Now, give me a kiss and go to your wife. Now!"

As *don* Memo turned toward *El Paseo de la Reforma*, he asked the question.

"As always, Ma'am?" her faithful friend asked, knowing that Susana's first duty upon her arrival in the city, regardless of the hour, was to report to her political mentor.

"Yes, *don* Memo. As always."

A half an hour later, the old man stopped the limousine in front of a rod iron gate in the *San Jerónimo Lídice* colony, and he blew the horn. The gate opened and he guided the limousine into the mansion's outer gardens. At the end of the long driveway, he stopped in front of a regal staircase which led up to another rod iron gate that opened into an inner garden surrounded by a edifice that looked like an old, restored hacienda in *provincia.*

But this *hacienda* wasn't old, nor was it a convention center like the great old haciendas of the countryside that were part of the National Historical Heritage Registry.

This hacienda had been built in the sixties, and it belonged to the most feared, yet respected ex-president of Mexico.

An officer from the Presidential Staff's Office ran to open the car door, and held out his hand to help Susana out of the vehicle.

"Mrs. Ambassador, how nice to see you. Mr. President wasn't expecting you, but he will certainly be glad for your visit."

"Thank you, Colonel, but it's my pleasure. I hope I haven't arrived at an inopportune moment, but it is imperative that I speak briefly with Mr. President."

"For you, there is no such thing as an inopportune moment," the Colonel assured her. "Do come in, please."

Susana followed the Colonel to the inner gardens. The night air had become a little chilly, but after the unbearable heat and humidity in Washington and New York, Susana appreciated the breeze, and she walked straight to a small gathering of rattan sofas and chairs where she always sat to talk with her ex-president and mentor.

"If you don't mind, Colonel, I'd like to wait for Mr. President right here. The night air feels so good and the garden is so peaceful, that I'd like to enjoy a few moments alone until Mr. President arrives."

"Of course, Mrs. Ambassador," the Colonel said. "Would you care for something to drink? A cup of coffee?"

"I would love a cup of coffee, Colonel, if it isn't too much trouble. You have no idea how much I miss our good Mexican coffee, but what I miss the most," She waved her arm in a circular motion with her hand out, "is all this. You are privileged to live here, and you can't possibly realize what a paradise you have here!"

Colonel Gordillo smiled at her, pleased.

"Please consider this your humble home, Mrs. Ambassador. And if you please, I will send your coffee out while I notify Mr. President of your arrival. I know he will be pleased."

"Thank you, Colonel, and there's no hurry. I'm very comfortable here."

Once the Colonel had disappeared into the interior of the hacienda, Susana crossed the enormous patio to sit in her favorite chair. It was cushioned and comfortable, and the foot of the chair lifted like a lounger.

She lifted her feet with the handle on the side of the armrest, and stretched out luxuriously; enjoying one of those extraordinary moments in life when one actually feels like a part of one's natural surroundings.

Her thoughts took her to an afternoon fifteen years earlier, when she had mustered all the courage she could find to come to this very same place accompanied by Carolina, to visit the ex-president considered to be the most powerful man in Mexico by all sectors and independently of any political party or schools of political thought.

Carolina had insisted that they sit in the garden to talk with Mr. President that afternoon, fearing that there could be an electronic or recording device somewhere inside the building, and ever since then, Susana had always preferred the gardens over the house.

Hey, Carolina, she thought. *I really need you today.*

The news that she had to give the ex-president of Mexico wasn't exactly good.

Susana had understood the concept of "unspoken understandings" from that day with Carolina in these very gardens, but she had never felt as adept as her friend at manipulating the information that moved the world. She had often thought that Carolina would have been better suited for the job of Mexican Ambassador anywhere in the world, but Carolina had never wanted any other political nor diplomatic appointment after her time in Washington when she was going to marry Arturo Durango.

Carolina had left Mexico filled with illusions, like any other woman in love going to join her future husband. *Las Chicas de Palacio* had gotten together at Carolina's house a couple days before her departure to give her a little bridal shower, and they had toasted to Carolina's happiness with their customary *Santos Albanist Mai-Tais.*

"To Carolina," Lorena had said. "May today be the least happy day of the rest of your life!"

The women had clicked their glasses to the toast, and had spent the rest of the afternoon talking about all their achievements stemming from the pact that they had made in Cozumel a few months earlier.

The shower had taken place less than a week after the meeting that they had organized in these very gardens, and Susana shuddered just remembering how nervous she had been that day.

The pact in Cozumel had been very simple, and the four women had entered it as a natural step beyond Carolina's discovery. After all the drinks they'd had in President Santos del Alba's suite, they had taken sort of a picnic to the beach, and there, Carolina had explain the details of what she had discovered and proved during all her years in the service of the Presidential Staff's Office. She had explained things eloquently, as a theorem. Her words had been etched into Susana's memory, as so with all the women:

"True power in this world has nothing to do with financial power. Financial power facilitates the manipulation of information, but one can have all the money in the world, but that doesn't mean that one has power. True power is the power of life and death, and I'm not only talking about physical death, but political, cultural, religious and existentialist death of the world's populace.

"Even the Spanish conquistadors that enslaved our ancestors could only do so by using their knowledge. Although culturally they may have been quite inferior to our native ancestors, they were infinitely superior in their knowledge of the technology of those times. They simply manipulated information to convince our indigenous tribes that they were inferior to these strangers, and they took control of our lands. In some ways, they're still doing it today.

"So information and knowledge will always be more powerful than mere economic power. And our beloved Mexico has a privileged place in this world. Our foreign policy of non-intervention is laughable; because the truth of the matter is that we indeed intervene in all world events however we please, because no other country in the world holds the trust of so many other countries in the world as Mexico.

"I have observed, for the last six or seven years, just how the information that Mexico has is used to mold and influence decisions made

by the great powers of the world in a way that is, well, convenient for the country that possessed the information. And I don't mean Mexico's best interests, because it really isn't so. The holders of the information and the way they manipulate it truly believe —or at least I feel they do— that they are working for their country's best interest, but when they wield that much power, the holder can't possibly do anything more than to blend their personal interests with the country's interests. Power on this level is by far the most seductive element in the universe, and no human being is immune to its seduction. It's uplifting. It can devour even the purest of souls.

"So now, my Chicas de Palacio, we have much more information than you can even imagine. I am absolutely convinced that if we share all of the information that each of us has, then we can become the most powerful women in the world someday.

"But we have to set precise goals for what we want, and never lose sight of the goals that each of us has set lest we, too, are devoured by power, just as it has happened to the men who have had it before us, and those who will possess it after us."

And from that moment, the women had discussed their true dreams. Carolina seemed to have a special tidbit of information to help each woman to achieve her particular goal.

And over the nearly fifteen years that had gone by, Lorena, Susana and Tanya had reached the goals set that day. Each of them had followed Carolina's suggestions, and Carolina had intervened at different times to help them.

They all knew that Carolina was holding back an enormous amount of documents, journals, recordings, photographs and videos that she had gathered over the years. However, for her friends' safety, she had never revealed their location.

And now she had died. Susana had decided to be the bearer of bad news to the ex-president, even though it could cost her everything if she couldn't convince him that she still had all the documentation and supportive information that Carolina had used originally to help Susana achieve her goals.

Deep in thought, Susana didn't even realize that the housekeeper had served her coffee, and was withdrawing into the house before Susana could thank her. She sat up in her chair, and put her feet back on the ground to reach her coffee.

"Thank you, *Señora,*" she said to the servant, raising her voice so that the woman could hear as she walked back into the house.

She drank a bit of the hot liquid, and it tasted wonderful.

I should have asked for a good shot of Tequila, she thought, *to calm my nerves. What if he tells me to go to hell?* She knew, deep down inside, that this wasn't an option, but she was overwhelmed by doubt. It was as if she were still that young woman who had come to demand help from the ex-president so many years before.

"Susana!" She heard the soft voice of the most powerful ex-president of Mexico, and she stood up after placing her cup on the plate on top of the table. "How nice to see you!"

Susana took a few steps forward to greet the man, and hugged him warmly.

"I just arrived on the ten o'clock plane, Mr. President, and I wanted to see you before anything else," she said as she kissed her mentor's cheek.

The ex-president returned her kiss, and took her by the arm to guide her to her chair again. She let herself be guided, and then sat down. Her mentor sat on the other chair, in front of her.

"Send us a bit of Tequila, please, Colonel," he told the Colonel before leaning forward to take Susana's hands in his. "You seem worried, Susana. Was there, by any chance, a problem in your meetings in New York?"

"No, Mr. President, there weren't any problems. Everything resulted exactly as you ordered."

The octogenarian smiled, satisfied. His indigenous features barely showed the passage of time. His light olive complexion showed a few expression lines, but except for those lines, his face was taut and healthy looking. His posture was straight and strong, and anyone would have thought he was a strong young man, if they didn't know that thirty-five years had gone by since his presidential term.

"So then, to what do I owe the honor of your visit? I would love to think that you're here because you have discovered that you are deeply and hopelessly in love with me, but at my age, dear, even pipe dreams are hard for me to believe."

At that very moment, his housekeeper approached them with a tray holding a bottle of Centenary Tequila and some shot glasses, and she placed it on the table as she removed the coffee that Susana hadn't finished.

The President served two shots, and handed one to Susana. He lifted his glass, and offered a toast to his guest:

"To pretty, intelligent women who are braver than bulls. God bless them!"

It was his customary toast, but Susana laughed good-heartedly.

"Thank you, Mr. President, especially for the compliment. At my age, I don't hear 'pretty' very often."

"Ah, Susana, you are not only a pretty woman, but a beautiful one, because you have a very special angel that keeps your spirit young. What more could a man want than eternal youth?"

Susana was beginning to think that her mentor was already informed about the news she was about to give him, because his unusual joy was making her suspicious. She pushed the thought from her mind, and decided to get to the point.

"It's not that I want to sadden the day, Mr. President," she said as she placed her shot glass upon the table, "but I have come because I just received some bad news."

The ex-president was already serving her another drink, and one for himself.

"Oh, yes. A terrible thing. May God hold her in his Holy Glory!"

Susana began to tremble. Was there anything at all in the world that the shrewd old man didn't know before anyone else?

"What? Do you mean that you already..."

"Knew about Carolina? Of course I did, Susana. They brought her ashes back to Mexico two days ago. My old friend Santos del Alba's —rest in peace— widow has them. It is a shame. A true shame, truly."

Susana knew the ex-president very well. She knew that when he said the words *true* and *truly* in the same sentence, he was lying. Her mentor was thrilled over the news. Susana shuddered for the second time that evening, and her trembling was not unnoticed by the old politician.

"Are you cold, Susana? We can go into the living room, if you wish."

"No, Mr. President. I think it's just that the news of Carolina's death just finally hit me. I really hadn't had time to deal with it, and the truth is that it really hurts. She was one of my best friends."

"Yes, dear, and one of mine, too. We'll both miss her."

Susana felt very poorly then, and she couldn't distinguish whether it was physical or emotional. The only think she knew for sure was that if she didn't get out of that place that only minutes earlier had seemed but a paradise to her, she was either going to vomit or faint.

She quickly drank the drink that the ex-president had handed her, and then she placed it on the table with far too much force. She knew that her nerves were betraying her, and he had to fight to hold back the tears.

She slowly rose to her feet, and her mentor did the same, smiling at her in a friendly way.

"Well, Mr. President, given that I didn't bring any news you didn't already know, I suppose I should go home and rest a bit. I am very tired, and I must admit that the Tequila has made me a little dizzy.

The ex-president seemed truly alarmed. He put his arm around her shoulders and squeezed her.

"And I'd bet anything that you haven't eaten, either, my dear. Wouldn't you like to have me order you something to eat?"

"No, Mr. President, it's not necessary. I think I am more tired than hungry, and the best thing for me would be a hot bath and bed, but thank you, anyway. I truly appreciate the offer."

The President accompanied her through the garden to the gate that led to the outer gardens.

As soon as Susana felt the burst of fresh air from the outer gardens, she felt much better. She turned to her mentor and gave him a warm hug.

"Thank you for seeing me, Mr. President," she said.

"We'll get together at the end of the week to decide how to proceed," the ex-president told her, and Susana felt herself trembling again. "What a truly terrible shame."

"Of course, Mr. President," she responded, and then she climbed into the car through the door that *don* Memo was holding open for her.

During the short drive to her house, Susana calmed down, and her nerves began to change into fury. It was more than obvious. The most powerful old goat in the country was enjoying her friend's death.

He probably thought that with her death, all the evidence that Carolina had used in her power game had been lost in the undisclosed location she'd hidden it. She had never told any of them where the information was hidden, for their own safety. Susana had never seen the documents. She only knew that they showed something so terrible that they could actually affect the sovereignty of the country. She never wanted to know any further details.

But, how did the old man know that the evidence no longer existed? Could he have had something to do with the natural causes of her friend's death? Susana was trembling so violently when she got out of the limousine at her house that she had to lean on her old chauffeur to get up the stairs to the front door.

When she entered the living room of her house, *don* Memo helped her to the couch, and then went in search of the housekeeper.

Susana felt lost in a sea of fears; fear over thinking that the causes of Carolina's death might not have been as natural as they had made them out to be; fear over having to become a puppet for the ex-president of Mexico just when she'd reached the peak of her diplomatic career; fear of everything.

Guadalupe, her housekeeper, appeared and she pushed all thoughts from her mind.

"Good evening, Ma'am," her servant said. "Would you like something to eat? To drink?"

Susana smiled at her and decided to enjoy her employee's attentions.

"Good evening, Guadalupe. It's good to see you. And yes, I think I probably should eat something, but in my bedroom. If you can ask them to fix me something simple in the kitchen... some scrambled eggs and toast would be fine. I think I'm going to soak in the Jacuzzi a while and then eat in bed and watch the television for a while before I go to sleep."

"Very well, Ma'am. I'll order your dinner from the cook and will draw your bath. Don't you want me to unpack your things?"

"No, Guadalupe, don't bother. We can do it together in the morning, if you'd like. But, thank you, anyway."

She wished her employees a good night, and walked to her bedroom. She felt at least one hundred years old... and a very drawn-out hundred years, at that.

Perhaps it wouldn't be so bad for her career to end. After all, she had traveled the world over as Ambassador of Mexico. She had lived in France, Germany, Belgium, and Spain... and now she was at the peak of her diplomatic career as Mexican Ambassador to the United States.

In a way, it might be the best time to retire: at the top of her field.

Chapter 12

"Cheers!" Tanya lifted her *Santos Albanist Mai-Tai* in the air. "To the *Chicas de Palacio!*"

"Cheers!" Lorena said, then added, "To Carolina!"

"Cheers!" Susana said. "May her spirit live in us forever!"

The three women had just entered Tanya's studio. There, waiting for them, was a replica of the table at which they had originally made their pact: two bottles of Havana Club Rum, the tropical juice mixture known as *Conga* juice, and the same hors d'oeuvres of cold cuts, caviar, smoked oysters, smoked salmon, crackers and breads that they had enjoyed that first time.

On the far wall there was a giant television screen, and at the head of the table was Carolina's place. The urn that contained her ashes was in the middle of her place setting, with three medium-sized boxes marked with the numbers 1, 2 and 3, along with a DVD that was propped up on her urn.

The three women sat at the table, and Tanya picked up the original letter that her brother-in-law had given her a week earlier.

She read it to her friends in its entirety, and the three cried together.

"And now, I think we should put on the video," the hostess announced.

"Haven't you seen it?" Lorena asked. "I think I would have died of curiosity if I had been you."

"No, I haven't seen it, and now you'll know why," she said, picking up the envelope containing the DVD. She read it aloud. "*Chicas,* don't even think about watching this until the three of you are together. You can stop it at any time, but at the end of the video it will automatically erase itself after being seen only once. The only thing that will be left is the beginning where the pictures are. And please, don't try to record it on another tape. If I have prepared it just this way, it is for your own good. If this were to fall into the wrong hands, it would be a disaster; and not only for us, but for our beloved Mexico.

Lorena and Susana were dumbfounded.

Tanya stood up and crossed the room. She opened the DVD player, and pushed the record button on the videocassette recorder at the same time.

"I know, I know," she explained to her friends, "but with all the mess over the people of Mexico suing, we can't risk the lights going out or something else that would leave us with no DVD. We'll destroy the tape later."

Susana and Lorena nodded their heads, and Tanya took her seat again.

With the remote control, she played the DVD.

On the black screen of the gigantic television, the title of Carolina's last production appeared: *Las Chicas de Palacio - Friends Forever.*

Lorena's sobs became audible.

"Ah, Lorena, you'll never change," Susana said, also crying.

"Shhh!" Tanya hushed them. "It's starting."

First, a series of photographs appeared on the screen. They had all been taken during the women's days in the Presidential Staff's Office; in Switzerland, skiing; in New Delhi at the open market; in Havana posing with President Fidel Castro; in London inside Westminster Abbey; at the Vatican; a few photographs in different summit meetings all over the world posing with thirty or more heads of state.

When one photograph flash of the four women in skimpy bikinis during a rest stop in Acapulco, Lorena burst out laughing, and Tanya stopped the recording on that frame.

"There is no denying that we haven't looked like that in many, many... pounds!" she said sadly, and the three of them laughed until they cried.

They would cry a lot that afternoon.

Tanya began the tape again, and there were more photographs. The last one was of Lorena, Susana and Carolina in bikinis and drinking beer in the Jacuzzi in the interpreters' lounge in the Hotel Melia in Cozumel during the very summit meeting where they had all become *Las Chicas de Palacio.*

Finally, the photographs stopped, and after a short pause, Carolina appeared on the screen seated at a desk in what looked like a library.

She was smiling at them with the same roguish smile that had identified her with them over so many years. Her eyes were shining mischievously, and on that huge screen, it was as if she were visiting her friends from beyond the grave.

"*Hola Chicas,*" she began, and the three women answered. On the video, Carolina raised her *Santos Albanist Mai-Tai*, and waved her hand toward the desk where the same hors d'oeuvres and drinks as Tanya's table. The three women raised their glasses, too.

"*First, a toast... To Las Chicas de Palacio!*" she sipped from her glass, and placed it on the desk. The three women did the same, whispering, "cheers."

"First, I'm going to tell you why you haven't seen me in so many years. As you surely remember, right after our pact, I went to Washington to marry Arturo. Well, once I was there, I realized two things: first, that Arturo was an incorrigible womanizer that only wanted me as a trophy to show General Porfirio that he, through his ques-

tionable personal charm, could still make things happen in the Presidential Staff's Office... even though they had kicked him out for being a traitor. And Second, because I discovered a world that was so manipulatively sordid within the hallowed walls of the gringo's Superior War College that I decided to devote the rest of my life to destroying all foreign control over our beloved country. You see, I found that our very sovereignty was, and still is, in danger.

Now, you're probably asking why I have called you together from the beyond, so I'm not going to leave you chomping at the bit. I didn't call you here to tell you about my trials and tribulations, because they are not important compared to the magnitude of the task that I am going to ask of you.

Marcelo, my husband, sent you three boxes with my urn... which, incidentally, I hope is with you, because I feel like I should be there with you.

She rose from her chair, and showed them box number one.

This is for you, Tanya. Please take it and open it. I'll wait for you.

Tanya stood up and picked up her box, and opened it. There was a package of photocopies of documents that looked very old, and many of them had the old Seal of the Presidency of the Republic, and many others had the seals of other secretariats, all from the same era. Tanya placed them on the table, and as if she were watching her, Carolina continued.

Now here goes, amiga. I know that you are going through terrible times right now. Everything the love of your life left you seems to be lost through lawsuits filed by his children and even more now, as you're facing a lawsuit by the People of Mexico. Right?

Susana and Lorena turned toward Tanya with shocked expressions on their faces, and Tanya nodded her head. She was crying openly, and she wasn't embarrassed to share her pain with her friends.

Well, don't even think that I would abandon you when you need me the most, amiga. That's what friends are for, isn't it? she paused for a moment, and took a big gulp of her drink. *Well, now I have to tell you all about something you didn't know about during Gallardo's term.*

Remember how they put me in an office that General Porfirio's brother had used during Santos del Alba's term? Well, there was an antique safe in there that was locked. No one had the combination. I ignored it for almost two years, but natural curiosity got the best of me, and I finally brought a guy I had defended many years before who was an expert locksmith. She laughed mischievously. *Well, that's a misnomer. He was actually a criminal, but a very talented and bright one, so I took him personally to my office, telling security that he was a cousin of mine that I hadn't seen in years and that I didn't want anybody disturbing us.*

Anyway, Carlitos-the-Criminal managed to get the safe open, and he gave me the combination for future reference. Then I took him out the way I brought him in, and I gave him a little money for his social rehabilitation. Then I returned to my office, and opened the safe again. The originals of the papers you have in your hand were in there, Tanya.

Tanya's mouth was hanging open. She had sorted through the papers enough to realize that they were copies of all of the invoices surrounding the construction of the presidential complex that was in litigation. She didn't quite understand how it was going to help her to have them, but she was sure Carolina was going to tell her.

Obviously, you aren't understanding yet, Tanya, but what you have is proof positive that your properties were not built with public funds like they say in Mexico. On the contrary. Your husband received that land long before he became a public servant. You will find the deed which traces the title right back to Colonial times. Your husband was going to build a middle-class residential subdivision there many years ago with a guy by the name of Arturo Pasos. The land belonged to the Pasos family, and at that time the family was in financial straits, so Pasos put the land in your husband's name. There was no monetary consideration because they were going to be partners in the subdivision. This all took place more than twenty years before your husband was President, and Pasos died of old age long before his term, also.

What you will also notice is that all of the construction invoices, material, labor, etc. are processed through the Secretariat of Agriculture and Water Resources, and show the provenance of every penny spent on the construction, referring to a personal loan by the Secretary of Agriculture and Water Resources. As you'll remember, the Professor, rest in peace, was very possibly the wealthiest man in the entire country, and the provenance of his money is unquestionable. His honor has never even been clouded by doubt. There are rumors out there that tie his children to drug traffic and organized crime, but the old man was never known to be involved in anything crooked. Carolina laughed. *Or maybe I should say, he was never caught.*

Carolina laughed again, and took another sip of her drink, finishing it. She served herself another before continuing.

At the very end of the papers, you will find two more invoices, and they are the most important of all. They are attached to two deeds that describe a world renowned soap factory in the Canary Islands in Spain, and then a Santos del Alba estate in Palma de Majorca. These two properties have been in your husband's family for over one hundred years, and he quit claimed them over to the Professor to pay off this debt. However, you will find, at the very end of the package, two new deeds signed only five years ago, that's to say more than ten years after the end of your husband's term. These are new deeds that his old friend had drawn up, returning the properties to your husband. There is a copy of the cover letter that he sent to your husband from Spain when he deeded the property back. He says that since your husband's children from his first marriage would inherit his businesses in Mex-

ico after his death, he wanted to deed back his family holdings in Spain so that your husband could leave them to your children, Tanya. In his will, of which I have a copy, he has left all of his interest, title and power over all his holdings in Spain to your children.

Tanya was sobbing by this point, unable to control her emotions. She looked up at the screen, and mouthed a silent "thank you."

As if she were watching her in person, Carolina said, "*You're welcome, amiga, but do me a favor, would you? Tell your brother-in-law that he is a total idiot as an attorney and an asshole of a friend and brother. All of these last documents are duly registered in the Public Registry of Property Ownership, both in Mexico and in Spain. If he had done his homework, he would have known this. As for the invoices, General Porfirio has had them for over twelve years. These are the documents that I found in the safe in my office in Los Pinos, and I sneaked them out of the presidency clandestinely. Using my ex-commander's birthday as an excuse to visit him as a courtesy and in representation of my new commanding officer, I took the package of documents —not without copying them first, of course— and I handed them over to him.*

But don't be angry at him. I don't think he concealed these out of malice, but rather out of stupidity. He would have been so worried about the personal loan that he thought had never been paid that he hid the whole package of documentation, fearing that one of your husband's old friend's kids might try to put a lien on your properties to pay off this debt.

Anyway, this is the legacy I have left you, amiga. I hope it brings you the peace you so deserve. And now, I need to tell you that Santos del Alba was no saint, and I won't say he never did anything crooked in his life. That would be ridiculous. We all know that he had ambitions just like any other president, and that he wasn't above a few dirty deals, here and there. He made millions of dollars in very dirty businesses, but that aside, he was first and foremost an attorney, and a good one. He knew how to keep things separate so as to never leave his family in a quandary.

Everything is in the information one has on hand, and how one uses it, she said with a giggle. *But don't worry, because the information about his dirty businesses is going to be used in another way that doesn't muddy your husband's reputation, nor anyone's, for that matter. It is just information to be used to achieve certain goals, and nothing more. It will never be divulged. There are some things that are better off undisclosed.*

The video was silent while Carolina served herself another drink and tasted a few hors d'oeuvres. The other women followed her lead. Tanya had returned the papers to her box, and she was still hugging it with tears in her eyes. Lorena and Susana were so anxious to see what their turns would involve that they could hardly eat, but they did, anyway.

Finally, Carolina tapped her glass with a knife and laughed at the camera.

And now, she said to the camera, *it's your turn, Lorena. And yours is a little more complicated, so please take box number two.*

Lorena picked up the box marked with the number two, and opened it. Inside there were other papers that looked like the political "jackets" that they used to receive during summit meetings back in the eighties.

Now, Lorena, I know yours is much more complicated, so listen up. You can come out on top of this thing. I promise you that. And Susana, please pay attention too, because all of this has something to do with you, too, so please take box number three, so I can explain it all.

The two women exchanged confused looks, but they did as Carolina said, but not before serving themselves another drink.

Carolina did the same thing while she hummed the Smurfs theme. Once she had her glass in hand, she turned back to the camera.

We'll start with you, Lorena. I know that your path has probably been the most difficult of all, because despite your many claims about being after the properties and money, you were loyal to Arnulfo even when everyone else turned their backs on him. And regardless of how good he was to you, Lorena, Arnulfo was precisely the one who did all the dirty business during Santos del Alba's administration. Do you remember those boxes in the Presidential Hangar? Well, before they could be put away and after you two got off the plane, I had them all the documents and photographs in the damned boxes copied.

"But how?" Susana and Lorena asked in unison.

Do you remember that I didn't show up for work the day after the State of the Nation Report because I had such a terrible cold? Well, everyone was so busy at our office in Los Pinos that they weren't paying attention to anything else. When I saw the order where they were sending a unit of enlisted men to put the boxes away, I took off for the hangar, walked right in, and made myself at home. I checked each and every box and had everything I thought could be important photocopied in the offices at the hangar. There was only one sergeant on duty and she was watching television, and she paid no attention to me whatsoever. So let's look at the pictures first, which I put on a DVD that is in your box, Lorena. But let's look at them together, okay?

Carolina turned toward her television screen, and moved to one side so that the camera could record the images. She snapped on the player, and a series of photographs began to appear on her screen.

Here, you'll see Arnulfo with the Attorney General of the United States, right outside the city of Irapuato, Guanajuato, just after the floods of 1972. Everyone knows that the Secretary of Defense under President Santos del Alba had been the Commander of the Military Zone in Irapuato back then, but very few people know that Arnulfo was his second in command, nor do they know that he was the one to do the dirty work for the First Lady's family. They owned poppy fields on their thousands of acres of land in Guanajuato.

Susana sat up in her seat, paying even closer attention.

Yes, Susana, this is part of what your mentor and benefactor knows I have hidden away. But it is only a part, and the least important part of what I have, believe it or not.

The video advanced a few frames, and there was a photograph of the ex-president with the Attorney General of the United States, with Arnulfo in the background.

Now you will see the Attorney General with our very esteemed ex-president, shaking hands and hugging each other. I wonder if it even weighed on his conscience to have killed more than six thousand peons when he had the dam that flooded his wife's family plantations blown to hell... but anyway, this was the first of the dirty businesses that I was talking about, Lorena, and they are all duly documented in your package of documents.

She took another drink from her glass, and continued.

Now, let's go to the next important stage, which was during the administration of Santos del Alba. Here you will see only photographs, but they say a picture is worth a thousand words...

Another ten pictures or so of metal boxes full of gold coins appeared on the screen.

Yes, Lorena, it is a blessing that you never had to take off in that plane, because it would never have reached enough altitude for it to clear the mountains around the Valley of Mexico. Only three of the twenty boxes were full of documents. The rest were metal boxes wrapped in cardboard. They were full of Centenary gold coins worth approximately fifty million dollars which all came from the bribes that the People of Mexico were giving all the police under Arnulfo's command. They were under a standing order to convert 50% of their take into gold for their commanding officer. In your box you will find the documents, and Susana, there are copies in your box too, that prove the final cuts on the gold. Arnulfo kept 50%, and the rest was divided between Susana's mentor and benefactor for another 25%, and the remaining 25% went directly and personally to that same Attorney General of the United States. There is a rumor, of course that out of his 50%, Arnulfo gave most of it to Santos del Alba, but there is no documented proof of this.

Now, here is some further photographic evidence you should find interesting.

On the screen there were three photographs of the U.S. Attorney General supervising the arrival of five of the boxes. It was perfectly clear that he was at Edwards Air Force Base, near Washington, D.C. In the third photograph, just in case there was any doubt as to the contents of the boxes, one of the boxes had fallen, and the content was visible.

And as far as I was able to investigate, those poor soldiers who witnessed the box falling, died of natural causes shortly after these pictures were taken.

Carolina took another sip of her drink, and then turned off the video.

There are many more, but they all describe the same thing: a disgusting network of corruption that starts on the lowest levels and reaches the highest hierarchy of not only our neighboring government, but others, too. And yes, everything indicates that Arnulfo and his second-in-command did all the dirty work for the Mexican government. Don't feel bad, amiga, because he was good to you, and when you get right down to it, he was always a good friend. However, what they say about him is the absolute truth. Now, put those documents away in a very safe place, girlfriend, because one very important Mexican has already died trying to safekeep them, and it was our beloved ex-Commander, General Porfirio Caballero Castillo, who had him killed. He had done a thorough investigation on the whole mess, as Director of the MIA, or Mexican Intelligence Agency. He was about to launch an investigation on an international level through the International Court of the Hague when Porfirio took matters into his own hands to shut him up. When General Porfirio sent a unit to clean out the MIA offices, there was a window of opportunity that I simply had to take. I carefully selected the most important documents, and kept them.

But all is not lost, I promise you, Lorena. But now, we have to go on to Susana's box, because her role in the final stage is the most important one.

The three women opened Susana's box together, as it was the biggest one of all. Carolina was staring directly at the camera, as if she was watching them open her legacy. She finally spoke.

Very good, Mrs. Ambassador. Or should I say... Mrs. President?

Susana turned toward the screen, with her mouth open.

Close your mouth, Susie, because a moth might fly in. Serve yourself another drink, and listen to me. Look, because in your box you will find copies of everything that I just showed Lorena, but there is more. I imagine you have already spoken with our dear ex-president, and you are probably feeling helpless. I also imagine that the old goat feels completely confident because he thinks that now that I am dead, everything that I was holding against him has ceased to exist, too.

Susana felt her heart pumping so hard that she was afraid it would jump right out of her chest, but she didn't say a word.

Look, the fact is that the ex-president has been losing his power for a very long time, but he just doesn't know how to accept it. So he tends to exercise total power over anyone he can, including you, Susana. But enough is enough, don't you think?

Susana nodded her head in the direction of the screen.

In your box you will find some papers that will render all the politicians, Mexican and American alike, to their knees. But you must know how to manipulate the information properly. What we need to be able to count on is that it is not in anyone's best interest for this information to get out. So now, I am going to tell you exactly how to use it.

In your box there is a series of photographs that I took from the photographic archives of the Chief of Staff's office that you should find very interesting. You see, there is a defect in their security system: the official photographers always take all the photos to the Presidential Chief of Staff, and he picks and chooses the ones he wants. But the photographers don't destroy the photos that aren't used. They file them away by date. It's very easy to find photographs of very interesting people with very interesting people. So I simply reviewed the journals that I have kept since I was a child, and checked the dates of all the summit meetings in Europe when I observed very interesting things. Among those photographs there are some Arabs that you will probably recognize, or perhaps you won't, but if you can visualize the guy with the President of the United States with a beard and a little thinner, then you'll know who he is. Then you'll see the same guy with our President in another summit meeting; and you'll see him with the presidents of Venezuela, Argentina, Costa Rica, Panama and a number of other countries, too.

Carolina threw her head back and let out a war hoop of laughter.

Ah, but they're looking for this guy all over the world and just can't seem to find him, right? The point is that politics worldwide is a very dirty business, and in Mexico we are not quite as non-interventionist as we say we are, and we haven't been in many, many years. There is nothing new under the sun, as my father used to say.

Carolina stood up and stretched, then shook herself, and then she sat down again.

Sorry, but I was getting stiff. She howled in laughter again. *I guess it would be better to say that I am going to be stiff, right? Now, Susana. Here goes the most important of all, and with this you will un-*

derstand why you will be the new President. There is a situation in Cuba right now that will affect Mexico much more than you can possibly imagine. The Americans will do everything in their power to keep this from happening, but Mexico must make it happen, anyway. It is very simple, but the future economy of our country depends on this happening. Of course, you are aware of all the recent acquisitions of the Beta Group, right? Well, since acquiring all of those European financial institutions, it seems that they have now become the second strongest financial group in the world. And together with a German company and another Venezuelan conglomerate, they are updating the Cuban refinery in Cienfuegos. Do you remember all the problems we had in the eighties when I had to go to Cuba? It was all about a similar situation, and what Santos del Alba did to the Americans worked. There is no reason for it not to work again, Susana, especially because Cuba has just discovered rather rich oil fields right on their island, and will no longer have to depend totally on imports. But this time you'll be doing it for Mexico, and not as a Cuban puppet or spokesperson. If you still don't understand how important this is, just think about what has happened in Mexico since the North American Free Trade Agreement. First, our economy has gone from bad to worse, because the only jobs that NAFTA has created are minimum wage jobs, since the Gringos bring their own executives, of course. Second, with all the chains coming from the United States, not only have they devoured our national chains, but Mexican small businesses cannot possibly compete in the marketplace. Beta Group Financial is just about to pull all its capital along with all its business concerns in Mexico, because up until now, Mexico has not supported its participation in the Cienfuegos project because of pressure from the United States and the U.S. obsession to control all the oil worldwide. I don't have to tell you what the consequences would be if Beta Financial Group were to withdraw all interests from Mexico.

And if you're worried about invasive retaliation from the United

States because of our support of the Beta Financial Group, don't worry about it. What you have with those photographs, added to the criminal relationship between the first family of the United States with regard to the petrochemical industry with partners and Mexican relatives, I can assure you that they won't say a word. With your experience as an Ambassador, you will know how to handle it, and I have all the confidence in the world in you, just as the Mexican People will. I promise you that, amiga.

For the following fifteen minutes, Carolina explained to Susana exactly how to handle the information, and with whom, but mentioning so many different things that now Susana was glad to know that Tanya had recorded Carolina's DVD in videocassette. It was just too much information, and even though she had the documentation right there, it was going to be a tremendous help to hear Carolina's tape over and over until she understood everything.

And then, if you handle things both in Mexico and in the United States exactly as I have explained it all to you, you will be ready to run for the presidency, my dear friend. Your dear mentor and benefactor will back you with the entire old school of Mexican politicians. The information that only you have will help you with the new school of politicians, and you will get one hundred percent support from the entire world on an international level.

Ah, and if any of you are worried about losing your boxes or them being stolen or whatever, don't worry about it. My husband will be around, and any time that he sees you losing strength, he will help you out with further documentation or more copies. He is of my absolute trust, and he will back you, amigas. But for obvious reasons, he will always remain behind the scenes.

Carolina stretched again, but this time in her chair. Then she smiled at her friends.

Ah, and Susana, here's another thing, in case it isn't obvious. One of the first presidential orders that you will have to give as Constitutional President of the Mexican United States is an Executive and Posthumous Pardon regarding everything surrounding Arnulfo "El Gordo" Mendoza's life. It's only fair, because he never did anything on his own volition. He was always just following the orders from Ali Baba and the Forty Thieves, and in a very sick way, if you want to call it that... his loyalty surpasses any other in Mexico's history. Even now, the current president would give him an executive pardon if you were only to suggest the mere existence of the evidence you have because of the current First Lady's ties to organized crime through her family ties to Gordo Mendoza's second-in-command, but this would be giving him far too much power. Just remember that SHE who has the information and knows how to use it, is the one in true power.

And now, my beloved friends, she said as she popped a bottle of Dom Perignon, and Tanya did the same at their table to serve three flutes of the liquid, *I believe this deserves a toast!*

The three women raised their glasses with Carolina on the screen.

To the Chicas de Palacio! she said, with a big smile. *When we decided to call ourselves that years ago, did we know, on some level, that we would end up at this decisive and important moment for our country?* She sipped from her glass. *I doubt it, but we are there, dear friends.*

I can just see you all a year from now: Susana, our beloved President. You, Lorena, seem an excellent choice as Secretary of Public Education, and you, Tanya as Secretary of Fine Arts and National Popular Culture. Yeah, I know, there is no such Secretariat, but don't forget that Susana can create any Secretariats she wants. The way I see it, it's not even us who are coming out on top with our power play. It's our Nation. Our beloved Mexico and all our compatriots will come out ahead with your presidency, Susana. And Tanya, when you become Secretary of Fine Arts and Popular Culture, my husband will see that you receive a package that will allow you to recover all of the treasures that were stolen from the Museum of Anthropology and History during the Gutiérrez administration. I have been investigating the case here in Europe, and I have the information that you'll need to recover it all for the People of Mexico.

The three women exchanged shocked expressions.

And now, about my ashes. You can do anything you want with them, because they are only ashes. You can scatter them in the ocean, or in my beloved Guanajuato. Or if you want, you can carry my urn around with you; after all, you'll remember well how much I loved to ride around. The ashes aren't important. I love you all, amigas...

And the screen went dark.

The three remaining *Chicas de Palacio* drank their flutes of champagne while they cried.

Tanya was the first to get up from the table. She crossed the room, and removed the videocassette that she had recorded to hand it to Susana.

"Take very good care of this, *amiga,* because you have a lot to do. But just know that you can count on me in any way I can help you, and if you'd like to, you can use any one of the houses as an operations command center. You know I have a huge security squad from the Chief of Staff's office to take care of it."

Even she realized how ridiculous her words sounded, and burst out laughing between the tears that had overwhelmed her. Lorena laughed too, but Susana didn't.

"I might just take you up on that offer, Tanya."

"Have you gone mad? With the security squad around?" Lorena laughed.

"It's the last place in the world that anyone would look for anything," Susana answered, "but I agree. We'll have to really think about it. For the moment, I am going to take my stuff to my son's business where he has a safe. That building has more security in place than the White House, and it will serve me well while I decide what my next step will be."

"That's a given," Lorena said. "You need to teach our ex-president and mentor of yours some manners. Don't you agree?"

"Everything has its own precise timing, *amiga*," Susana said, "but at the moment, the only thing I want to do is to rest... to sleep and think about things tomorrow."

Tanya stood up, hugging her box against her chest.

"Then, it's off to work we go! We only have four short months to announce your pre-candidacy, *amiga.*"

Epilogue

The waters of the Gulf of Biscayne had a turquoise tint under the morning sky. Sandra Bolaños was enjoying her third cup of coffee on the terrace of the little condominium where she lived with her husband in Santander, Spain. She was anxiously awaiting her husband Marcelo's return from going out to buy her the newspapers from Mexico that always arrived at the corner news stand at around ten thirty in the morning.

She had already read the new online, but she wanted to see the news in print. She was dying to savor every one of the photographs and every written word about the first woman president in Mexico.

Her first joy had come in July, when her dear friend had won the popular vote in Mexico for the presidency. She had followed all the news that came out in the Mexican newspapers and in the rest of the world on the course of her friend's career and her preparations for the most important job in her country, and the bookshelves in her studio were full of newspaper clippings and photographs of Susana's activities, from the beginning of her presidential campaign to date.

The breakfast plates were still on the table. Marcelo's plate was empty, but Sandra had barely touched hers. She got up to clear the table, since she would need the entire table to spread out her papers.

She carried the plates to the little apartment's kitchenette, and while she washed them, she decided to make another pot of coffee.

Just as she was turning the coffee pot on, her husband returned home.

Closing the door behind him, he walked straight out to the terrace, and placed all the newspapers from Mexico on the table.

"There you have them, except for the *Uno Más Uno*. It hadn't arrived yet, and I didn't want to wait for it any longer."

"It doesn't matter. It doesn't have a lot of pictures, anyway."

Sandra ran to the terrace, and tripped on the rug that was in front of the glass doors. She caught herself just in time, and didn't fall.

"This damned thing is going to kill me one of these days!" she said as she picked up the little rug. She carried it over to the railing, and looked below. One of the students who lived in their building was talking with some friends on the sidewalk, and Sandra yelled out to him. "Hey, could you use a little rug? It's pretty... I bought it in Marrakesh last year, but it has homicidal tendencies!"

The young man happily accepted the gift, and Carolina let it drop on the ground. The boy picked it up, calling out a sincere thanks.

Sandra sovereignly ignored her husband's teasing laugh, and she sat down at the table. She opened the *Universal de México*, and lovingly looked at the photo of her dear friend at the very moment that the presidential banner was transferred. Susana looked radiantly beautiful. Sandra picked up the page with the photograph, and kissed it.

Her husband was still laughing.

"You could have been that woman, Carolina," he said.

"Sandra!" she exclaimed furiously. "If we have spent more than Spain's foreign debt to change my face and buy me a new legal identity, the last thing we need is for you to keep calling me Carolina!" she said with a gesture that showed her dislike for the name. "I am Sandra, and we had better not forget it, my love. But getting back to your comment, I can assure you that there is nothing in this world that would interest me less than to return to politics in any form. I am a writer, and I hope to die someday with my laptop on top of me."

She continued paging through the newspaper, and then suddenly let out a war cry that made Marcelo jump. The young student's voice could be heard from down below.

"Miss Sandra, are you all right?"

Marcelo leaned over the balcony to assure the boy that he hadn't struck the friend and voluntary cook for all the students in the building, and then he turned to his wife.

"Calm down, will you? I understand your joy, but if you keep this up, someone is going to call the police."

Sandra was pointing at the second page of the newspaper with her finger, laughing like a fool. "You have to see this, my love. It's just too freaking incredible!"

Marcelo picked up the newspaper. There was a photograph of Susana sitting at the grand presidential desk in National Palace. Beside her was her newly appointed Secretary of Public Education, Lorena Araujo. On her other side, the newly appointed Secretary of Fine Arts and Popular Culture. The ministry had been created that very day by the President especially for Tanya Monteblanco de Santos de Alba.

Marcelo read the entire note in which the first presidential foreign trip to Brussels was announced, where the Secretary of Public Education would be meeting with her counterparts from the European Community in the seat of the United Nations in Brussels to discuss the educational future of the children of the world. On the other hand, the new Secretary of Fine Arts and Popular

Culture would meet with her European counterparts to discuss Mexico's recovery of the archeological treasures that had been missing from the National Museum of Anthropology and History of Mexico for fifteen years; the same ones that currently filled a major part of several private collections in a number of European cities.

"From what I can see, Tanya received the package that you sent her with my letter to her," Marcelo said, "and she has the guts to carry out the recovery plan."

"Yes, I liked that part a lot," Sandra said, "but you haven't seen the most important part of that photograph."

Marcelo still hadn't seen anything, so Sandra picked up a pen from the table and pointed at the object that she found most important in the picture. Behind the three women, on the bottom level of the bookshelf, in plain sight for the entire world, was the little urn that Marcelo had sent in March.

Just then the phone rang, and Sandra ran to answer it. This time she didn't trip.

"Hello?" she answered.

"Carolina?" Her agent's voice made her jump, but then she was mad.

"No, Angel, this is not Carolina. Do you need a lobotomy to erase that name from your vocabulary?"

"I'm sorry, Sandra. It's just that I'm having a hard time getting used to it," her agent responded meekly. "It's just that I have the copy editing for your last book, and I wanted to send it out to you today. Should I send it where I always do?"

Sandra softened her tone, and felt badly for blowing up at the other man in her life who knew who she was and had kept her secret for almost a year. Thanks to him, she could continue writing as long as she wanted, and her books had been very successful even with her name change. No one in the literary world connected Sandra Bolaños with Perla Dosamantes, her former *nom de plume*.

"No, Angel. You'd better send it to the post office box in Brussels.

"Why?"

"Because my husband has a very important date with some old friends of mine, and if everything works out as planned, I may even collect on an old bet I made years ago with one of them... in Paris."

About the Author

Erica Fuentes

A successful attorney and author of several non-fiction books before bursting into the world of mainstream fiction, **Erica Fuentes** has delighted her readers with tales of intrigue, romance and international politics beginning in 2000 with her release of *Island Dreams*, followed by *Miguel's Cantina (First Love)*, *A Window To Paradise*, and *Hearts Ahoy!* in 2002. ***Shakedown***, released in Spanish in June 2007, with the title *Las Chicas de Palacio* is currently being adapted into a screenplay and holds fast on the best seller list in Mexico. All of Erica's novels have been published simultaneously in two versions: English and Spanish.

Her latest novel, *Salve Regina*, the first of a three book series co-authored with Annemarie Stonewater, was released by **Casablanca** in December 2010 and it promises to be another best-seller by the author.

Erica's *The Hunt Club*, on which ***Salve Regina, the Series*** was inspired, will be published by **Casablanca** after the series' third book.

After many years abroad carrying out diplomatic and corporate assignments, Fuentes currently lives in her beach home somewhere…

Salve Regina, the Series

by Erica Fuentes & Annemarie Stonewater

Salve Regina

(At your favorite bookseller now!)

During its one hundred year reign as one of the best Roman Catholic boarding schools in the country, Villa Vistamar was home to many young women —particularly politically vulnerable, but wealthy young women— from all parts of the world. Brought back by a class reunion, two former resident students haunted by the unexplained mysteries encountered in their youth, have set out to expose the secrets of the old Southwestern estate and the strange relationship between the Sisters of St. Thomas and their benefactor. Convinced that the key to the mysteries must be hidden away in the macabre old trunks that fill the basement of the old convent, a late-night escapade into the catacombs of the old abbey literally swallows them into —and past— the point of no return from their journey into Church history and intrigue. Several frightening encounters with Church Sentinels guarding the very secrets that the women have determined to unshroud, along with the death of an elderly nun and former Mother Superior of the order, leads the women to the discovery of a cache of priceless jewels that protect a far greater treasure; that which the Church has shielded from the world for nine decades of Eastern European history, under the ecclesiastical code name of *Salve Regina*.

Unholy Trinity *(Available March, 2011)*

Unholy Trinity, loosely based on an intriguing true case, evolves from Marisa's pro bono defense of a purportedly innocent man accused of murder, into a frightening journey through a labyrinth of evil and deceit, the nucleus of which seems to point to an obscure parish church ministered by an enigmatic old priest with a special fondness for his young acolytes. Marisa involves her coheroine, Erin, who brings in their unique clan of recurring support characters, including a semi-retired Jesuit monk licensed by the Vatican as an exorcist. This terrifying and spellbinding tale affirms the predominance of true power ever prevailing over the overt corruption and vying struggle between the powers of Church and State, but only after many unexpected twists and turns into realms that shake the characters' veritable core of truth and faith.

Sacred Secrets *(Available July, 2011)*

The story begins when Marisa finds herself in a quandary after bringing a few pre-Columbian artifacts back from Mexico; their provenance questionable, at best. What begins as a prank evolves into a highly suspenseful escapade into the world of clandestine art trafficking that eventually leads the group to the unexpected discovery of the treasures amassed during the Jesuit missionary era in the Californias before their expulsion from New Spain in 1867. The historical provenance and international treaties inherent to the questionable ownership of such treasures throw both countries into a legal battle with each other and against the Jesuits, while the group of characters follow their own agenda. This novel is laced with the customary bantering among the cast of characters and humorous moments found throughout the series.

www.ingramcontent.com/pod-product-compliance
Lightning Source LLC
LaVergne TN
LVHW091045080826
845145LV00002B/627

* 9 7 8 6 0 7 8 1 2 5 0 0 5 *